SAINTS AND SOLDIERS

Saints and Soldiers

10 9 8 7 6 5 4 3 2 1

First printing 2005
Published by Majestic Distribution, LLC
Printed by Banta in the U.S.A.

Scott, Jeffrey
Saints and Soldiers/Jeffrey Scott 1st Edition

Summary: The Battle of the Bulge, December 16-19, 1944. Fictionalized as the events turn the tide of WWII in Europe.

ISBN: 0-9723311-3-1

1. WWII-Fiction 2. Battle of the Bulge-Fiction

SAINTS AND SOLDIERS

by Jeffrey Scott

Based on the movie
Saints and Soldiers

Based on the story
by Geoffrey Panos

DECEMBER 16, 1944

Winley on the Ridge

Captain Winley stood alone at the broken window, staring into the dark forest. He craved a cigarette, but hiding in a dilapidated barn less than a mile from the German front demanded caution. He flipped the collar of his dull green overcoat against the night air, his shallow breath marking each tired exhale in the waning moonlight.

He looked at the three privates sleeping in the far corner and shook his head. Despite trying, he couldn't forget they were his responsibility. Outside the glassless opening, the clouds thickened. Winley knew that snow would soon fall over the Ardennes. The limbs on the pines and firs already hung heavy with the weight of moisture. The Captain hung heavy with thoughts of his sister.

He took off his glove and slid his hand through the slit in the army-issued overcoat, reaching deep into his left pocket. His lungs filled with the icy air as he touched the silk. Turning his back to the window and leaning against the framing, Oberon

Winley removed the white handkerchief and held it up to the last brush of moonlight. The initials JAW stitched into the corner with fine blue thread allowed his mind to wander.

"Shh! She's in the other room," Oberon cautioned his sister.

"We're gonna get caught."

"Not if you stop talking."

The two children crouched behind the kitchen island counter. On the other side, large French doors led to the dinning room where their mother sat drinking tea. They stared at the remaining few feet in the open until reaching the pantry.

"I don't really want any anyway," whispered Josephine.

"You know we're not getting any at the party. We can't even come downstairs when they have people over. We won't get caught. So, shh."

Oberon, who was an inch shorter than his twin sister, moved first. He scuffled across the tile floor, watching his mother's back. He reached the pantry and breathed.

Waving at his sister, he mouthed, "Come on."

Josephine peered around the corner of the counter. Her mother was stirring her tea with a small spoon. An open book sat next to the cup. Squatting, Josephine pulled her dress to the side and into a knot which she fisted. She crossed the kitchen unnoticed.

"See," he whispered.

Oberon stood inside the large pantry. He took out his pocket knife and began to cut. The thick frosting and cake sliced easily. He laid a thin piece of ruby red cake with white frosting in his palm and looked down at his sister.

"Here," he said rolling the cake into her hand. He cut another small chunk. Oberon then used the knife to spread extra frosting into the gap in the cake. He made little swirls in a failed attempt to camouflage his misdeed. Licking the blade, his mouth began to water. He folded the knife and put it into his back pocket.

Oberon sat back down, cake in hand. With a large grin, he bit into the sweetness and ran his tongue across his upper lip. "Mmm," he muttered.

Josephine didn't say anything while she licked sticky frosting off her fingertips. The two thieves sat on the floor next to each other and savored the confection.

"Ready, Jo?" the boy asked.

"Yeah."

Oberon looked out the pantry door. "She's reading her book. It's all clear."

The siblings scooted back across the kitchen. As they reached the island counter, they heard a chair scrape on the dining room floor. They paused and exchanged frightened glances.

"Come on," he whispered. Oberon grabbed his sister's hand and ran with her out of the kitchen.

They entered the foyer breathing heavily. At the base of the broad staircase, Oberon looked around and said, "In here." He led his sister through the entryway and into the music room. They momentarily hid underneath the black, grand piano.

"Oberon Winley the third, you get in here immediately! Where have you taken off to?" his mother yelled from the kitchen, her voice echoing through the spacious home.

"I think we're in trouble, Obee," Josephine said.

"No we're not. Come on!"

The two children ran through the music room and into their father's study. They had discovered long ago the secret staircase behind one of the bookshelves. Together they pushed against one edge forcing the other to swing open. They didn't turn on the light but just sat in dark on the first tread, heaving with the rush of adrenaline.

The steps led upstairs to a similar bookshelf in a sitting room off the master suite. An ancestor of the Winley's had been a commissioned general in the revolutionary war. He built the home and installed the passage as an escape route from night marauders. Although the residence had remained in the family, the general was the last soldier to occupy the seventy-acre estate nestled on the hills just outside of Boston. The last until Oberon III joined the army.

"What do we do, Obee?"

"Nothing! We're fine if we stick together."

"I don't think I can," Josephine admitted.

"Look, if she doesn't catch us inside the house, she'll blame one of the servants."

"Obee!" Josephine looked at her brother even though she couldn't see him in the darkness.

Oberon felt the glare.

"The cake was for her big party tonight. She'll be so mad I don't know what she'll do. We have to say something. We shouldn't have done that." Josephine began to cry.

"Don't worry, Jo. I'll tell her. I'm used to the whippin' anyway."

"No you won't."

With that, Josephine Alice Winley leaned against the bookcase and ran out.

"Hey, Winnie, what's out that window that's got you so interested?" Private Larsen asked, chuckling from under his bedroll in the corner of the abandoned barn.

Opening his eyes, Captain Winley stuffed the last tangible memory of his twin sister back into his pocket. He didn't hear the Private.

Larsen continued, "Close the window! It's freezing in here! Can't you see I'm trying to get some sleep."

"I cannot close it. The glass has been blown out."

Larsen smiled. "Winnie, you've got no sense of humor."

Larsen's head emerged tortoise-like from his roll.

"Refer to me again by that appellation, and I will see to it that you receive a court martial for insubordination."

"Huh?" Larsen only understood the words court martial. He held his large and growling stomach underneath the bed roll. "It's, like, early, or something. What time is it, anyway?"

Winley pulled on the cuff of his overcoat and glanced at his watch. "0600."

Larsen pulled the cover tightly under his neck. "A little earlier than I would normally eat, but would you order some breakfast. I'd like eggs, flap jacks, real maple syrup, please, and a whole lot of hot coffee. And could you turn up the heat in this room."

Winley heard nothing cognizable from the comedian in the corner. He considered Larsen large on weight and small on wit and had learned to ignore him. Besides, the case of the stolen confection still lingered in his mind.

His sister had immediately confessed to their mother, relieving him of his father's belt. He couldn't remember if he felt guilty back then, but he certainly did now. That episode had occurred just before Christmas, exactly twenty years ago. The two were only seven.

Currently, Captain Oberon Winley, an officer with the 395th Infantry Regiment, led three inexperienced and incompetent privates through the Belgian woodland on what he felt was a meaningless fishing expedition.

The day before, the Captain and the privates were sent on a reconnaissance assignment to the Elsenborn Ridge on the eastern edge of the Ardennes forest, overlooking the German border. On their way to the ridge, chance favored the small group not only with shelter in a large clearing but a couple of enemy bedrolls. The farmhouse had been burned leaving only the stone foundation and walls, and the sheep had long since wandered on to friendlier pastures. The barn, although crumbling from the rafters, still provided some relief from the cold, northerly wind.

"I said could you turn up the heat," Larsen repeated.

"Be quiet, Larsen." Winley turned his ear to the wind outside the broken window.

"Wah, wah, be quiet," Larsen replied in muted breath. "Nothing's going on out there. We haven't seen a thing since we left. The rumors were just a bunch of paranoid locals, old folks gossiping in cafés because they have nothing better to waste their day on."

"I said please be quiet."

"There's nothing in these woods but these comfy bedrolls. By the way, thanks, Jerry," Larsen said staring at the cold air above his head.

Winley now squinted. Flakes of fresh snow began to flutter to the ground, and shadows seemed to shift with the passing clouds. But a dark figure moved between the trees.

"Well, we've got to take off at first light anyway. Might as well get up." Larsen emerged and stretched his broad chest like a bear after hibernation. His breath only frosted the damp air as he blew on his hands for warmth.

"Ouch!"

Larsen kicked another bedroll. "Get up, we're taking off."

The bundle barely moved.

"Larsen, shut up and get down!"

Larsen reacted quickly to the uncharacteristic language from Captain Winley. The only familiar intonation in the command was the New England "R" in Winley's accent, making the private's last name sound more like Lawson.

The Captain ducked beneath the open window. From a crouched position, he motioned above his head. The others, instantly alert, crawled over to the Captain, sliding their rifles along the bare ground.

"How many?" whispered one soldier.

"I saw only one. Do you have your mirror?"

Larsen pulled out a square sheet of metal he used for shaving from his field glass case. However, the disappearing moon provided inadequate light. In another uncharacteristic move, Winley dared a personal observation. Behind a snow-covered fir tree, a dark figure brandished a shred of cloth.

"I believe he is waving a flag," Winley informed the others.

"A white flag? The international symbol of being a pansy?" responded the comic. "What? You give the Kraut that stupid hanky of yours so he could give himself up?"

"Quiet." Captain Winley stood up.

"What are you doing? There could be others! You don't know what he's up to. Winnie, hold on." Larsen shuffled toward the barn door. The door had detached from the hinges, and a three-inch gap formed between the door and jamb.

The two other soldiers also took strategic positions. The first man skirted to another broken-out window opened to the front, and the second snuck out the back and around the side of the barn.

From his vantage point, Larsen watched the figure emerge from behind the pine tree and slowly make his way forward. The man was thin and wore a German officer's gray, double-breasted, wool overcoat. The insignia on the right collar revealed him as part of the Waffen-SS. On his head he placed a cap of the high command, not a helmet. He held out his arms spread eagle, the white cloth prominent in his dark gloves. Larsen saw no weapon as the man continued toward the barn.

Winley, Larsen and the private at the other window presented their rifles. Three barrels from three angles were aimed directly at the man's chest. The fourth American remained hidden outside and scanned the forest. The German officer acknowledged the weapons and proceeded forward.

Standing to the side of the window and tracing the German with his gun sight, Winley could see this was no foot soldier. The man was a first lieutenant. Winley suddenly realized that the officer must have known they were in the barn yet took no aggressive action.

Accordingly, Winley took no action. Many Germans were deserting, so he watched.

The SS officer reached the barn door, less than two yards from the tip of Larsen's barrel. Winley re-aimed inside the barn. With arms still raised, the German pushed open the leaning slab of wood with his boot. The private outside the barn, too apprehensive to notice the sub-freezing temperatures, tried to recon the meadow: nothing but darkness and falling snow.

The moon, now fully covered by clouds and floating low in the sky, withdrew its light. Inside, the wanderer became nothing more than a faint silhouette in the doorway.

"Halt." Winley didn't know what else to say. Although his university education allowed some measure of invention, it was no substitute for experience. He despised relying on instinct, and not knowing the answer made him uncomfortable. He held his rifle raised in caution, and fear.

The officer stopped and said nothing.

Larsen, legs wobbling, pressed the muzzle into the back of the intruder's neck. Winley went for the gas lantern. He propped his rifle next to a small shelf. He reached inside his overcoat and removed the matches next to a pack of cigarettes. He really wanted a smoke now. In a single flick he lit a match, and the lantern produced a pale, blue-white glow.

Larsen hid his fear from the artificial light.

Winley and Lucht

Holding up the lantern, Winley paused on the German's features. Thin lips without upturn appeared solemn but relaxed. He was clean-shaven with no sideburns. High cheekbones seemed to indicate birth into a refined family. The bridge of a long, straight nose separated dark eyes, intense under the brim of his hat. He was handsome and strong, almost statuesque with his arms still in the air; a white handkerchief hung in his right hand.

In his pocket, Winley perceived his own folded, white symbol. He felt a connection with this German officer. They both had lost something.

Without speaking, Winley motioned for the officer to move into the center of the barn. He looked to Larsen and flicked his head toward the door, an instruction to push it closed. The first soldier remained a sentry at the far window and confirmed no movement to the Captain.

With the barn door shut, Winley moved behind his captive. He instinctively pressed his worries to the back of his mind.

"Do you speak English?"

"Yes." The German's voice was deep and clear.

"What are you doing here?" Winley succeeded in keeping the nerves bubbling in his gut from vibrating his speech.

"I surrender," he replied, slowly, with emphasis on each consonant.

With that answer, Winley looked again to Larsen, now back to peering through the slit in the door, and the soldier by the window. Both nodded negative.

"What's your name?"

"Obersturmführer Frederich Lucht, SS-Panzergrenadier-Regiment 25." Although his speech was heavily accented, Lucht had obviously been educated outside of Germany.

"Turn around."

Lucht obeyed.

The officer's regiment was part of the famed Hitlerjugend, the division thus named because it recruited mostly from the ranks of Hitler's Youth, young men born, bred and trained under the auspices of the Nazi party. General Josef Dietrich of the 6. Panzer-Armee had assigned Lucht's regiment the assault on Elsenborn Ridge.

As he nodded for Larsen to come and search the officer, Winley removed his .38 pistol with his free hand.

Larsen unclasped Lucht's gun belt, sans sidearm, and unbuttoned the thick, wool overcoat.

Lucht lowered his arms and allowed the coat to fall to the ground. "We have little time. They are coming."

"Who's coming?" Winley asked as Larsen continued the search.

"My regiment, and another from 12. SS-Panzer-Division."

"They're coming this way?" Winley asked, looking the German in the eye.

"Yes, to take the ridge, then down to Elsenborn."

Surprised, Larsen found no weapon of any kind. "Clean," he reported. Instinctively, Larsen held up the man's coat.

Winley never moved his eyes off Lucht's. They faced each other like pawns across a chess board. Lucht responded in kind. Unbeknownst to either man, they both enjoyed and excelled at the strategic board game.

"How long until they get here?"

"Orders are to leave at dawn. Very soon."

Larsen glanced out the open window where Winley had lost himself in memories of his sister just minutes earlier. Below the clouds, the sky was beginning to lighten with daybreak. He looked back to Winley with large pupils.

"Who's your division commander?" Winley asked the question to test the German even though he didn't know what the correct answer should be.

"Standartenführer Krass. We must hurry."

"Is this a German offensive?"

"Wacht am Rhein." Lucht physically relaxed, confident the Americans were beginning to trust him. He kept his tone serious.

"Larsen, check outside on Macon."

The remaining private relieved Larsen as guard at the window as the big guy went out the back door.

"I don't understand. Wacht what?" Winley motioned for Lucht to move over to the side of the barn. He placed the lantern back on the shelf.

"Wacht am Rhein." Lucht paused, thinking. "Watch, uh lookout, on the Rhein River. Hitler's codename for the offensive. Two divisions are coming here. Three full armies in the Ardennes, others, I believe, all along the Belgian border."

The American reconnaissance group, now all back inside their vulnerable refuge, stood stunned at the revelation. Larsen nervously began scratching the side of his leg, his round face sweating. The two others went pale.

Through the pines and mist, the sun brightened the eastern horizon from black to dark blue. Then they heard the faint rumble, barely audible but clearly recognizable to even the inexperienced soldiers. Had the Americans left a day earlier, they would have seen the Germans amassing below the ridge.

Outside the towns of Wirtzfelf, Rockerath and Losheim, mortar began falling on the western side of the front. The German Wehrmacht was moving.

"Forget the Kraut! Let's get the hell out of here. Back down to Elsenborn." Larsen nearly yelled, becoming increasingly agitated. The others appeared to agree. One went to grab his gear.

Lucht remained fixed on Winley, neither flinched.

"Slow down! I will not allow you men to do anything imprudent. Just ready your gear."

"There's more that you must know."

"More than three armies!" Larsen yelled. "We've only got a few divisions in these parts and even those are spread thin as a cobweb."

Winley turned and glared at Larsen, finally taking his eyes off Lucht. Larsen didn't comprehend the possible leak of information to the German officer.

"We've gotta get back and warn the C.O." Larsen now let his rifle droop, aimed at the ground.

"Private!" Winley lost patience.

"Where's your radio?" Lucht calmly inquired.

All the Americans except Winley exchanged embarrassed glances. Larsen looked at his feet in shame.

"Broken," the Captain replied without any intonation. Although Winley reinitiated the staring contest, he struggled to restrain the impulse to shoot Larsen for the not-so-comical incident earlier that evening that had resulted in a broken transistor, rendering their only mode of communication useless.

Lucht reached inside his shirt pocket and removed a thick

fold of papers, his turn to make a move. He quickly unfolded the maps and documents and placed them next to the dim lantern.

He spoke fast for broken English, and the Captain struggled to follow. In less than five minutes, Lucht had precisely divulged Hitler's plans to retake Europe, including routes, troop and artillery strength, and most importantly, Operation Grief, the key to Hitler's success.

"Is your gear ready?" Winley asked his men with less authority than the situation demanded. His thoughts were too preoccupied on the recent events to pretend to be a leader. He came from a long line of New England aristocrats, educated and wealthy. He had mastered the etiquette of using dining utensils before his first day of grade school. Military leadership skills were not prized attributes in his home, and war was a vulgarity to his liberal parents.

Oberon Winley had his own reasons for conscripting after graduating from Harvard. His current rank was due to his education, and he possessed no intention of climbing the army ladder any further. The only reminder of his Boston home was the white handkerchief in his pocket. The only one he wanted.

The five were ready to set out for Elsenborn. With luck they would be back at the regiment camp in a few hours where Winley could unload the vital information he now carried unwillingly on his shoulders. Snow began falling more densely as Larsen opened the barn door to the cold morning-and a single gunshot.

"Larsen!" Captain Winley's warning came too late.

"Ugh."

With the single, throaty utterance, Frederich Lucht stumbled a few feet and collapsed to the ground, face down in dirt.

A second shot ricocheted off an iron hinge. Larsen slammed the ten-foot, wooden closure back to its insecure position, his face white beneath his heavy, dark beard.

Three more bullets sliced the stale air inside the barn. One found the private standing next to Winley, dropping him instantly.

Winley grabbed the maps from the ledge as the two remaining privates flew past him towards the rear exit. His pistol reholstered, Winley stuffed the documents into a breast pocket of his dark green uniform and scooped his snow cape and rifle off the ground.

Out back, a small, snow-covered pasture meant fifty yards in the open until the three Americans would reach the forest wall. A platoon from Lucht's regiment swarmed around the barn.

Outside, all three men moved in slow motion, their speed hampered by the wet snow blanketing the field. Surprisingly, Larsen's large torso led the escape, followed by Winley and Private Macon.

The platoon had been dispatched soon after the German officer's disappearance. They had found the officer's gun conspicuously placed at the head of his cot and decided to leave early.

Schütze Heinz Sandig belonged to that platoon. Despite being sixteen years old, fair-skinned, blonde and not having reached puberty, he still could not have looked less of a soldier. He never wanted to be in the army nor a member of the Hitlerjugend. But there was nothing else left for him.

Heinz followed the other boys around the barn as the Americans escaped across the field.

Obediently, he kneeled by the rear corner of the barn. With the butt firmly pressed against his right shoulder, he lined the sight of his Mauser Kar 98k rifle at another human being for the first time in his life. He thought of his little sister and his mom back at home. He thought of his father killed during the air raids of Berlin. The boy hated the war and himself. He closed his eyes and squeezed the trigger. The gun exploded. In the snow-covered field, an American soldier running for his life fell dead, sliding across the pasture.

Heinz began to cry, never knowing that his bullet hit a tree ten feet to the right of his target.

The Medic and the Lieutenant

"Medic!"

"All right! I hear ya!"

"Medic!" a boyish private screamed again at no one, hunched over another soldier, who didn't appear much older. The Private appeared agitated but resolved. His uniform doubled the bulk of his body, and sprayed blood pimpled his pale skin and wire, military-issue glasses.

The Medic, Corporal Stephen Gould, glanced up toward the cry and witnessed chaos. Some men were fleeing into the forest while others were still emerging, bewildered, from foxholes. A moment earlier he had been fleeing with them.

Scattered gunfire hit a few of the soldiers before they took their second breath of the cold, morning air. All of them appeared young, too young. A few months earlier, these guys would have been chasing girls at a football game pep rally or at worst running from the local truant officers for ditching school. However, at 0730 in the middle of the Belgian Ardennes forest near the German border, it was tragic.

"Medic!"

The immature urgency of the boy's cracking voice snapped Gould back to his reality: he was a medic, whether he liked it or not. "I'm coming." He paused; then, barely above a whisper and shaking his head, he repeated, "I'm coming."

The veteran Medic grabbed a small, green duffle bag and skid across the slush. He kept his torso and low, the dirty snow cape trailed behind, ghost-like in the early morning light and fog. Despite the constant rattle of gunfire and flashes from German muzzles, Gould only heard the crackle of crisp snow under his feet and saw a thin blond boy with glasses.

The young Private sat motionless, apparently compressing the shoulder of the other soldier. Gould sidled next to him.

"He's my boss, uh, Lieutenant."

"And I'm fine," the officer replied, irritated at the unnecessary attention. "Who are you? You're not with our regiment."

"No." Gould pulled a pair of scissors from his duffle and cut away a small part of the officer's uniform. He probed the wound with his finger and felt no foreign object. The bullet must have ricocheted off the bone. The skin was torn and the muscle slightly injured.

"Is it bad?" the blonde boy asked.

"No. More blood than real damage." He then ripped open a small packet with his teeth and poured a gray powder into the Lieutenant's small wound at the shoulder. Gould wedged his last sterile 4x4 inside the opening of the man's shirt and wrapped a long length of dirty bandages, quickly but meticulously in a figure eight around the officer's arm and shoulder. The Medic was proud of his ability to work quickly and without emotion, even under fire.

"We need to get our men back into their holes," the Lieutenant ordered the soldier with glasses. "Walker, do you hear me?"

"Yes, sir!" he replied "But . . ."

"GO!"

The young blond jumped and ran with an odd strength for his frail body, nimbly keeping the glasses perched on his nose.

Gould began organizing the few remaining pieces of equipment in his bag. "I think they're moving off, probably following the ones that ran into the woods or back to their platoon. I'm surprised they came out this far. It's quieting down; but it won't last. Best I can tell they're headed this way. We better hurry and get out of here. See if we can get to Honsfeld, or hopefully further west."

"We're not going anywhere." The Lieutenant spoke with an authority far beyond his age and glared Gould in the eyes. "I asked you who you were. And where did you and all these other soldiers come from?"

"Name's Gould. I'm part of the 2nd ID. We came up from St. Vith to help you boys take the Roer River dams. We were less than a mile from here when it all started."

"What started? What's going on? I swear I was just having my morning coffee and bam. Shots came from everywhere at once, and soldiers I've never seen before were leaping over our foxholes. We're even an I&R, and we knew nothing was supposed to be coming down. This is impossible!" the Lieutenant exclaimed as he got up without Gould's assistance. His voice just began to reveal his age. "What are you doing here?"

Gould explained, "The Krauts broke the line and hit about an hour ago, outside of Losheim. The regiment there was nearly decimated. Everyone scattered. I was chased and ended up here. Part of the 106th was there as well, platoons from three divisions mixed and men scattered in all directions. Nobody was sticking around for orders, if you get my drift. It came too fast."

The Lieutenant stood quiet for a moment. "We shared rations with a Colonel transferring out that way just last night. He headed off late. I hope he realized what was going down before he got there." The Lieutenant then muttered something more to himself as he walked back towards a foxhole.

Picking up his bag and following behind the Lieutenant, Gould commented, "There were more Germans than I've seen since St.-Lô. Hell, since Omaha. Someone was yelling something about multiple Panzer-Armee units. If it's true, we don't have much time to get out of here. You need to get your men and leave!"

Walker arrived running and out of breath-and finally wiping the blood from his glasses, creating smears rather than clean lenses. "The men are ready for orders, all eighteen are accounted for. But, but there are dead guys everywhere. Some are Jerries and others I don't recognize. I saw a few running into the woods. Where'd they come from?"

"Apparently, from the front line," his boss replied.

"I thought we were the front line?" Walker asked himself out loud.

"Walker, right now, we've got to get ready. Sounds like we're gonna have our hands full."

"Everyone back into the holes and ready weapons!" The Lieutenant suddenly aligned his demeanor and barked orders like a drill sergeant at boot camp, almost more for show than effect-his men always followed his command. "Search the casualties and grab any artillery you can find," he yelled, holding his Garand M1 semiautomatic rifle at the end of his injured right arm. "Get me the phone!"

Men obeyed and began crouching into foxholes dug into the south side of the road from Losheim. Unbeknownst to the Americans, it was the beginning of the German Army's Rollbahnen D, one of five lines of attack started that morning in what would become known as the Battle of the Bulge.

"Lines are cut, L.T.," a soldiered informed the Lieutenant.

"Then get me the radio! Someone has to know what's going on."

Gould began to head west, his nearly empty medical bag slung over his shoulder.

"Where're you going, Corporal?" The Lieutenant emphasized the rank as age was meaningless at this point. The young Lieutenant had lied about his own age to enlist in the army before the war even started-he kept his reasons to himself. Commissioned second lieutenant by age eighteen, he was now head of an Intelligence and Reconnaissance platoon with the 99th Infantry. Although informal in manner, older soldiers followed this young officer's commands without hesitation.

"With everyone else, outta here," replied Gould without turning around.

"I've got a feeling we're gonna need a medic and we don't have one. All we've got is a brand new medical kit in the foxhole, and nobody knows how to use the stuff in it. You're staying!"

Gould stopped. In a moment, he mentally reviewed the faces of death he had seen since landing in Europe, horrific flashcard images flipped in his mind, hundreds of men, soldiers, women, children. Even Madeleine's face appeared. Nothing seemed to matter. When a shard of metal no bigger than a small fingernail pierced a lung, the aorta or the brain, the result was always the same: death.

The Medic wasn't a doctor-at least not yet, the army saw to that-and, despite his best efforts, there was nothing he could do to stop the inevitable. Nothing mattered: not to the injured; not to God; and certainly not to Gould.

With reservation, Corporal Gould turned and jumped into the cold, dank hole in the ground with the Lieutenant and the skinny soldier with glasses.

The morning continued as the week had begun. Bitter air flowed through the supposed winter gear the infantry divisions were issued as if it were made of cheesecloth. Freezing wet penetrated to the skin through snow-soaked boots, socks and trousers. Wool hats, gloves and coats provided little warmth.

The sky never blued as the gray clouds hovered relentlessly overhead. When snow wasn't falling, wet mist, damp fog or the enemy prevented fires for drying out. Mushy snow covered the entire forest except for the brown, muddy roads that webbed their way between towns. Deep ruts carved out by jeeps, truck and tanks measured up to three feet deep, becoming physical barriers between opposing troops and causing men to become state fair shooting targets if they tried to cross.

The young Lieutenant's regiment had camped along side one of these roads, if it could be called a road, that came from Losheim. The entire division was spread thin, north to south, along the front line through the Ardennes. They were mistakenly told that it was not an area of strategic importance.

"Now what?" Gould inquired of his new Lieutenant. He had become accustomed to the constant change, officially or unofficially, in leadership.

"That depends on how much you can tell me about what's going on here."

"Not much I'm afraid."

Walker squatted across from his L.T. and Gould, his weapon resting on his thin thighs. He looked almost calm despite the events of the morning. Gould eyed him with curiosity.

"You've got to know more than we do. We landed at Le Harve a little over a month ago. Took us almost as long to get here. We haven't seen a Jerry, let alone combat. At first we thought it was just the outgoing mail that we heard this morning."

"That wasn't outgoing. It was incoming." Gould replied.

His curiosity deepened. "You telling me all these guys are that fresh." To Gould, this regiment certainly didn't act like untested soldiers.

A few men moved in the woods behind the foxholes. Muffled voices told their story as they headed west. Snow began to fall again.

"Yep. Almost the whole 99th is just a couple of months old. The few that aren't replacements are in command now." The L.T. sensed Gould's curiosity. "And no, I've been in the army a long time, longer than most, anyway." He ended the conversation with his standard explanation: "I'm older than I look."

Just then a soldier jumped into the foxhole carrying a large radio like a football halfback.

"Found this in the back of that jeep. I can't believe it, but it works."

"Get me battalion H.Q."

"Already got 'em. Here ya go." The soldier delivered the handset to the Lieutenant and kneeled next to Walker. The two younger men began chatting with a feigned composure.

"Don't tell me that! I've got eyes!" The L.T. screamed into the handset. "I'm telling you that it's happening right now. There's a German column coming up the road from Losheim. We need artillery, and now, damn it! Look, it's my job to report intelligence and that's what I'm doing. We were under fire minutes ago and we've got reports that the Krauts are coming straight at us. Yeah. We need artillery!"

He stood, handset still at his ear, and looked above the hole. Visibility measured in feet. His men, all eighteen, were still alive and hunkered down in a series of holes alongside the road. Each hole, originally meant for two or three, contained five to eight men, most from other platoons. Others had disappeared into the fog or woods. Scores lay dead on the road, now half buried by snow and mud.

"You really haven't seen any action?" queried Gould, still staring at the thin soldier across from him.

"Six weeks ago we were in England. German bombs from those unmanned things smashed the hell out the place, but things have been basically quiet since we got here. What about you?"

"You could say I have." Gould intentionally concealed information he'd been trying to forget. But Walker looked on with such simplicity that Gould felt compelled to continue. He kept his explanation as brief as he could. "Landed at Omaha in June, pushed on to St.-Lô in July, then to Paris and towards the German border, and now here, sitting in this damn hole as perplexed as you are."

Unphased by the obvious brevity, Walker furthered his investigation. "How were the beaches? I've only heard second-hand stories and some of the news reels. Was it that bad?"

The soldier next to Walker now looked on, youthful faces from under the hoods of their snow capes beamed like school children listening to their teacher, hoping for words of inspiration, or at least distraction.

"You wouldn't understand." Gould said, abruptly ending the conversation. The soldiers looked dismayed and slightly wounded. Gould took a deep breath as the nightmare of the last night before capturing St.-Lô began to play in his mind, the night he lost Madeleine. He squeezed his eyes shut in a metaphorical attempt to squeeze out the memory. It wasn't enough. He tried to replace the thoughts with better ones.

"I'm not a doctor, just a medic," Corporal Gould replied to the nurse in charge of the surgical ward.

"You're not just a medic," Madeleine said in return as she led the Corporal down a row of cots. "You boys in the field do as much, if not more, than the doctors here."

Madeleine Béart, a French-American, worked as a nurse at the Hotel Coeur en Hiver. After the Normandy invasion, the hotel north of St.-Lô had been transformed into a makeshift Divisional HQ, hospital, barracks and staging area as the Allies pushed further into France.

"I don't know about that." The Corporal scanned the beds. While his eyes searched for his friend's face, his mind searched for words to ask Madeleine.

"I do," she said.

Without hearing her, the Medic sighed. "I don't see him." He stopped walking.

"He was your friend?"

"The last, I think."

"Certainly not the last." Madeleine turned and faced the Medic who appeared distraught. She lightly touched his arm.

Gould tried to look the woman in the eye but dizziness prevented the contact. He stared at his feet. "Actually, he was the last."

"I don't understand." Madeleine's face looked serious but empathetic.

"He was the last original member from my company. They're all dead now. In only one month, everyone I came over with is officially gone. The entire company is nothing but replacements, including the officers."

"You are not a replacement," Madeleine pointed out.

Raising his head, Gould thought back to himself, I've never been anything but a replacement.

Madeleine continued to smile at him.

Gould finally found the words. "Would you like to have some coffee? It's army-issue but not too bad."

"I'd love some."

The pair proceeded down the stairs to the hotel lobby. There were hundreds of soldiers and officers drinking coffee, casually talking or merely standing around. Gould guided the nurse through the congestion to a table with a large metal canister with a spout at the bottom and rows of cups. He poured, and she smiled.

They took their coffee out large glass doors to the veranda on the side of the lobby. The sky was gray and rain fell heavily. Water ran off the canopy in large drops as the two silently watched and thought the same thoughts.

With another extricating breath, Stephen Gould stood up and turned his back to the other soldiers. "What's the word, Lieutenant?"

"They have less of a clue than we do. And unless the weather clears there won't be any air support. Sounds like we're on our own for at least the rest of the morning."

"Retreat?"

"Negative. We hold the road. Those are my orders." The L.T. faced Gould with a look of resolution and fear. To him, Gould still possessed experience, combat experience, and that often accounted for more than rank or years in the service. He hoped Gould would offer some words of encouragement, some advice.

"Against an entire Panzer-Armee?" Corporal Gould tried to sound convincing, not scared.

Disappointed, the L.T. said, "What ever portion comes down that road."

"But you're intelligence, not combat. Your men aren't ready for this. That's why you guys are behind the lines. They weren't supposed to see that kind of combat. It could be . . ."

The L.T. cut the Medic off. "They did this morning. We hold the road. Take a look at this and keep whatever you want." The Lieutenant tossed Gould the medical kit that the arrogant Colonel had hastily left the night before.

With that the Lieutenant leaped out of the foxhole and started an inventory of men, weapons, artillery and the terrain. He moved with confidence, and his men responded. They had little in the way of heavy artillery, but there were a couple of Browning .30-caliber machine guns, a .50-caliber on that Colonel's flipped-over jeep, some BARs and numerous submachine guns.

The platoon's position, however, was their greatest strength. The dense forest would force the German spearhead along the center of the road, which would be slow moving in the slush. Their foxholes, hidden in the snow and mist, would flank and entrap the advance.

Gould searched through the medical kit and couldn't believe his luck. No real medic would have left that stuff here, at least not intentionally. There were supplies that Gould hadn't been able to get for weeks, and some he had never seen. He sighed in relief as he pulled out the packets of morphine and held them in his hand.

In the field, medics were revered as saints and soldiers handed over rations, especially cigarettes and other personals, as gestures of appreciation. That admiration, however, always escaped Corporal Gould. From his experiences, he always felt useless.

Winley and Larsen

Oberon Winley and "Big" John Larsen sped without guidance through the dense forest. The heavy onslaught of snow, thick fog and pine branches nearly blinded the pair. Only gravity indicated that they traveled downhill.

"I can't go any farther," gasped Larsen, clutching one hand at his large chest.

Winley turned his head and tried to look behind. He saw nothing, but he also knew that that meant nothing. The Germans could be a few feet away in the current conditions.

Larsen stopped, nearly collapsing, and Winley ducked behind a tree trunk barely wider than his own thin frame.

"Winney, I'm gonna heave." Larsen bent over at the waist with his hands on his thighs and his mouth opened like a caught trout.

"Quiet!" Winley tried to listen for the sound of a moving platoon: voices, snapping twigs, crunching snow or even trucks. The forest returned nothing.

"Maybe they've given up," Larsen barely coughed out. "I

think I could really use your hanky." The big man wiped his lips and began choking.

"Sorry. You are on your own." Winley placed his hand over the cloth in his pocket. "And I doubt that they have given up. They have certainly located Lucht's body, and they are now aware of what he has done. They are either behind those trees, or trying to head us off from the front. Either way, they are certainly pursuing us."

Trying to control his breathing, Larsen looked to the line of firs, then back to Winley with terror in his eyes. "Do you even know where we're headed?"

Winley already had his compass in hand and began calculating in his head. "We are moving south. Unless we deviate from the current course, Elsenborn should be just down this hill and rather close." The truth was that Winley didn't know where the town was located. "We must keep moving," he ordered as he reinitiated his journey.

"Hold on, I'm coming." Larsen had barely regained his breath and began moving his body again when he started to ask, "What about . . ."

"You must forget them," Winley interjected, knowing what Larsen was about to inquire. "Dwelling on the loss will only slow you down. Concentrate on returning to the regiment." Winley didn't realize his own hypocrisy. "Save your strength. And would you please be quiet, if not just for one blessed moment!" Winley's impatience rang out through the storm.

Like a punished puppy, Larsen trudged forward, wiping the snow that had frosted on his thickening beard but had melted on his broad forehead. He moved well for a large man. As much strength as gut, his father always reminded him. Larsen's torso more than tripled that of Winley's, and the big man possessed the physical ability to overpower any man or officer. His personality, however, belied his prowess.

On the ridge, heavy snow dropped in torrents of wind and quickly accumulated as the pair had fled the barn. Larsen's back steamed from sweat and melting snow on his wool jacket. The large Private could barely see his Captain even though only a few feet in front. Their progress slowed to a crawl and then to a walk. Each step required tremendous energy to lift their soaking wet boots out from the drifts of heavy slush. Larsen lagged behind.

"Captain Winley?" Larsen spoke as if he were chatting to a friend during a picture show, barely audible enough for the Captain to hear.

"What?" Winley kept moving.

"I think I'm stuck."

Winley turned around. "What!" He felt the anger fill his chest as he began to backtrack. He saw the Private buried up to his neck in snow, arms raised in surrender and trapped against his head. "What happened?"

"I just took a step and fell in."

"Good hell, Private. You think you are stuck?" Winley again listened for any movement and heard nothing but the howl of wind. The snow continued to fall in sheets. "You had better hope the Germans are rutted as well, or you have placed both of us in peril." He stepped back up to Larsen's position. Looking down at the large head Winley inquired, "What is this?"

As the Captain began to dig around Larsen's shoulders and shake his head, Larsen said, "I think my feet are wet."

"Mine are, too. The white material we have been traveling through is snow, just in case you are too ignorant to realize it."

"No, sir, I think I'm standing in water."

As he scooped handfuls of snow, Winley realized that they had been running through a narrow ravine, probably carved by a small stream coming off the ridge. The v-shaped terrain had filled in with cubic yards of new snow.

"I'm sorry, sir. I guess I was just too big."

"Quiet, Larsen." Winley eased a bit. Seeing such a large head helplessly sticking out of the snow made the Captain smile through the thoughts of his sister and current mission. "I will try and free one those tree trunks you call arms. Then, you can dig yourself out."

Larsen began twisting his shoulders to loosen the pack. The snow fell so quickly, however, that nature reclaimed much of the progress the two mortals made. Some forces were too strong to fight against, they both thought.

The two men struggled for nearly half an hour before Larsen had freed both his arms enough to gain full mobility. He waved them in exhilaration.

"Halleluiah! Let the angels sing!"

"Quiet St. Nicholas. You are not out yet. And Christmas cheer is still a week away."

"I'll get myself outta here in no time now, sir."

Winley looked up. "I do not believe you will. Shh." Winley pressed his hand to Larsen's mouth. "I hear something."

Larsen's eyes darted back and forth in panic above his red, swollen cheeks.

Very faintly through the storm, Captain Winley heard voices. Quickly, he began shoveling snow from the hillside back on top of Larsen. The Private, although bewildered, remained quiet and obedient. As soon as his body was hidden, Winley lightly covered the top of Larsen's head with snow. Now, he really looked like Santa Clause. Winley used a few tree branches to sweep the snow and place on top of Larsen's head. The raging storm finished the camouflage.

Winley took a couple of steps up the hill and jumped down into the ravine at an angle similar to the slope. He was instantly submerged up to his chest. He finished covering himself in the snow as if he were burying himself in sand at the beach. He heard the first crunches of footsteps as he wedged his head underneath the cold, white blanket.

Six German soldiers tracking the escaping Americans made their way down the ravine. They had managed to follow two pairs of boot prints until the storm covered any further markings. Now they were lost. The young members of the Hitlerjugend were well-armed but grossly inexperienced.

The German posse followed down the notch in single file toward Winley and Larsen. The snowfall had almost erased any sign of their predicament. The Captain listened while Larsen began sweating.

The leading German held up his hand and stopped. "Halt." The soldier's boot set down a few yards from Winley's own.

Winley disappeared in thought.

"You're dead, Oberon!" Jackie Martell yelled across the school yard. The school's star rugby player and two other seniors chased after the young boy.

Oberon had been studying in the library with his sister when the trio of athletes stormed in. He managed to escape the building, leaving his jacket at the table. Outside, snow had been falling all day. He raced across the snowy field and into the woods beyond. His pursuers were not far behind.

"There's no use hiding. We'll find you."

Oberon knew why he was being hunted. Someone ratted on a group of seniors that had cheated on their midyear examinations. They mistakenly believed it was Oberon.

Although sixteen years old, Oberon was still small, lagging behind the other boys his age in development. He was thin and angular, especially in the face which appeared almost gaunt. His school uniform never fit right. Inherited from his mother, Oberon's blonde hair disappeared into his pale but blotchy skin. His blue eyes stood out as his only prominent, and attractive, feature.

Josephine, in contrast to her brother, was beautiful. On her, the thinness complemented her gentle personality. And it would be another year before the boy exceeded his sister in height. The darker hair, eyes and complexion of her father looked almost Mediterranean despite the family's nearly pure English heritage. Only their noses revealed the familial relationship of the twins. It was thin, slightly pointed and dimpled on the end.

In the woods, Oberon stopped at the crest of a small hillside. He looked back as the three bullies approached, and his heart pounded. Obee had succeeded to his sophomore year unnoticed. Now, the undue attention terrified him. He felt lightheaded and dizzy.

Just as Jackie and his buddies reached Oberon, the thin boy passed out and began to slide down the hillside. His body lightly bounced off a few trees before it finally stopped rolling. He was buried in the snow.

When he regained consciousness, Josephine was standing over him.

"Are you okay, Obee?"

"Yeah, I think. I'm cold." He stood up and brushed the snow off his wool uniform.

"Here," Josephine said holding out the jacket.

"Where's Jackie?"

"They left. I guess they thought that crashing down the hill was enough punishment. We need to get back up to school. Mother will be here to get us any minute. You sure you're alright?"

"Yeah, I'm fine."

The two walked silently up the hill. Although the siblings never discussed it, Oberon later found out that Josephine agreed to kiss Jackie Martell on the lips in order to convince him of her brother's innocence.

The boot moved away from Winley, rousing him out of

the daze.

"Ihr Zwei steigt auf der seite!" the leading soldier ordered and pointed up the hillside to the west. Then, pointing to the other hillside, "Und Ihr Zwei auf der anderen Seite."

Begrudgingly, the inferior soldiers obeyed, and the group spread out. Two moved up each hillside, difficult enough in the snow, while the remaining pair stayed true to the center of the ravine, and straight towards Larsen.

Larsen began thinking about Lucht and the other privates back at the barn. He thought about how quickly they dropped with just one bullet. He was a replacement with the regiment and hadn't seen any combat. After this morning, he firmly concluded that he didn't want to see anymore.

He began to shake as a foot landed inches away from his head. He closed his eyes hoping to elude his reality. Sweat had melted a portion of the concealing snow, and only the branches kept his head in disguise. Had the big man opened his eyes, he would have seen a pair of new American combat boots beneath the German field pants.

"Ich kann nicht weiter gehen. Der Schnee ist zu tief." A soldier standing on the hillside near Winley yelled back down to the others. It was obvious they couldn't climb the hill any further and were giving up.

Private Larsen squeezed his eyes harder and began to silently pray. He wasn't a church-going man, but the oration seemed appropriate for the circumstances, and he remembered a few from his childhood.

His body temperature rose in direct relation with his fear, and sweat from his face finished melting the shroud of snow. He prayed faster as a few branches slid off his head and exposed half his head above the snow pack.

"Dies ist verrückt. Wir kommen weider runter." The soldiers attempting to scale the other hillside began coming back down.

They slid on their sides in the soft powder.

The boot near Larsen's face lifted, almost scraping his nose which was now fully visible. Without noticing, the soldier moved towards the others coming down the hill.

Larsen sighed.

The search party met a few meters above the Private and heatedly discussed their options. The boys appeared and acted more like a football team losing a game than a group of soldiers. They resolved to return back to their platoon. Turning up the ravine, the former leader now trailed behind the others, quiet. Soon their voices disappeared into the fog.

Neither Winley nor Larsen dared move. They remained frozen and oblivious to the passing time. The sky brightened overhead as the snow stopped falling.

"Winnie, I'm getting cold," Larsen eventually reported as a matter of fact and without trepidation.

The storm had now completely faded, and Larsen's face bobbled on the snow like a decapitated puppet.

The Captain pulled himself out of the wet coffin and shook off the snow. He slid back to Larsen and reinitiated the task of extricating his ward. This time around proved quicker than the last.

Winley soon had "Big" John cleared down to his waist. Then, with a worried look on his face, he asked, "Can you feel your legs, Private?"

"I think so, why?"

"They are encased in ice."

Larsen looked down and saw that the snow had melted with the heat of his body and refroze in a fairly solid block of ice.

"Can you wiggle your toes?"

"Uh, huh."

"Thank God you are well-insulated," Winley muttered more to himself than to the Private.

"I did," Larsen replied

"Did what?"

"Thank God."

"Wonderful. Now, did He tell you how to get you out?" Winley removed a glove and scrubbed at the ice with his fingers. He realized it would take all night to scrape the man out. He sat down next to Larsen. "I think I will just have to leave you in there."

"No, please, don't leave me here." Larsen began struggling to push himself out of the snow.

"I am kidding, Larsen."

"Oh." He paused. "I didn't know you had a sense of humor."

"Wait. This might work." Winley stood and walked behind the Private. He unhitched his belt and lowered his drawers.

"Winney, what are you doing?" Larsen tried twisting around.

Captain Winley let a small sprinkle of piss fall around Larsen's back. The packed snow began to melt. "That will do it!"

"What? Tell me! What are you doing? It stinks."

"Urinate!"

"What?"

"I said, urinate, now."

"In my pants? What are you crazy?"

"Yes, start, uh, peeing, as you say. And yes, in your pants. As much as you can."

"I have been holding it since I woke up this morning. We've been sort of busy. But . . ."

"Do not speak, Private, loosen your bladder!"

"I can't. Not with you standing there."

"Larsen!"

"You promise you won't say anything to the guys when we get back?"

"Good grief, man, I promise."

"Okay." With a great sigh, Larsen relaxed his bladder and urinated with bravado.

Winley covered the rear, literally. A foul steam rose from around the extra-large green uniform protruding from the snow. The heat from the urine began melting the ice.

"Very well done, Private. Now, shake as much as you can. Try jumping, or kicking, whatever, just move!"

"I am. I am." Larsen squirmed like a deformed belly dancer, twisting and gyrating his large midsection

Dressing himself, Corporal Winley came around and squatted on the snow in front of Larsen and grabbed him around the chest. He arched his back and lunged with his thighs. It looked as if Winley was pulling a tree stump out of the ground with his bare hands.

Larsen pressed down with his arms, writhing his lower torso in the yellow, crusty snow. The warm fluid had melted just enough of the ice to allow some movement.

Then, with an audible thup, the Private popped from his ice box, and all two hundred and fifty pounds landed chest to chest on Winley's scant one hundred and forty.

"Thanks, Winnie."

This time Winley ignored the nickname. He could barely breathe. "Now, please get the hell off me. You reek."

Saints at War

The clouds momentarily thinned just enough to allow the low winter sun to infiltrate the small meadow. Light blindingly reflected off droplets of moisture in the air. The snow fell lighter and mostly blew in circles. The air had been quiet for less than an hour, dampened by the heavy moisture, but that would soon change.

Men, shivering in their icy bunkers, nervously fingered their weapons. A few relieved their anxiety with vulgar jokes. Walker appeared more on edge; his eyes scanned back and forth from behind the wire rims like he was watching a tennis match. For a moment, Gould thought that that the boy seemed older, his brow more furrowed, more aware. Then, Walker's back straightened.

Corporal Gould and the others now heard it, too.

The faint rumble of engines grew louder. Gould recognized the sound as the slightly higher pitch of smaller vehicles, probably jeeps or light armored, but no tanks. The greener soldiers assumed worse.

Gould remained hunkered down while the Lieutenant and

Walker peered over the edge of the foxhole, their eyes barely visible from under their white hoods. The sky quickly darkened, somehow in anticipation. The sun hid its eyes from the coming slaughter; the snow fell harder, now slanting in the increasing wind. The L.T. observed his men well-camouflaged in their holes. He silently thanked God for the usually irritating damp, foggy air. The Germans saw nothing.

The L.T. turned and displayed four fingers and waved them towards the east.

A band of nearly three hundred Germans, walking linearly four abreast, marched up the road. Their long Mauser rifles hung unready over their shoulders. Slush and ruts slowed their advance. A few yards behind the regiment trailed a handful of American jeeps draped with Nazi flags. There was no armored support.

Walker rested his M1 on a solitary rock, the barrel draped with his snow cape, and lined his sight on a German soldier.

"This Kraut's getting one hard between the eyes," he quietly remarked, glasses pressed against the site of his gun.

Just before firing, the Lieutenant gently pushed Walker's weapon down. "Wait," he whispered.

Walker didn't understand. The Krauts are sitting ducks, he thought to himself and squinted at his commander.

"Not yet," the L.T. mouthed without moving his eyes off the column. He motioned with his hand for the others to stay low.

As the first group of Germans passed in front of the hole, he saw the target. Just behind the column and before the jeeps, three officers marched with maps, binoculars and a radioman. He silently signaled to Walker. Walker silently understood.

The young soldier again lifted his rifle and quietly placed it on the rock. He aimed at one of the officers.

"Passuaf!" a German officer yelled and pointed directly at Walker's M1.

The gray morning disintegrated.

Walker fired and hit the officer in the chest, dropping him instantly. He took aim again and a second officer fell.

Dark slivers randomly popped up from every foxhole. Small flashes and puffs of smoke dissolved into the fog and snow. The dark threads then disappeared to reload and emerge again.

The odds were impossible: hundreds of Germans versus a mere score or two of Americans. The young platoon from the 99th Division, however, seemed not to notice.

Walker fired off his remaining six rounds. Then, amid the onslaught he sped across the road and leaped into the Colonel's stranded jeep. He took control of the .50-caliber M2 mounted on a pole where the passenger seat should have been. He felt a guilty gratitude for the accident the night before.

The soldier that had brought the radio shadowed Walker, artillery rounds draped around his neck, over his shoulder and on his arm. He seemed to move with ease despite the weight of his cargo.

The jeep lay almost on its driver's side. Walker had to torque the gun on its joint as much as possible to shoot through the door opening, which provided more than adequate protection from incoming rounds.

Fumbling, the German infantry scattered and dropped to the prone position, their Mausers blazing aimlessly.

"Under fire, send artillery!" the Lieutenant screamed into the handset.

The single word "Hold!" barely vibrated back through the earphone's speaker before

Crack!

the handset shattered in his hands. Fluidly, the L.T. threw the broken radio behind him, grabbed his weapon and began firing. His shoulder wound throbbed but didn't weaken his aim or his concentration.

"Walker, left flank!" the L.T. yelled as loud as he could over the rattle of gunfire.

Walker spun around, his body barely remaining in the jeep; his spectacles never slipped. On the road's edge, three Germans attempted to set up an MG42 machine gun on top of a dead American soldier, already half buried. Walker's M2 roared in reply.

Seconds later the infiltrators lay in a pool of blood, staining the snow a deep red and mixing with the sludge beneath.

The others, protected by foxholes, held the German column in the middle of the road, literally stuck in mud. With their backs protected, the Allies resolutely pounded the Wehrmacht infantry.

The "acquired" jeeps, bringing up the rear, careened and slid off the rollbahnen, slamming into the thick clump of bodies stalled in the clearing. The vehicles turned their occupants onto the bank of the road. The following trucks stamped those bodies into the snow, some never to get back up. Soon a massive entanglement of metal and man blocked the entire width of road.

Officers shouted orders but few seemed to understand, or failed to follow. The German soldiers drifted around like the falling snow, and Walker kept dropping the wet flakes to the ground.

Corporal Gould remained in the foxhole and fought his own battle as he anticipated the call for medic, which always followed the first gunshots. He listened to the clatter above his head.

The Allied automatics sounded in full rhythm. Gould found the sounds almost hypnotic, harmonious. But experience taught him what was really happening above his head. He had seen these engagements countless times before; he had seen enough.

Any symphony the sounds afforded disappeared in a bloody cacophony.

He had personally witnessed how automatiçs wrecked the human body. Multiple rounds ripped through flesh, tearing and shredding organs and tissue until little remained for a medic. Tensing with his thoughts, Gould clung to his duffle of medical supplies and slowly peered over the edge of the hole.

In slow motion, he watched bullets criss-crossing the road, leaving dark, thread-like trails of smoke impressed on the fog. Lips mouthed words he didn't understand. A frenzied stampede of gray and white camouflage uniforms darted from side to side, searching for refuge. In the foreground, a grenade victim hobbled on one leg towards what was left of his Kampfgruppe.

With few options, the living piled the bodies of the dead like sacks of sand to absorb the spray from the automatics. Hundreds of rounds stopped short of their intended targets, each with a splatter of blood and frayed cloth. The snow darkened in a soup of dirt, blood and bodies until nothing clean remained. Many attempted to turn back, but the clog of forwarding troops prevented any retreat; others fled into the woods. Most never accomplished their objective in either direction.

The German column kept advancing. Hundreds of men marched right into the middle of a slaughter, as if dazed or blinded. The Allies fired not at individuals but at a solid wall of men. One row tumbled after another, like timber hewn down by swift chainsaws. Still they marched on. Gould couldn't decide if it was by command or from stupidity. To him either answer proved a senseless waste of life. But what else was new with this war.

Corporal Gould thought the scene redundant. Whether on sand, snow or in a French hay field, the movie played-and ended-the same: loss.

Sitting back down, Stephen saw Madeleine in his mind but felt the tightness of bereavement in his chest. He held onto his bag.

For an hour, the rattle of small artillery echoed off the forest wall without pause. Some of the Lieutenant's men crawled on all fours from their protected positions to steal ammunition, rifles, grenades, even clothing. However, their scavenging was methodical, at opportune moments, and seemingly with experience.

Walker spent the .50-caliber rounds effectively. Hundreds of German infantry fell. The bodies formed mounds for almost two hundred yards of road.

Suddenly, the L.T. flew from his cover and sprinted across the road.

A lone schütze had crawled past and taken position behind a fallen timber not twenty-five feet from the fallen jeep. He conspicuously unscrewed the cap near the handle of a steel stick grenade. The German infantry often used the dreaded StiGr39 with a seven-ounce TNT charge as antitank mortar. It contained more than enough explosive power to obliterate Walker's metal cocoon.

With each stride, the Lieutenant's boots sank deeper into the sludge. He picked his knees up like a seasoned sprinter and continued his drive.

Gould stared from the foxhole. A bit of originality amid the cliché, he thought.

The enemy had just pulled the porcelain bead attached to a silk cord. This started the four-and-one-half second delay.

Walker continued to target the line while the radioman fed rounds into the chamber, neither realizing the danger from behind.

While eyeing the small, can-like charge on top of the stick

handle, the L.T. made his final lunge at his troops.

The canister blazed through the air, on a solid trajectory of smoke and light to its target.

Gould, still in the foxhole, raised his rifle and took steady aim.

The officer's right foot landed on the rear jeep tire, just behind the gunner. His left shoulder tackled the radioman and his right arm clothes-lined Walker. Thrusting his body with his legs, the boss catapulted his human projectiles nearly ten feet off the side of the jeep.

The mortar landed in the driver's seat just as the threesome landed face first in the snow. Instinctively, Walker stood, fisted the snow capes of the other two and charged further away from ground zero. Six legs then spun frantically in the slush without much traction but moving forward.

Gould fired his weapon.

The incoming mortar blew. The damp air reflected the red and white flash. A ball of smoke expanded and swallowed the entire jeep. Suddenly, glass, rubber and contorted metal exploded from the epicenter like a starburst firework. The boom shook snow off the limbs of pine trees for fifty yards. The other gunfire paused in the recoil.

As the debris landed over the entire meadow, Walker, the L.T. and the radioman were already heading back to their foxhole, unharmed.

Behind the jeep, blood streamed from underneath the lone German's right eye, still open and fixed on the jeep. Gould's bullet, the first he had shot since St.-Lô, found its way just underneath the man's helmet.

Peace Outside Elsenborn

Captain Winley wiped his forehead with his handkerchief as the two men exited the woods. He had meticulously kept the white cloth clean but noticed that it was beginning to yellow. There were also a few frays in the blue stitching.

The afternoon passed rapidly, and the storm had faded. Unfortunately, with the clearing sky came colder temperatures, and both Winley and Larsen were soaked through. They cared less about the Germans and more about finding some shelter in which to dry out.

They made better progress as they moved off the ridge. Even Larsen quickened his pace to the point of jogging. Winley kept his compass in hand and their direction at south. The forest, once thick with cedars and firs, evolved into more hospitable terrain. Aspens and oak now dotted the flatter slopes.

They saw short, stone walls surrounding a multitude of pastures, creating a patchwork of neatly arranged squares until completely dominating the landscape. Each plot was studded with a farmhouse, stable or barn that was lit like a tiny star in a darkening sky.

Emerging from the forest felt like breathing new air. More than fog had lifted from their midst. The gray clouds sped by, retreating from the setting sun. As they turned toward the west, the orange glow from the sun briefly warmed their faces. No sound escaped the freshly fallen powder. For the moment, peace reigned in the valley near Elsenborn.

"We had better keep moving," Winley noted, looking down at his compass in the fading light.

"Let's check out one of the homes down there. Maybe they'd let us dry off. My clothes are beginning to freeze up on me." Larsen spoke with a reanimation.

"Do not forget what is happening. The Germans already have one day's advantage. I only hope the storm delayed their plans to break through." Winley lifted his head. "That road should lead us straight to Elsenborn."

"And our regiment. Let's go. Anything is better than being up on that ridge." Larsen took a deep breath and started across the field ahead of Winley.

They marched in solitude across a few farms. Winley felt inside his overcoat. The thick wad of maps and papers was still there. The temptation to leave them behind percolated inside his head. The Captain had succeeded in avoiding any real responsibility in the army, using it as an escape and nothing more. But by fate or ill fortune, he now carried in his coat pocket probably the most important piece of information at this juncture in the war. The Germans were headed to the Meuse River to retake Europe. Unless he could get this information to Allied Command, they might make it.

Winley and Larsen ran across quiet fields like two evening sentinels, neither realizing that they could have been target practice for a sniper's Mauser. In the last minutes of daylight, they arrived, in horror, at the road to Elsenborn.

Larsen stopped first with Winley nearly colliding from behind. Then Winley noticed it as well. The road was heavily rutted with tank tracks. Thousands of footprints lay everywhere. Every few yards, tire marks broke off from the road and headed to farms, the woods or elsewhere. The tracks led west, to Elsenborn.

Larsen turned around, shocked pallor on his face from the realization. "Winnie, I think we're behind enemy lines."

Neither man spoke for what seemed like hours. They simply stared at the road in disbelief. The Germans had already pushed through and probably taken Elsenborn. Hitler was marching to the Meuse, and quickly.

"What do we do?" Larsen broke the silence.

"We cannot press forward. That is clear. I surmise that our best option is to go south and try to meet up another regiment. We will have to stay off the roads. With fortune, someone will have held their position. We will find a radio and all will turn out well."

Larsen didn't buy what his Captain was selling.

Winley looked at Larsen's face. "But for now, I suggest we proceed with your initial proposal of finding a warm place to dry off." With a slightly lighter tone Winley added, "And getting away from this road."

"Amen to that, sir."

Winley surveyed the area as best as he could in the waning light. There was nothing to be seen or heard. The tracks followed the road west for a few hundred meters and then around a small hill. He could see nothing beyond that.

At the far edge of the clearing, near the ridge they had just descended, a small, dark farmhouse stood in contrast to the others with lights. They headed towards it. Either no one noticed or no one cared that two Americans were walking through their fields.

When they arrived, the home was apparently empty but not abandoned. Larsen shouldered his way through the bolted door, breaking the hinges clean off the posts, with mixed emotion. He hated destroying someone's home, but he desperately wanted to get out of his clothes.

They found the building hastily deserted. It was sparse, but clean. A bundle of wood was stacked next to the cold stove, and a few dishes were piled in the sink. There was no running water but a bucket full of melted snow sat next to a large wash basin. Larsen's eyes bulged in relief. Immediately, he started undressing.

"Relax, Private. Let me investigate the rest of the house before you lower your drawers. And see if you can repair the door first." Winley began to look around. There was only one other room, a parlor, really, with one bed, two soft chairs and a fireplace. A second door led to the outhouse. Wool blankets were heaped at the foot of the bed. Wood shutters covered the only window. Winley shook his head. Of all the luck, he muttered.

"What's that?" Larsen yelled from the kitchen.

"I cannot believe our luck."

"It ain't luck, sir. I prayed for it." Larsen had accomplished setting the door back into its frame, a perfect fit, and was undressing.

"Here, take the blankets. I would rather that I not see you disrobed. I found matches near the fireplace. If we keep the fire small, I do not believe anyone should notice from outside. We are situated far from the road. Sleep will occur in two hour shifts. I will take the first watch. We should leave before daylight in order to cross the road in the dark."

Before Winley had finished speaking, "Big" Larsen had completely undressed and stood like a St. Bernard wrapped in a brown blanket.

Winley looked on in mild humor and shook his head as he

removed the handkerchief from his pocket. "You had better hope that we are not rushed out of here, or you will be one cold soldier."

"I don't care, I just wanna be warm now. It'll be the first time in over a month that I'll have dry clothes." Larsen carried his wet socks and gloves and placed them on the hearth. He returned to the kitchen to finish rinsing through his soiled trousers and army-issued long johns.

Winley entered the small kitchen and removed his socks. He held the white handkerchief in his hand.

"I'll do that for you, sir." Larsen took the clothes and made no comment about the piece of silk cloth that looked like women's underwear.

Winley appreciated the reverence. Then, he began relating a story. "Awhile ago, before you arrived, when the regiment was outside Paris, the soldier had a rather severe case of dysentery. We had been stuck in this foxhole for days, and he was so scared to leave that he released right in his drawers. The smell was fouler than anything you can imagine."

"I don't know about that. After today, I can imagine a lot of foul smelling stuff," Larsen replied, squeezing ice cold but clean water out of his clothing.

"Rather than remain in his soiled uniform, he took his under-garments off and cut out the stain with his bayonet. The ordeal required hours. I was amazed at all the trouble he went through rather than leave the foxhole." Winley sat down on the bed.

"I don't know, sir. Fear makes a guy do a lot of stupid stuff."

"I suppose you're right, John."

A White Flag

"We'll have to pick the rest of the Krauts off one-by-one," proclaimed Walker as he landed next to Gould in the foxhole. "You still here?"

"I'm amazed, not one cry for medic," Gould replied. He said nothing about his marksmanship. "What's that?" Gould noticed a small red spot on Walker's neck. "Let me take a look."

"We didn't let 'em set up. They were helpless." Walker tried to brush the Medic off. Turning toward his commander, "Any word from H.Q. on backup?" he asked.

The Lieutenant, pressing his back against a cold, dirt wall, picked up his weapon. As he crouched to replace his clip, he nodded to the far side of the foxhole.

Walker turned and recognized the remains of the radio. "Guess not."

"Looks like a shard of metal just scraped your neck. You're lucky. Any deeper and it would have sliced more than skin."

Walker rubbed the wound. "Feels like a mosquito bite."

"Good work out there, Walk." The L.T.'s fingers nimbly

manipulated a full cartridge into his rifle. "I'm proud of you boys."

"Boys? Look who's talking," Walker quipped.

They looked at each other and smiled. Their eyes spoke what their mouths wouldn't. Nothing else remained to be said. It was the same with most soldiers during war. Medics, however, always worked independently, alone. They didn't belong to platoons-they were attached to them, like armament. Gould preferred it that way.

Gould listened to the gunfire taper off until only a few random pops echoed through the air.

The Americans remained quiet in their foxholes while the Germans began forming a line at the east end of the clearing.

"That's got to be at least a full battalion," Walker commented, still breathing heavy and still wearing his glasses, despite the exploits that morning.

The radioman broke in, "This can't last. We can't keep this up forever. I'm near out of ammo." He delivered these statements not out of despair or fear, but rather of fact.

"H.Q. knows what's going on. Someone will have to be here soon. We've got position. We'll hold." The Lieutenant spoke without any vocal quiver but knew inside that help would come too late, if at all. "How're we doing on casualties?"

"No deaths as far as I know, but everyone's down in the holes. Hard to tell." Walker began counting his clips.

"How's your ammo?"

"I've got a couple of clips. I doubt anyone's got much more considering the amount we've sprayed on the damn Krauts. They're like flies."

"The story was the same earlier this morning. I swear I'm having déjà vu," interrupted Gould, uncharacteristically. "They've obviously started a major offensive." Gould began to see a crack in Walker; his youth started to emerge again.

"I thought we'd know something if they tried something this massive." Walker looked toward his commander.

"Help will be here soon." The L.T. sensed Walker's growing trepidation. "Why don't you take any man who wants to go and get out while it's still quiet. Lanzerath is not far. Even in the snow, you could easily reach it in less than an hour."

Gould straightened up.

"What about you?" Walker asked.

"I've got my orders."

"Then I've got mine."

Gould listened with interest but realized it would probably be suicide to leave on his own. Besides, despite his increasing lack of faith, he was not a coward. He sat motionless and said nothing.

Walker turned to Gould and asked, "What time is it? I lost my watch a few days ago."

"Don't know. Mine broke this morning."

By 1500 hours on December 16, hundreds of German bodies littered the road to Lanzerath. Yet only one American of the Lieutenant's regiment had been killed. The men had held the road for almost an entire day and inflicted a casualty rate of nearly fifty percent. History would remember them as heroic despite their inexperience in combat. Other platoons within the fledgling 99th Infantry Division had performed similarly that day-seriously, yet unknowingly, disrupting Hitler's plans.

Corporal Gould hopped from hole to hole as much to illustrate his confidence as to do his job. To his shock, most soldiers required only minor attention. When he returned, Walker held his rifle with its last clip perched on the same rock that provided the stability for his first shots earlier that morning.

It won't end as it began, Gould thought to himself.

"They're building forces, boss." Walker kept the informality with his commander. "The Krauts have got a bunch of MGs ready. And I can make out a couple of Tigers coming down the road."

Walker squinted through his dirty but trusty spectacles while a few shots rattled off between the newly-formed front line.

"Correction. Make that a bunch of Tigers. Boss, what do we do?"

The Lieutenant thought about the morning. In just a matter of hours he would turn twenty-one. The realization that he probably wouldn't see his birthday tightened the muscles in his face. He had no wife or children, nor any attachment to his parents. His only real relationships formed among the men with whom he served. He wasn't ready to die, however. Just before speaking, he thought to himself that there was only so much a man could hold inside.

"We surrender."

Gunderson and Deacon

The morning repeated itself throughout the Belgian Ardennes forest. The German offensive was swift and, initially, effective. From Monschau to Bastogne, multiple Panzer-Armee groups forged their way towards the Meuse River. While some Allied regiments disappeared in death, retreat or capture, others passed the day completely unaware.

"Café, monsieur?" Marie St. Clair asked a quiet, unassuming soldier sitting alone at a corner table. She tilted her head downward to look the boy in the face.

"No, thank you," he whispered as he raised his head.

Something touched the woman by what she saw. His blue eyes sank deep in whirlpools of dark rings, and the creases at the corners extended further than expected for a man of twenty-four. Each facial muscle seemed to pull outward, taught, stretching his mouth thin and dissolving any attempted smile. The man didn't appear scared, as she had observed on the faces of many young soldiers that came through her small town. He gave the impression of working on a complex problem that demanded too much from his faculties, and for far too long.

She removed a rare cookie wrapped in wax paper from her pocket and placed it in front of the soldier. Without waiting for acknowledgment, Marie tended to her other customers. She had been serving coffee at the small café in Baugnez since she was old enough to carry a tray. Now, she was its proprietor. The few remaining residents in town met, drank coffee and discussed the latest war news daily at the St. Clair café.

Outside, armored vehicles filed past on snow-packed roads en route to Malmédy or St. Vith. The locals had grown accustomed to the constant rumble of tanks and artillery passing through the small village. So small in fact that Baugnez made the maps only as the crossroads to other, much larger towns.

Whether German, American, British, or Canadian, all the armies had been through Baugnez at some period of the war, rarely stopping for more than a quick glance at a road map or a hot cup of java. And quietly thriving on the corner of these crossroads sat the St. Clair Café.

"Banjur, Marie." Sergeant Gordon Gunderson strolled through the huge, arched doorway to the café. Despite his attempts to learn French, his accent was far from perfect.

"Bonjour, monsieur. Please sit," Marie giggled. Her English wasn't much better than his French. She and the Sergeant had been innocently flirting since he arrived with Deacon the day before. She felt comforted by the rare consistency in her military patrons.

"A cáfe, si vus ples."

Marie smiled again and slid around the serving bar for a tray of cups and an old, army-issued, tin coffee pot. Her beautiful porcelain sets had been looted early on in the war. The pot had been a gift from a Brigadier General, so her story went. But everyone knew the Americans always proved more generous with supplies than the Germans.

Gunderson pulled a chair from a nearby table and moved it over to the corner. "Hey, Deac. How ya doing?"

"Fine." Deac stared at the table and gently touched the ball of dough made from oatmeal and molasses.

Gunderson thought not to press his friend further. He understood that everyday for the last week had been touch and go with the Corporal.

"Uh, le voila, monsieur." Marie placed a cup on the table and skillfully poured it full of coffee. Faint steam and an acrid scent rose from the hot black liquid.

"Please, sit with us, Marie. I know my buddy Deac here and I could both use the companionship of a beautiful woman. Don't let that timid nature of his fool you. He's really a tiger." Gunderson winked with hyperbole.

Marie couldn't translate every word, but she understood the meaning. Her smile brightened. "J'ai d'autres clients," she replied and pointed to her other customers around the large hall.

A handful of soldiers and numerous residents dipped cold and stale bread into their coffees and conversed amicably. In better times, there would have been pastries, croissants, jelly rolls, varieties of rustic breads made with dill and oregano and rosemary, and even torts aside their café. Even chocolate, melted and creamed with fresh dairy, would have been posted on the menu.

The commodious, square room sported dark brown brick and wood plank flooring. Dried mud swirled in random patterns around the tables and bar. Small, round wooden tables, cut from old barn doors, rested on wrought-iron pedestals. The two windows, on either side of the arched doorway, glass shattered and removed, framed a constantly moving picture of the world outside the café.

In the foreground, jeeps, tanks and soldiers, all clad in dull green, paraded back and forth, seemingly forever, like ducks lost on a pond. Behind the convoys a thick grove of aspens, tall and slender like Marie, changed their colors with the seasons but only by nature's command.

Marie spent her days gazing out the window, wondering if the rest of the world moved in the same, monotonous ways, the same year after year. Occasionally, she watched her childhood through the windows, the games she played in the streets with her friends. She took comfort in knowing that every spring the scents of wet grass and lavender permeated the grove under a canopy of green foliage. The smells would return, she always reminded herself. No war could take them away; no matter who won.

"Hey, Deac," Gunderson whispered.

"Yeah." The soldier looked up at his Sergeant.

"You worried?"

"Not really."

"I spoke to the C.O. We can catch our ride to St. Vith tomorrow afternoon. When we get there, things will be easier. I swear." Gunderson attempted to ease his companion's thoughts.

Deac didn't reply to the proposed itinerary; he merely sighed and looked back down at the table top and toyed with the cookie.

"Whatta ya hear from your wife?"

"I haven't gotten any letters since we left. But she . . ."

Gunderson waited for his friend to finish. "But?"

"No, nothing. She's great." An image of a dead woman flashed in his mind. Deac's face pulled tighter.

"What? Deac, it's okay. Maybe it'll help to talk about it." Gunderson noticed the furrows on Deac's brow deepen.

"I just saw her again."

"The same one?

"Yeah. The one from Thurs . . ." Deac stopped short and paused. His right arm, his shooting arm, started to shake; he accidentally dropped the cookie to the floor.

Gunderson realized his mistake in pursuing this line of conversation and seized the break to change topics. "Tell me about your farm."

As he reached down to pick up the cookie, Deac visualized the expanse of orchards his family owned in northern Arizona. His chest relaxed, and his breathing slowed. The air seemed lighter now, maybe even warmer. He looked around the café and noticed, for the first time, the others engaged in jovial banter. Deac smiled. He looked at Marie. She was too slender, and by tying her long, dark hair at the back of her head, she appeared bony in the face, and her very delicate features couldn't compensate for the worn skin. Certainly, she was younger than she now appeared. Perhaps an easier life would have produced a much different version of the woman who now owned the café.

Marie wore a brown, wool smock, gathered into deep pleats at her thin waist and held by a black belt. The lacing on her black boots disappeared far underneath the skirt hem. Over her blouse a green, GI issue waist coat with the insignia torn off hung on her wire shoulders. Her small, freckled hands barely snuck out from the cuffs, her fingernails cropped short and unpolished.

What her appearance lacked in attractiveness, her smile and wit compensated for. Marie moved easily among the men that frequented her establishment. They spoke openly with her, and she returned the gesture. Many even sought her advice. She occasionally smoked a cigar and often played cards with them. She would have made a fine soldier, Deac thought as he remembered his Sergeant's question.

"Most of the work would be done by now. Apples were picked in August, mostly johnnies and goldens; most of the honey during the fall. My father may be taking my younger brothers hunting, if the weather isn't too bad. The elk and deer will be coming down from the mountains. It'd be a good time for a four point." Deac's conversation smoothed.

"A four what?"

"A buck."

"A dollar?"

"A male deer, you fool!" Deac intentionally held back a smile.

"Oh. Is your farm like the ones around here?" Gunderson asked, feigning ignorance.

Deac actually laughed out loud, his first hint of levity since the pair had left Elsenborn almost a week ago. "Not at all," he replied. "Don't you know anything about the West? This place is a tropical rain forest compared to where I grew up."

"That much of a desert, huh." Gunderson felt a warmth as he watched his friend forget his nightmares.

"A mountain desert, yeah. Our farm is on the benches of the mountainside. But it's really dry most of the year. The winter snow pack melts and we irrigate the orchards from streams that flow out of the canyons. If we didn't, we'd never make it through the summer."

"Okay. The bee thing. I don't get it. Why would anyone actually want to keep bees around?"

"You city boy. You figure it out." Deac had finally dismissed the images that plagued his head.

"You have a honey fetish. I don't know. I'm from New York A bee means an allergy attack to me. But, to be honest, I don't think I've ever really seen one. Does the sting hurt?"

"No. Not really. You really don't know why we keep bees? I mean, the honey's nice. But that's not the reason we keep 'em."

"I really don't know."

Before Deac could answer, a local man yelled out "they're coming" in English. Both Gunderson and Deac turned their attention to an elderly Belgian who had just come in through the archway, trailing after an American officer.

"Yes, Yes. I know. They are coming." The officer tried to shake the old man, obviously irritated.

The man went by the name Luc Gavrote. He wore simple farm clothes, and an old felt hat shadowed a heavily wrinkled face and large, pimple-marked nose. Luc had the reputation in town of missing a few cards from his mental deck; to the soldiers he was the local idiot.

"Luc, Il ne faut pas deranger des clients!" Marie said sternly, her smile gone and trying to detach Luc from the officer.

"They are coming." Luc waved his fingers and left.

The patrons went back to their coffee and conversations. Marie went about business.

"Hey, Sarge. Do you think there's any truth to the rumors?" Deac asked, his tone quickly returning to serious.

"Brass doesn't seem to think so. They would have passed on any credible information. Hitler would be foolish to begin an offensive on the west. He's getting his butt kicked in the east, and I doubt he's got anything left to attack with. He can't retake Europe." Then, trying to lighten the mood, Gunderson shot out, "Besides, me and you are here, buddy. Hitler wouldn't dare touch us. Your aim and my good looks. Boy, we're unstoppable!"

Sergeant Gunderson held out his hand for the young corporal to slap. Deac hesitantly complied and broke a grin.

The Sergeant and Corporal Nathan "Deac" Greer left their company in Elsenborn a few days earlier to rendezvous with a battalion from the 285th field artillery on their way to St. Vith where an army medical facility was located. Along the route, they had heard locals gossiping about a new German invasion. After decades of war, the older locals had become paranoid about the Germans coming back.

"What about your farm?" Deacon suddenly inquired, as if

subconsciously altering his thought patterns.

"My farm?" Gunderson snapped. "What farm? I grew up in a row house with paved streets. I could spit on my neighbor's house from my bedroom window. Usually did, too. Fifty families on one city block. Stickball in the streets, hot as hell summers. Ah, Queens, the best damn borough in New York."

"We've got burrows, too."

"You're kidding. I didn't know that. I thought you had to ride your horse for an entire day to see another farmer."

"Very funny. Yeah, we've got lots of burrows. Possum burrows, beaver burrows, ground hog burrows, even rat burrows."

"Enough already. I get it. Now who's being the wise guy."

Deac stared at the cookie in his hand, blew some dirt off and broke it in half.

"Here, it's not everyday ya see one of these." He handed the bigger half to Sergeant Gunderson.

"Thanks, Deac." Gunderson popped the whole piece in his mouth and took a long drink from his cup. He closed his eyes, sat back and allowed the sweet warmth to fill his body. Then, with a deep breath and a shudder, he exclaimed, "Wow, I can't think of the last time I had anything with that kind of sugar."

"That's 'cause you give all your lemonade packets to me." Deac rolled his piece of balled molasses like a street magician's coin in and out of his fingers.

"Lemonade?" Then a little louder Gunderson repeated, "Lemonade? That stuff is nothing but the citric acid from lemons pulverized to dirt. I swear they invented sugar specifically to try and sweeten that stuff. You can have it. Just give me my morning cup of joe and a cigarette, and I'm as bright as the Chrysler Building."

"Healthy breakfast, Gordon," Deac replied with a hint of sarcasm. He rarely called the Sergeant by his first name and only did so in private. "Here, you can have this half as well."

"Don't be stupid, Deac. Eat it. You need it. Hell, you deserve it."

"Sugar's not my thing. Take it. Besides, I've got all that sweet lemonade to drink when we get to St. Vith." Deac was beginning to accept the purpose of their detour from combat.

"Thanks, buddy."

Gunderson finished the cookie and his coffee. They prepared to leave. "Mercy, Marie!" Gunderson yelled as he left a few coins on the table.

Marie smiled back and shook her head.

Gunderson and Deac left the St. Clair café and turned north. On the corner, a sign read: Malémdy, 3km. The day had been heavily overcast, and the snow was just beginning to fall. It appeared as if it would soon worsen. Deac pulled at the collar of his overcoat, tightening it around his neck. The temperature was falling; it would soon dip below freezing and the roads would ice over. They both heard faint booms from the east.

"More outgoing mail," Gunderson stated, half to reassure himself as much as Deac. In truth, he wasn't sure.

They walked along the side of what was barely discernible as a road. The pavement had been torn by years of tank tracks until all that remained disappeared in the wet earth. Snow had been plowed to the shoulders, almost three feet deep, by military vehicles leaving muddy grooves covered by freshly fallen snow. To Gunderson, it appeared like a bowl of chocolate ice cream dusted with powdered sugar.

An M3 half truck, overloaded with soldiers rushed past, splashing the brown mess just behind the pair. The men in back huddled close to keep warm, with rifles to their sides and despair on their faces. They wouldn't know where they were going until they got there. Then, they would move on to somewhere else.

"Thanks, guys." Gunderson waved and glanced down at his

coat to inspect the damage.

Deac hardly noticed the near miss, looking only at his feet in the mud.

They headed to the edge of town, where the 291st Engineer Battalion had sent up a small camp headquarters, barely visible now. Most of the vehicles had been covered by white camouflage netting while the white tents in uniform rows appeared as nothing more than snow drifts. A few men stood outside and smoked.

Feeling his chest tighten, Deac stuffed his hand into his pocket and grasped a small book. His breathing relaxed. He pulled the book from his pocket and removed a small photograph wedged flat inside the front cover. The image measured only a couple of square inches, and was heavily worn at the edges and fading. But, to Corporal Greer, it was as precious as any famous portrait that hung in a museum.

Deac's wife had been his high school sweetheart, something he didn't tell the other soldiers. He gently placed the picture back in the book and in his breast pocket, the proximity of being close to his heart served as more than a metaphor.

"God willing, you'll be back at home before that photograph wears out."

"Amen to that."

Gunderson, while only a few years older and without any sons of his own, felt a strong paternal bond developing for his friend. He put his hand on Deac's shoulder and gently squeezed. Deac lifted his head and smiled.

The Colonel

Corporal Stephen Gould intentionally lagged behind the others from his foxhole. He stayed back to remove his snow cape and reveal the white arm band with red cross; his medical bag and medic's helmet were prominently displayed as well. Then he fell in line with the Lieutenant and the other prisoners.

Just over one hundred American soldiers, most captured near Losheim earlier that morning and the rest from the Lieutenant's regiment, solemnly marched toward the end of day.

A fresh layer of snow white-washed the meadow, innocently covering the stains of the morning. Behind them, bodies became nothing more than wrinkles in a blanket thrown lazily on a forest lawn. The setting sun cast a warm blend of pinks and oranges across the sky, reflecting off the low clouds, a friendly hearth burning in the horizon.

The evergreens, needles sparkling with the freezing moisture, glowed like tiny candles in a field of Christmas trees. In the distance, winter shadows played their evening games, running from the light in long stretches. It appeared to the

Lieutenant like one of the Norman Rockwell paintings he had seen growing up.

That pastoral scene, however, faded with the evening. Bulbs flickered and died; the shadows swelled and consumed the light. Nighttime doused the fire. For the men staggering along this lonely roadside, thoughts of the coming holiday froze in the cold, dark air. He didn't know why, but the Lieutenant couldn't stop thinking about the previous night and the dinner he had with that arrogant Colonel.

A jeep slid into the Lieutenant's camp around suppertime. The jeep had a .50-caliber M2 mounted in front but no one behind the gun. They entered from the west and were trying to make it to Losheim before dark, but the weather conditions had held them up.

The jeep sped half on and half off the road, the left tire stuck in the wrong rut. Seeing the camp straight ahead of him, the soldier behind the wheel tried to steer left. The jeep began to skid, and the driver, being from Florida, overcorrected the vehicle, spinning it to the right. The jeep careened, plowing the snow in its path, and rolled onto its side. The passengers bailed out like rookie paratroopers. With the exposed tires still spinning, the driver roared out a list of obscenities.

"Think he's mad?" Walker rhetorically asked his boss. He and his Lieutenant had witnessed the entire spectacle from a safe vantage point.

"Yep." The L.T. smiled with diversion. "Think we should go over and help?"

"Nah, it's too cold. Let's eat."

"Come on, Walker. Could be fun. I think that one's a colonel." The Lieutenant pointed to one of the ejected soldiers.

Others in the regiment now stood and laughed-ironically-at the overturned jeep.

The Lieutenant and Walker made their way across the sludge to the castaways. The driver, a sergeant, cussed in a heavy southern accent and kicked the hood with his boot. A private sat dazed while the Colonel brushed snow from his collar.

"Anything we can help with, sir?" The Lieutenant addressed the superior officer.

"Get me a new driver." He looked over at the Sergeant who stuffed his hands in his pockets and looked embarrassed. "Sergeant, are you going to flip this thing back over before midnight?"

"Ain't gonna do no good. It's got a broke axle. See." He pointed near the tire that had finally stopped its rotation.

With reserved anger, the Colonel simply replied, "Great," and turned back to the Lieutenant. "Well, if you have any food, I'm hungry. We should have been in Losheim an hour ago."

"Absolutely, Colonel. We were just about cut through some frozen rations. You're more than welcome to join us." The Lieutenant's formality was unusual but easy.

Turning to the bewildered Private, the Colonel ordered, "Steadman, collect the ammo and gear and put it back in, well, by the. . . . Oh hell, put it anywhere. But bring my bag here."

Obediently, the Private scrambled over the ten yards of debris that had been ejected from the jeep during its demise. He collected boxes of ammunitions and artillery, some weapons, field bags and a small medical kit.

"You're packing a ton of heat, Colonel," Walker exclaimed, looking around the jeep's carcass. His boss scowled.

"I suppose they needed the ammo. It was already in the jeep. I'm Colonel Ridgeway." He extended his right hand.

The Lieutenant introduced himself and Walker, who felt like a little kid just invited to hang out with his older brother. They led Ridgeway back to their foxhole.

"What, not even any tents?"

"Not this close to the front. Besides, the quartermaster hasn't even made it yet with our bedrolls. The roads are terrible. But, I guess you know that." The L.T. and the Colonel shared a quick laugh. Walker bounced ahead.

"What about the night? How do your survive? I don't see any fires."

"We sleep like dogs on canvas half tents. The men are used to it."

Ridgeway surveyed the camp. The men appeared jovial and content, squatting like gophers in a series of holes about ten feet off the road. He wondered how long it took them to dig through the frozen ground. The Colonel had been assigned mostly office duties well behind the lines, in the rear echelons of the war. He had never paid attention to soldiers living in conditions like that.

Men of the Second World War disappeared into the earth at night, sometimes close enough to the enemy to eavesdrop on its conversations or hear a blown nose. No one dared leave the sanctity of his hole; any movement could result in a quick death.

The foxholes of most divisions spread over hundreds of yards and were occupied by only two or three soldiers each. Gone were the continuous trenches of the First World War. Men along the German line in 1944 spent their nights in relative isolation, alone in their hand-dug coffins rather than with their comrades in arms.

When luck didn't allow commandeering an abandoned German foxhole, digging one in the Ardennes became its own major offensive. Tree roots, frozen ground and rocks rendered entrenching shovels almost useless. But, with incredible determination, they built rectangular holes up to six feet long, five feet deep and wide enough for one man to get around another. When available, logs, branches and soil were used as camouflage.

If weather and fighting permitted, the quartermaster would jeep-in bedrolls to the front line. The rolls consisted of half of a canvas pup tent and a couple of wool blankets. Two men would sleep huddled under the blankets while the third kept watch. A good night's rest came in discontinuous bouts of twenty minutes of sleep. Fear, cold and one's thoughts prevented anything more. During the Belgian winter, nights lasted up to sixteen hours and temperatures often dropped below zero degrees Fahrenheit. Most times, men couldn't decide which caused more mental agony, the shelling or the dead quiet.

Hot food rarely made it to the front lines. A cook with marmite cans appeared as frequently, and as welcomed, as Christmas day. Lining up for hot chow proved an expensive lesson on the front; German 88s traveled so fast that soldiers would never hear the incoming, and some entire companies were destroyed with their forks still in hand. Most soldiers sat on the frozen dirt and ate cold C rations.

The L.T and Walker shared their rations that night with Colonel Ridgeway. The combat rations included biscuits, premixed cereal, candy-coated peanuts, soluble coffee, lemon powder, sugar, cocoa powder, caramels, meat and beans, vegetable stew, ham, lima beans, water purification tablets, chewing gum, toilet paper, matches and, most importantly, cigarettes all neatly wrapped in wax-covered boxes.

"Speaking of smokes." The Colonel stuck two fingers into his breast pocket and gently removed a thin, European cigarette. "My last of the good ones," he said as he flipped it to his lips. Then he fumbled around his uniform with his hands not finding what he was looking for. "Anyone got a light?"

Walker, hoping to impress the superior officer, presented the first match. With a quick scratch, he lit the splinter of wood. The Colonel bent forward to receive the flame. Walker cupped his free hand around the match instinctively to hide the glow. Ridgeway took two short puffs and then one long drag.

"Ah. Such simple pleasures."

"Just sit low in the hole; you never know where Jerry's looking. By the way, where'd you get that?" the L.T. inquired.

"A woman back in Paris gave me an entire box. That was only a few weeks ago and look, it's my last. My habit has gotten out of control since this campaign began." He emphasized the word campaign. He sighed, "A woman back in Paris."

"They had be to better then these issued ones." The L.T. joined the Colonel and lit his own cigarette.

"The blend is sweeter, and they last longer." As the Colonel pulled, the tip burned a faint orange, and a thin line of pale smoke rose into the dark night. The smell of cloves and herbs filled the foxhole. "I would rather be anywhere than here." He looked around and smiled, then said, "No offense to the present company intended."

The Lieutenant grinned back. "None taken. We'd all rather be somewhere else."

"I'd be out chopping wood for my parents," Walker volunteered. "We live on the outskirts of Des Moines, near the woods. Every night in the winter we build a big fire in the fireplace and sit around listening to the wind outside. That and the radio."

"Really? Walker, I had no idea." The Lieutenant looked incredulously at the Private. He couldn't visualize this skinny, blonde kid chopping anything. But he also watched in awe every time the boy fired a gun. I guess I should get used to him surprising me, the Lieutenant thought to himself, he does it enough; I guess there's more inside all of us than others see on the outside.

"About now, my mom'd be cooking dinner."

"Don't go there," the Colonel ordered. "I'm still trying to chew my M unit."

"Sorry, Colonel. But thinking about that stuff is what gets me through the night. I try to concentrate on my parents, my mom's cooking, the smells of food coming from the kitchen, my warm bed, looking at the stars from by bedroom window. I put myself a million miles from here. I'd go crazy if I didn't have all that to think about. Shoot, just about anything is better than thinking about this place. About all I've done since I got here is think about home."

"Well, Private, that's where you and I differ. I haven't seen my wife in years. I'm not even sure I still have one." Ridgeway winked at Walker who couldn't figure out if the Colonel was kidding. "The way I make it through is to forget all about home. Pretend as if it doesn't even exist.

"I'm a career man and this uniform's my suit. As soon as I put it on, there's no home but my CP pillbox and no family but the Army. What I do here, stays here. I like it that way and it seems to like me, if you know what I mean."

Walker looked on in bewilderment.

"Give yourself a couple of days on the front, and I think you'll be singing a different tune, Colonel," the Lieutenant broke in.

"Oh, I won't be here that long. Already got a friend working on a transfer back to the rear. Sending me upfront was a mistake. Guys like me don't belong here."

The L.T. was beginning to loathe the Colonel. He glanced at the boy in glasses. Walker eyed the same feeling back.

The Colonel enjoyed the last drag on his cigarette, took it between his thumb and first finger and flicked it just over Walker's head and out of the foxhole.

"Colonel!" the L.T. exclaimed as quietly as possible.

"What?"

He paused and looked at the Colonel's face. Ridgeway honestly hadn't realized the possibly fatal mistake he had just committed. I don't know if it's better for this guy to see the front line or get transferred the hell away from here, the L.T. wondered, and all he said was "nothing."

maps and papers. Engel unclasped the brief and butterflied it open. Soon the entire tabletop was covered with documents. The Captain stared at the papers and shook his head.

A second captain entered the farmhouse yelling. "This is ridiculous. We've only come a few miles. We should be at the Meuse by now! Captain Engel, Peiper will not be satisfied!"

Captain Engel continued his survey of maps while Captain Hans Beyer joined him in the kitchen. "The Meuse. There is no way any army could have made it to the Meuse in the plan's time frame. The objective was impossible from the start."

Captain Beyer stopped and grabbed Engel's shoulder to turn him around. "Do not question the Führer's plans." The men looked each other squarely in the eyes. "Be careful what you say, Georg." As Beyer spoke these last words, he gently touched the four gold squares on Engel's left collar, the mark of a Sturmbannführer.

Hans Beyer had rapidly stepped his way up the ranks in the German military and had become the right hand of Lieutenant Colonel Joachim Peiper, leading one of the many Kampfgruppe pushing through the Ardennes. Beyer had a strong, round face and wore a short, Hitleresque mustache. Nearly clear, blue eyes stood in contrast to his other predominately dark features; the disparity was almost mesmerizing.

"The roads are tight and almost impassable, and we meet with the Americans at almost every turn. We lost . . ." Engel didn't finish his sentence.

"No excuses, Captain. Let me see the maps."

"We are less than fifteen miles from Stavelot if we stay on course. Through here." Captain Engel traced a thin line on the map. "The roads from Stavelot are better, but it will take days to fight our way through to there."

"We won't have to fight our way. The Führer has taken care of that. The Americans will be in chaos. We will move as fast as

"What about you, Lieutenant? You haven't said much. How do you get by up here living so close to the Krauts?"

"Lately I've been thinking about Christmas. I used to really enjoy the holidays. But it's been hard to focus lately."

"That's my point." The Colonel spoke with an air of superiority, almost as if he were ordering his audience to believe him. "If you don't think about it, it doesn't exist. Then you don't miss it. To me, next week will just be another week. Same in, same out. That's what I say."

"Didn't you enjoy Christmas back at home?" Walker asked.

"Sure my wife decorates and does the whole party thing. I was never a big fan. Seemed like a waste of money and time."

"Not to me," Walker joined in. "My mom plays music on the piano, and we all sing along. My dad dresses up as St. Nick. One year I even played one of the shepherds in the town play."

"How old are you, Private?" The Colonel was digging something out of his teeth with his pocket knife.

"Eighteen, Sir."

"That's why."

Walker didn't understand the Colonel's sarcasm and continued his detailed description of Christmas in Des Moines, Iowa without a hitch. The innuendo, however, didn't escape the Lieutenant who began dwelling on his own memories of the holiday.

His parents always took him to mass on Christmas Eve, the only sermon they attended during the year. In a pew up front, he sat between his parents, shoulder to shoulder, watching the pastor looming behind the pulpit.

The L.T. loved hearing stories of the Wise Men, Mary and baby Jesus, seeing the church all decorated, taking communion with the other parishioners. He even enjoyed wearing his brown wool suit that scratched his neck. He especially loved the choir, pretending that they were angels singing from heaven. It was the only night he felt like he had a family; it was the only night his father didn't come home drunk, and swinging.

Just then, the Sergeant that drove the ill-fated jeep discreetly dropped into the foxhole with the Colonel.

"Hey, another truck's come through, headed our way. They'll give us a lift if ya wanna get out of here tonight."

"Absolutely, the faster I get there, the faster I get out."

"Could be dangerous, Colonel. I wouldn't travel these roads at night. We're only a few miles from the line."

"I'll be fine. Let's go Sergeant."

The Colonel grabbed his gear and pulled himself out of the foxhole. Just as he cleared the hole, Ridgeway stood and turned back around.

"Merry Christmas, Lieutenant," he pronounced and tossed the medical kit into the foxhole. "You'll need this before I do." The Colonel turned his back on the Lieutenant and left.

The Colonel didn't number among the column of prisoners that the Lieutenant found himself leading. His men marched despondent and unaware of their destination. The L.T. was surprised to be moving west.

Determined but obviously fatigued, Walker strode next to his boss. His face had lost whatever color it once may have had, and he appeared to have lost weight. The thin wire rims of his glasses seemed to float around his sunken eyes but somehow remained attached to his head.

Night fell on the POWs.

Two German Captains

After they had corralled the Americans under guard in a nearby pasture, the Germans forced a family from their home and converted it into a command post. More soldiers, tanks, trucks and provisions arrived in a steady stream from the rear.

Captain Georg Engel arrived in a Kübelwagen shortly thereafter. Holding a large, leather satchel in his right hand, he dismounted the bucket car with a spare tire on the hood.

"Hiel, Hitler," a soldier saluted the Captain in the obligatory manner as he made his way toward the farm house.

"Hiel, Hitler," Engel instinctively responded and quickly moved past the sentry.

The newly dedicated headquarters of the 1. SS-Panzerkorps consisted of a small kitchen, two bedrooms and a living room. A gas lamp and table in the kitchen designated it as the control room. The black, iron stove in the corner still burned. The family's dinner, a pot of meatless stew, bubbled on top.

"In here," the Captain ordered and set the satchel down on the wood table in the kitchen. Others followed with additional

our trucks and men can. That is your assignment," Beyer stated with decisiveness.

Engel looked perplexed. "Once we reach the river, the Americans will blow the bridges and we will be trapped. If we cannot cross, we cannot take Liege and we will be cut off from behind."

"Captain! I am tired of your insolence and cowardice. You will follow orders!" Captain Beyer pulled his pistol from the holster and aimed it directly at Engel's face. "Do you need reminding, Captain?" Beyer tensed his shoulders and began shaking, his round face reddening. He couldn't hide his bluff.

"Relax, Captain," Engel calmly answered. Experience gave him the upper hand against his counterpart. "I'm only saying that I cannot follow orders that I do not know." Georg Engel, nearly forty years old, had served in the German Army his whole life and throughout its many incarnations. He had worked with men like Beyer before: young, idealistic and overzealous to follow the leader who was quickly becoming, in Engel's opinion, Germany's greatest liability.

Beyer relaxed and lowered his sidearm.

"What are the orders from Peiper?" Engel asked.

"We must clear the way for Skorzeny. He and his men must get through tomorrow. It is imperative." Beyer began speaking more deliberately. "We are to preoccupy the Americans while Skorzeny slips past them."

Engel held his attention on the word preoccupy. He also wondered what Skorzeny's mission might be. He knew Skorzeny to be a renegade and fearless commando-style soldier who had been part of Mussolini's rescue in 1943. Engel further understood that both Skorzeny and Peiper were ruthless leaders and must have been hand-picked for this mission.

"We will leave at day break and head directly for Stavelot, as ordered, Captain Beyer." Engel, in at least the appearance, now presented the obedience demanded of an SS officer.

Beyer, with a look of concern, asked, "This road, here. Is it maintained?"

"No, it is nothing more that a country road. Very much covered in mud. But it is the most direct route to Stavelot."

"What about here?" Beyer continued his query, pointing to the map with a short finger.

"Yes, we can detour through Baugnez. It is a better road but will add a few miles to our route."

"Than I shall advise Peiper that we change course at Thirimont and reroute through Baugnez. The better roads will make for faster travel."

"What about the prisoners? They will slow the column. Should we not be moving them back to the camps at Stadtkyll?" Engel half asked, half stated to Beyer.

"The prisoners will be taken care of by Peiper soon enough. They will not slow us down." Beyer then saluted, nearly knocking Engel's hat off, and left the farmhouse.

Those last words echoed in Captain Georg Engel's head as he stood alone in the kitchen watching the family's cat scratching at the window from outside.

Saints and Soldiers

Captain Winley stood by the shuttered window and finally lit a cigarette. He pulled the dry smoke into his lungs. Closing his eyes, he leaned his head against the wall and exhaled. He disappeared into the earthy smell.

"Oh, Obee. You're in love. And I think it's wonderful," Josephine exclaimed. She took another drag of the cigarette before giving it back to her brother. The Winley women didn't smoke, but Josephine took advantage of the opportunity alone with Oberon to steal a few puffs before returning to the party.

Oberon took the wrapped tobacco in his fingers. "You know father will not approve, and mother . . . well, she'll have some sort of nervous breakdown and blame her demise on me."

"Don't bother with them. I think she's simply wonderful. I never would have dreamed of this when I introduced you two. It all makes me very happy, you know."

"Jo, you don't understand. Do you realize what would happen if I brought her into the house as my guest? What if I had brought her to this party, mother's famous Christmas party with all their friends?" Oberon took the last drag of the cigarette and snubbed it out with his foot.

"You worry too much. I hate those people in there anyway. They're all so stiff. I feel like I'm at a wake, not a Christmas celebration. Light another one and tell me about the first kiss."

"Jo!"

"Oh, Obee, get over it. That's the part I like to hear. Do tell, please." Josephine placed her hands on her knees and turned toward Oberon.

The two sat shivering on cold, iron chairs near the covered pool. The night was dark and clear. Inside the Winley home, dozens of guests sipped from glasses of champagne and antiseptically discussed the latest developments in Europe.

"You know just off campus, near my dormitory, the bridge over that little river."

"Oh, yes. I remember from my visit. Please tell me it was on that bridge. I can just see it now. A beautiful, fall night. The stars and a crisp wind. The two of you are all alone."

"Yes, Jo. I was just such an evening," he confirmed, lighting another smoke.

"How wonderfully romantic." Josephine spun in her chair. "I can't wait to fall in love."

Oberon took a puff. "Just pick someone more suitable to the Winley name." He handed the cigarette to his sister.

"Obee, you tire me with your pessimism. Everything will be fine. I just know it. Mother and father will see how simply marvelous she is. Just like I do." Josephine looked her brother in the eye. "Here," she said, pulling a small wrapped box from underneath her chair. "An early Christmas present."

Oberon took the gift. "Jo, we don't exchange presents until Christmas eve. You know that. I'm not prepared. I feel awful."

"Don't worry. You still have a few days. I finished it just this morning and didn't want to wait."

Oberon carefully tore at the wrapping around the small, cardboard box. He lifted the cover. Inside was a piece of white cloth. "Oh, Jo," he sighed. Oberon lifted out the silk handkerchief and held it up to the moonlight. It nearly glowed in the blue light. Delicately stitched on one corner were the initials JAW. "It's beautiful, Jo, thank you."

"It's so you'll always remember me. And when you get married, I'll make another with her initials on it, and you'll have a pair. You'll see." With that Josephine kissed her brother on the cheek and reentered the party inside.

Oberon held the handkerchief. Maybe she's right, he thought to himself.

Captain Oberon Winley fell asleep slumped in the corner of a small room in a Belgian farmhouse.

Stephen Gould and the other prisoners sat disconnected and alone on the side of a snow-covered road. The Corporal wrapped his arms around his medical bag and listened to the silence in the air. He didn't feel the gratitude to still be in possession of his precious supplies that the young guards allowed him to keep.

As the wind pushed gently on his face, he tucked his head inside the jacket collar and his eyes peered from underneath the brim of his helmet. He saw only formless gray bodies, clumped and quiet. They appeared dead except for the wisps of warm breath occasionally rising from the dark mounds.

Death was not far from the thoughts of any man that night. But Gould felt as trapped in a mental cage as any real confine imposed by the Mauser rifles at his back. This night, in his eyes, appeared no different from any other. Except one.

"I'm very grateful for the rain," Madeleine said. "I have never much cared for it. But now, I'm grateful." The nurse stood partially disrobed by the window of her apartment. "It's so beautiful."

Stephen watched the silhouette of her body move across the room. Her dark hair glistened with silver threads in the scant moonlight. "It won't last much longer. The weather will clear and St.-Lô will eventually fall. I'll have to move on. There's another push in the morning."

"They try every morning. Let's not think about that. You're here now. Let's just enjoy the moment." Madeleine slid back into bed, her body brushing against his. She laid her head on his chest. Overhead, a fan whirred.

Stephen stroked her hair. "It's hard to believe," he said.

"What is?" She turned her head to face him.

"That you're here."

"I live here. You know I moved back before the war." She propped herself on her elbows to look Stephen in the eye.

"That's not what I mean."

"Don't worry. I'll always be here." Madeleine snuggled against his neck. "I'll always be here," she repeated. She knew his fears.

Stephen Gould held his lover in silence. He lightly touched the fine hairs at the base of her neck. Her skin was smooth and warm. He ran his fingers down her spine, feeling each bump of vertebrae. He felt a solidity with Madeleine. She was real, tangible somehow, in a way he hadn't felt before, not just in the six weeks since landing on the beaches, but in his entire life.

Madeleine tried to cuddle even closer. He smelled the roses in her perfume and the lavender from her shampoo, each scent magnified by the evening and registering deep inside him. All of his senses seemed heightened. He heard the rain drops splatter on the roof and the hum of the fan's old motor. Their lungs filled in rhythm. Every muscle in his body relaxed. He hugged her tightly.

Only his head fought the moment. Within hours he would leave her, again, and despite the rain. This time he knew he would not be back. They had discussed the eventuality, but he doubted the success of their plans. "That's not what I mean," he whispered.

"Did you say something?" she asked, nearly asleep.

"No."

Only after he knew she was asleep, he said, "I love you, Madeleine" and stroked her hair again.

Over in the corner of the room, he looked at his medical bag sitting crumpled on the floor, waiting for its next mission.

Corporal Gould held to his bag and looked over to Walker and the Lieutenant sitting among the other prisoners. They faintly broke smiles and nodded. It'll be okay, they implied.

No it won't, Gould thought to himself.

DECEMBER 17, 1944

The Prisoners March

The POWs awoke to kicks in the ribs before the sun had risen over the Fatherland. Walker moved quickly over to Gould.

"How'd ya sleep?" Walker asked, adjusting the wire arms on his glasses around his ears.

"How do you think?" Gould felt no compulsion to be cordial. He stood, stretched and rubbed his lower back. He had lain in the fetal position for hours, drifting in and out of nightmares. He dreamed about the battle outside St.-Lô the morning after making love to Madeleine. The scenes played like a dark, bloody Wagner opera. He still felt a part of it, clutched by it, as he squinted in the darkness at the other prisoners.

"Hey, Walk, check on the other guys. See how they're doing," commanded the Lieutenant, appearing unusually alert. He approached the Medic.

Gould raised his arm to shield his eyes from a pair of headlights coming from a nearby truck.

"You don't have to 'Heil, Hitler' me, Corporal," the Lieutenant teased and rubbed his right shoulder.

"Huh? No, the lights. How's the arm, Lieutenant."

"Pretty stiff, but I don't think it's infected. Thanks."

"Thanks for what?" Gould slung his bag over his neck and replaced his helmet. "I didn't do anything."

"No, thanks for asking."

"Oh." Gould staggered, groggy from the restless night and damp air. He didn't really comprehend what the Lieutenant had said. "Any idea where we're headed?"

"That's actually got me worried."

"Worrying you more than our current circumstances? We're already prisoners."

"The convoy's going west and I think we're going with it." The Lieutenant took off his helmet and rubbed his scalp. He looked at the trucks and tanks that had amassed during the night.

"Sounds good to me. That's where our boys are at. Maybe they'll give these damn Krauts a good old fashioned whipping."

"Medic, look around." The L.T. spoke with a dead tone.

Gould rubbed crust from his eyes and scanned the soldiers milling all around him. Thousands of Germans had arrived during the night, maybe more. The clearing looked like a Boy Scout jamboree with all the uniforms, tents and vehicles, but the mass of heavy armament dispelled any further agreeable extension of the metaphor.

Pak antitank guns lined the north edge, a host of 105mm howitzers the south and a few Nebelwerfer rocket launchers thrown in. A pair of new Panther V tanks, like the lion sentinels at the gates of Luxor, led a long line of Tiger and Sturmgeschütz assault tanks, half-tracked motocycles and a myriad of jeeps, all beginning to crawl forward. In the confines of the clearing and to the weary eyes of the POWs, however, the German force appeared larger than it actually was.

Gould could not articulate a response.

"After yesterday, I think someone figured out that they had

better lead with the armored divisions this time."

"I think you're right," Gould replied, still in dismay.

"I just don't know why they're dragging us along with."

"I'm afraid I can't help you there, either, L.T. Enemy strategy is not my area of expertise. I try not to think about the Krauts." Gould really didn't know what his area of expertise was.

"I just don't want to worry the men," The Lieutenant admitted.

"I think it's a bit late for that."

A guard yelled above the clamor of vehicles. "Zurück in die Reihe! Zurück in die Reihe!"

There was no language barrier, and the prisoners quickly fell in line. Just after sunrise, the time had come for them to follow their captors down the road to Stavelot.

Again, Walker stood next to his commanding officer, like a faithful companion, at the forefront of the parade. Corporal Gould stepped up as well and walked alongside the Lieutenant.

The day broke no clearer than the previous one. Gray overcast skies deepened the feelings of despair. Snow didn't fall, but a stiff wind rushed in from the north, nearly knocking some of the weaker Americans over. Their socks froze overnight, and many hobbled bootless, victims of trench foot, leaving bloody footprints in the crispy slush.

The original guards had been replaced by younger soldiers, some teenagers. The new guards paid less attention to the Americans and merely kept watch for stragglers and occasionally yelled obscenities.

These young boys called their commanding officer Captain Engel. He walked at the head of the group of POWs, straight-backed and rigid. He wore the gray, double-breasted, officer's woolen overcoat, buttoned clear to the collar. His pistol hung belted on his right hip. While the brim of his cap shaded his eyes, the angular face of a Hauptsturmführer clearly shined through: stern, worn and obedient.

The Captain's thin, colorless lips never parted. His only directions came through brisk signals with his arms. He appeared as a man distracted by weightier matters. Only he knew how difficult this march was going to be.

Walker's managing remarkably well, Gould thought of the thin waif walking next to him. "How you holding up?"

Walker seemed to brighten with the attention. "Fine, I suppose. I haven't really made sense of any of this yet."

"Don't waste your time. It'll never make sense."

"What do ya think they'll do with us?" Walker asked.

The Lieutenant shot a glance of friendly admonition at the Medic.

Gould understood and complied. "Nothing but bore the hell out of us. They'll march us around and pretend to be superior. Then, they'll stick us in some camp. It won't be a summer vacation. But they can't hold this front for very long. Once the big wigs get a hold of what's going on, they'll be over these guys like sour on kraut."

The L.T. and Walker smiled.

What Gould really wanted to say is that they'd probably all be dead before nightfall, either from the cold or the cane.

They marched on for hours, passing a few tiny villages. The locals never ventured out of their homesteads. They had seen all this before, and the Germans left them alone.

Past Hepscheid, Schoppen and Faymonville, the POWs sauntered through, led tirelessly by the young soldiers of Kampfgruppe Peiper. The morning warmed but not enough to aid the beleaguered prisoners. Their only rest came at the town of Thirimont.

The Americans were ordered to sit on the side of the road while the German officers met in discussion. The guards watched over them as many relieved themselves by a row of trees.

The column ahead had veered north toward Malmédy, causing some confusion. The junior officers had been ordered to head straight to Stavelot.

Engel explained that they would be traveling through Baugnez because of the better roads, and would soon be back on track to Stavelot. Satisfied, the guards ordered the Lieutenant, Gould, Walker and the other POWs back onto the muddy road.

"Not much of a coffee break, huh boss," Walker tried to jest, setting the glasses back on his nose.

"Nope, Walk. Not much of break."

Luc's Warning

"Hello, Marie. Banjur," Sergeant Gunderson hollered from outside the café.

"Bonjour, Sergeant. Entrez, s'il vous plaît," Marie returned with a welcome gesture and a grin.

"I think we'll sit outside today. It's such a beautiful morning." Gunderson and Corporal Greer pulled two chairs up to a small table just outside the café's arched doorway and sat. Deac said nothing.

Marie looked up at the sky, shook her head and laughed. It was not a beautiful morning. "A moment, monsieur, your café, Sergeant." Then, turning to Deac, she said, "et un cookie?" She winked at the young soldier.

The day dawned gray, cold and damp, and the remainder didn't hold any more promise. Gunderson and Deac sat on the wood plank walkway that extended the length of the café's façade.

Just off the landing, the river of mud and ice flowed nowhere and the street appeared deserted compared to the day before. A few soldiers sauntered past and nodded. A jeep went by, headed to Malmédy about two miles up the road.

The café, however, was full, mostly locals and a few holdover G.I.s. The 291st Engineer Battalion that had camped just outside of town moved on earlier in the morning toward Malmédy. As usual, Marie busied herself with her customers.

"You didn't sleep much last night," Gunderson said with empathy.

"No, not at all really."

"The shakes again?" Gunderson tried to catch Deac's eyes, but his head hung too low. "I'm not sure how that body of yours makes it through the day without collapsing."

Deac didn't respond.

"Votre café, monsieur, et un petit gâteau pour le garcon," she said, turning to Deac and setting another oat and molasses cookie down on the table.

Deac removed his green wool cap, looked up and genuinely smiled at the woman's generosity. He popped the entire cookie in his mouth. She placed a hand on her hip and laughed in surprise.

"Un café?" Marie asked before turning around.

Deac pulled out a packet of lemonade from his coat and replied, "No, thanks. Just some hot water, please."

The matron understood and left.

"Glad to see you're a bit more chipper this morning." Gunderson was truly happy to see Deac begin to interact with others, something that the soldier had been avoiding lately.

Deac took a corner of the lemonade packet and shook the contents to the other end. He tore the empty corner with his teeth. Gunderson sipped his coffee in silence, watching the gray clouds and worrying about his friend.

Marie came back with another cup, a small spoon and a pot. Steam rose in the frosted air as she poured the hot water. Deac emptied the yellow powder into the cup and stirred. The two soldiers sat across from each other in front of the crossroads café and warmed their bodies with hot liquid.

Back inside, smoke from cigarettes, cigars and pipes filled the St. Clair Café as Marie tended to her regular customers.

The large room had filled early that morning, all men, mostly older. The younger males of the village had left a long time ago, been recruited into service or were killed the last time the Germans marched through. Marie knew and called all her customers, past and present, by their first names.

The men spoke quietly and with reservation. Decades of war had been waged in their small village, and that reality escaped no one. Everyone left in the village carried some form of scar. They neither trusted nor aligned with any army that that had occupied the town, including the Americans. These men learned to keep their thoughts as well as their conversations inside the village.

With the other buildings in ruin, the café stood alone at the crossroads as a testament that some part of the town would survive. As long as Marie served coffee, the town of Baugnez lived.

"I tell you, they are coming." Luc Gavrote stood in the far corner yelling in both English and French, ignored by the other customers. "I saw the tanks at Thirimont. The Germans are headed this way."

Luc waved his arms in the air and pretended to fire a weapon as he spoke. He wore typical wool, country trousers and coat, both a faded brown, a scarf about his neck and a cap on his head. He was the oldest man in the café, and although he looked his age, he moved with the agility of someone much younger.

Darting around the tables like a soldier in the woods, Luc continued his ranting. He spoke convincingly, but few paid any attention. Even Marie ignored the old man.

In his early years Luc went by the nickname of Gavy. He had run away from home at thirteen and befriended a crowd of young and arrogant aristocrats in Brussels. While not of the same socio-economic status as his cohorts, his good looks and athleticism opened numerous doors. He cheated his way through school and soon became a manager of a bank owned by the father of one of his friends. He spoke fluent French, German and English never seemed to communicate to anyone.

The group frequented nightclubs, bars, restaurants and brothels, sometimes partying until dawn. Then, in drunken stupors they would wander the streets, break windows and harass children on their way to school. Their mischief was overlooked by the local authorities, who also happened to be their fathers.

Gavy's carousing ended, however, when he met his wife. She was the daughter of a French diplomat, wealthy and beautiful. Knowing Luc's reputation, her father disapproved of the matrimony. Nonetheless, the two had fallen in love and married.

No one in town knew any more than that, not even her name. Luc returned to his parent's farm during the first Great War-a widower. He never spoke about her, or about anything else, and slowly sank into senility. The townspeople left him alone.

Suddenly, he slammed his fist down on a table, knocking two cups of coffee onto the floor.

Marie stormed over to Luc with a broom in her hand and yelling in French. As she neared, she held the straw weapon overhead and swung at the old man, intentionally missing.

Luc ducked in fear.

"Bande d'idiots!" Luc stomped through the café and out the archway, stopping at the table occupied by Gunderson and Deac.

Gunderson instinctively stood in a defensive posture. Gunnie, as his high school buddies used to call him, had won the state championship wrestling title. Since then, he meticulously maintained his upper body strength with pushups every morning, even in foxholes on the front line. His forearms measured as thick as his calves and no other soldier has bested him at arm wrestling. Despite his physical strength, however, he always lost at cards.

Gunderson took the man by the collar, careful not to break the fragile collar bones, and led him off the porch.

"You'll wish you hadn't treated me this way," Luc warned this time in his native tongue as he hobbled down the muddy road.

Gunderson's French didn't allow him to understand this last warning.

The mood altered among the other patrons of Marie's café. The men quickly finished their coffee and extinguished their cigarettes. They placed a few coins on the tables, wrapped up their quiet conversations in their scarves and left.

Marie followed them outside, wiping her hands on the front of her smock.

"Is there anything wrong?" the Sergeant asked.

"Uh, wrong? No. No, monsieur. Drink, s'il vous plaît." Marie refrained.

"I've got a bad feeling, Gordon. Those men were scared of something." Deac now stood and looked to where Luc had disappeared in the fog.

"Yeah, buddy, me, too. But I'm not sure there's much we can do. I don't hear anything. Besides, the 285th should be rolling in here soon. We'll catch our ride and be on our way in a couple of hours. I'll get you to St. Vith. Don't worry."

Deac didn't respond. His right arm began to shake.

Larsen's Prayer

Just before daylight, Winley and Larsen woke refreshed from the first decent night's sleep either had had in months. They dressed in dry uniforms and optimism. Winley peered through a crack in the shutters but couldn't identify any movement across the dark fields.

"Man that felt good," Larsen said coming in the back door. "Sitting on a pot while doing your business is definitely the way to go. It's almost relaxing. You see anything out front?"

"Nothing. But remember where we are. We will just have to take our chances. Are you ready?" Winley gently folded the clean handkerchief and slid it into his pocket. Then he checked to verify that the papers were still in his breast pocket and finished buttoning his coat. The fire smoldered itself out.

"Yeah. Let's go."

Larsen gently removed the door and set it aside. "Sorry, folks," he apologized.

"Just move." Winley pushed Larsen from behind.

The cold air rushed inside the farmhouse. The night had been clear and the temperatures dropped below freezing. The other farms in the valley still slept in darkness. The pair headed toward the road. With Larsen's first step, the iced snow crunched under his weight.

"This won't be quiet, sir. We might wake the neighbors, or worse. You sure that you don't want to stay. That fire's awfully warm."

"We have no choice. Move soldier."

Larsen and Winley began stepping across a field of ice. Accustomed to moving in quiet, the crackle from breaking the surface of the snow seemed deafening as it echoed through the still valley.

As they traveled, Larsen silently prayed that no other German regiments were coming this way. Winley's thoughts, oddly, were centered on Hitler's Operation Grief.

Reaching the road, they stopped at the barriers in their path. The mud ruts had frozen overnight, becoming stone-like fences. The two sat low in a drainage ditch on the north side of the road. The sun peaked over the ridge, and the air reflected it with just a hint of light.

"I would certainly rather see their location before moving forward," Winley whispered.

"I'd rather not see 'em at all."

Winley took out his compass. After a moment of thought, he explained his plan to Larsen.

"Do you see those two homes, across there?" He barely lifted his head above ground level.

"Yeah."

"We must proceed straight between them and maintain the course through the woods. When we are well secluded, we will turn west, paralleling the road until we arrive near Elsenborn." Winley paused.

"Then what?" Larsen asked.

"We reevaluate."

"Reevaluate what?" Larsen appeared confused. "We meet up with the regiment, right?"

"Correct. We meet up with the regiment." Then Winley thought to himself, if the regiment's still there. "Are you ready, Private?"

Winley conducted an instinctive inventory, checking his gun and personal gear, which wasn't much, his handkerchief in his left pant's pocket and the wad of papers in the breast. He unfolded his snow cape. The sky was brightening and he wanted all the camouflage he could get. Just short of throwing the cape over his head, Winley held out the white covering to the Private. "Here, you're a bigger target. You need it more than me," he tried to joke.

"Nah. I left mine back on the ridge. Besides, you need it for warmth. I've got all this blubber to keep me warm." Larsen grabbed his belly. "I'll be fine. Keep it."

With that Larsen stood and made his way over the rutted road. Winley donned the cape and followed.

The men placed every step with caution. The road was so chewed-up and slick that each step risked a broken ankle. On the opposite edge of the road, a mound of frozen mud and ice ran the length of the road and measured almost three feet high. Larsen reached the obstacle first.

He placed his hand on top of the mound and pushed his body up enough to get one foot over the hump. As he straddled the earthen barrier, a ray of light broke though the trees on top of the ridge and spotlighted the soldier, his dull green uniform almost glowing in the early morning light.

A few feet behind, Winley stood in dismay, paralyzed by what he saw. He stared at the large frame in front of him, eyes wide open and fixed. Stupid was the only word that went through his mind.

Larsen turned around with the same realization. His fear froze him on his perch. He looked like a green porcelain plate at a county fair shooting gallery. His eyes searched the valley for the puff of smoke he knew was coming.

Winley began to run.

Larsen's foot slipped.

The Captain charged at and tackled the Private as he fell off the mound. They twisted in the air and landed on the other side, Larsen on top. They waited but heard nothing.

"Good morning, honey," Larsen finally whispered in Winley's ear.

"Remove yourself immediately." Winley didn't feel the humor of the situation.

"You okay? I know I'm kind of heavy." Larsen smiled and rolled off his superior officer.

"I think you broke a rib. Satisfied?"

"Hey, if at first you don't succeed."

Winley rubbed his chest. "The next time, I shoot you. Understood, Private?" Winley knew he was reacting to his own guilt.

"Sorry, sir."

The morning remained quiet. The soldiers easily made it through the last fields of the valley and into the woods. The forest on the ridge paled in comparison to the jungle they now marched through. The trees grew so densely that barely any light, or snow, found the forest floor. The walking proved expedient without the snow pack, and Larsen utilized his arm as a machete, hacking his way through the firs and spruces like an experienced explorer. Larsen began talking.

The weather lingered gray and cold. Although no new snow had fallen, the fog-frosted evergreens stood tall and white. Despite the conditions, to Larsen this was turning into a great day.

"How far do ya think it is to Elsenborn?" Larsen asked, confident in communicating.

Keeping an eye on his compass, Winley replied, "Perhaps one mile. Perhaps longer. Keeping a due course through all these trees is proving difficult."

"I know you'll get us there."

"And how have you arrived at that conclusion?" Winley wasn't actually attentive to Larsen's words. He maintained his focus on the thin, magnetic needle in his hand.

"Because everything I thought would happen has happened. You know, when I was stuck in that ice, I prayed . . ."

This caught Winley's attention. "What?"

"I prayed to get out of that ice, and that happened. I prayed to be dry and warm, and we found that great house. And then I prayed that you'll get that information you're carrying around back to the regiment. So, that'll happen, too."

"You urinated in your trousers to get out of the ice. The Germans scared, or killed, a family that left their house vacant. And we are not back to the regiment yet."

"Wah, wah." Larsen waved his arm.

"I never took you for a Christian, Private."

"I'm not. Haven't been to a church since I was a kid. Just thought I'd give it a try. See what happened, you know."

"Well, do not ascribe to God what is attributable to hard work or plain luck."

"Huh?" Larsen didn't understand and shook his head. "Don't you believe in God?"

"Yes. I was born and raised a Lutheran. My family attended church every Sunday."

"So, you pray then." Larsen kept the pace up and trotted just ahead of Winley. His head bounced and bobbled on his large shoulders.

"Right now I am praying that you will shut up. It is the same thing that I have been praying for since we left two days ago. And that has not happened." As Winley chuckled at his own humor, he thought about the handkerchief in his pocket with the initials JAW embroidered in blue thread. The levity passed.

"Well, all I know is that we'll get back to the regiment with those papers or whatever that German gave you. You've had this worried look on your face ever since he gave them to you. More serious than your usual. I wanted to ask about them, but now I don't think that I want to know."

The two walked on, Larsen chatting and Winley worrying.

"Have you tired yet?" asked Winley.

"I never get tired of talking," Larsen replied, turning around with a big grin on his face.

"No. I mean tired of walking."

"Yeah, a little."

"We can rest now. The diet of melted snow has left me a bit weak."

"I'll carry you." Larsen sat on the snow and laughed.

"Shut up."

As soon as those words left Winley's mouth, a shot echoed in the forest. Stunned, Winley instinctively lay prone and readied his rifle. He looked around. There was nothing but dense forest.

"Larsen, do you see anything?"

No reply came.

Winley turned his head and saw "Big" John Larsen slumped over onto the snow, blood flowing from a wound to his chest. His eyes were open, and his mouth formed a grin.

Another shot rang out, hitting a tree just behind Winley. He could now tell that the sniper had probably come down from the north, from Elsenborn.

Winley scrambled on all fours, his legs catching in the snow cape. In the snow cape, he thought. Then he cursed to himself.

He managed to scurry behind a thick clump of pines. Without thinking, he stood and ran as fast as his weak legs would carry him. No more shots came from the rear.

Winley's rifle lay half buried in the snow just feet from Larsen's body.

Massacre at the Crossroads

1210 Hours

"Hey, Kendrick, run ahead and see who those guys are," Sergeant Bowen ordered the eager Private.

"Yes, sir!" he instantly replied. Private Kendrick, who held his rifle in his hand, slung the weapon over his shoulder and ran off ahead of Battery B from the 285th Field Artillery Observation Battalion.

The Battery had left Holland the day before and was headed south to Luxembourg. They had stopped for chow just outside of Malmédy when Sergeant Bowen noticed American soldiers coming up the road.

Bowen watched as Kendrick sprinted through the muddy canal with the excitement of a ten year old child. His body bounced from side to side as he searched for solid ground to place his footsteps.

Sitting on the hood of a jeep, Bowen lit a cigarette from his rations and looked upward. Although overcast, no snow fell from the sky. Any light that penetrated the clouds reflected off the white ground, and Bowen regretted losing a pair of sunglasses in a card game last summer.

Kendrick returned with the Commander from the 291st Engineer Battalion.

Bowen hopped off the jeep. "Sergeant Bowen, sir," he said, saluting the Commander.

"Where're you men going?" The Commander asked the question like a math professor rather than a military leader.

"Luxembourg, eventually. Things are slow moving through this muck. We've got to get to St. Vith by tonight. We're only stopping for a few minutes' rations and we'll be on our way."

"There are rumors of German combat units to the south and east of here," the Commander informed Bowen.

"We weren't told about any activity along this route. It's supposed to be all quiet."

"We don't have anything confirmed either. Just talk from the locals ahead of you."

The Sergeant stood quiet for a moment. "We'll keep our eyes opened. Thanks for the tip."

The two saluted each other.

"Don't worry, Sergeant. We can handle any Krauts in our path," Kendrick blurted out, holding his gun again in his hand.

"Well, don't get too excited, Kendrick. I'm betting that nothing is there." The Sergeant turned around and yelled, "Let's move on."

Sergeant Bowen, Private Kendrick and the rest of the men loaded their gear onto their backs and lined up in the middle of the road. They marched toward Baugnez.

1255 Hours

Corporal Nathan "Deac" Greer stood pensive against the wall of the St. Claire Café, his right hand placed over his chest pocket, gently squeezing the small book inside. His mind, cluttered with images, struggled to maintain order. Faces in shadows and streams of light fluttered intermittently, emerging and disappearing. Sporadic images materialized then faded in undulating waves, making him dizzy and nauseous.

Deac braced himself against the cold brick exterior. His vision clouded by anxiety and air, he barely remained standing. He always felt it first in his fingertip, his shooting fingertip. It tingled, then cramped, locking at both anterior knuckles, as if to prevent him from shooting.

The fasciculation traveled through his hand and up his arm. If it reached his shoulder, it really took over. His chest would tighten. Respirations became labored and shortened. He felt like he was buried alive in a foxhole, panicked and helpless.

A few days had passed since his last major episode which prompted the transfer to St. Vith. Deac knew that he could no longer serve his unit. He feared letting his comrades down more than the attacks themselves. He first informed his Sergeant who later took the predicament to the other officers. Gunderson, who had witnessed that last attack, volunteered to escort him. Deac was relieved to have the company.

Sergeant Gunderson sat just inside the café, drinking a cup of coffee at a round table and watching his friend. They were the only soldiers around. Marie worked behind the bar at back.

"One more round," Gunderson yelled back to Marie. He gulped the last bit of coffee from the tin cup and stood up. He turned his wrist to view his watch, and a few drops of black liquid hit the floor, creating a small, star pattern in the dried dirt. "Any time now, Deac."

Deac said nothing and stared down the road.

"They're supposed be rolling in about now, if they're on time. We'll hop into a jeep and be gone."

"How long to St. Vith?" Deac asked, almost incoherently.

"In this mess, hard to say. Maybe four hours, or the whole day. It's only about twenty miles." Gunderson tried to maintain a normal conversational tone with Deac. "We should be there by chow time anyways."

"Here he comes again." Deac pointed to the south.

"Who?"

"That old guy. Here he comes."

Coming up the road Luc Gavrote flailed his arms as if he were scaring away crows from his field. The wind blew his scarf horizontal behind his head. In French, Luc gave his final warning. "They're here. You fools. You didn't listen. They are already here. I told you. I told you!" Luc's voice crackled with a dark excitement. "You should have listened. You'll regret it you fools! You won't ignore me anymore."

The old man ran straight up to the café's front porch. He stopped shoulder to shoulder with Deac and looked him in the eye, unaware of the warning. Luc only laughed and took off across the muddy road.

1301 Hours

From the north, Sergeant Bowen and the 285th came rolling into the Baugnez crossroads.

Just to the south, Captain Beyer and Kampfgruppe Peiper charged through the mud and slush.

As the entourage came around a bend in the road, from behind a thick row of trees, Deac and Gunderson finally understood everything that Luc Gavrote had been ranting about.

German soldiers quickly dismounted the jeeps and set up a dozen MG42 machine guns on the side of the road and began firing. The gun could spit off twenty rounds per second and its barrel changed in less than five. It was incredibly reliable and accurate.

Behind the jeeps and a column of soldiers, the Tiger and Panther tanks growled as they came to a halt, almost appearing to be heaving in anticipation of a meal.

The 285th stopped in alarm. Before any man could turn and retreat, the machine guns' rattle echoed in the crossroads. Scores of soldiers dropped to the earth, some nearly torn in two by the bullets.

Sergeant Bowen stood helpless, and without words. He glared forward at the line of Germans gunning down his men. Sparks and flashes burst through the cloud of smoke rising from the artillery. Bowen fell dead.

Deac immediately raised and aimed his rife. The emotional clamp on his mind released and his instincts resurfaced. With the images gone, he focused his sights on the advance. He shot off five rounds and hit five German infantry before Gunderson was able to grab his arm.

As Gunderson pulled the Corporal into the café, Deac finished his eighth round of the .30 caliber weapon and killed his eighth German.

"Let's go!" Gunderson yelled.

The two ran through the café. They headed toward the back where Marie hid behind the bar, shivering and crying.

Gunderson and Deac hurdled the bar top on their way toward the rear door. Before they landed on the other side, shots whizzed past their heads, one just scratching Deac's helmet. The men stopped, both realizing what trying to escape meant: the Germans would find and possibly kill Marie hiding behind the bar.

Simultaneously, and without speaking, they dropped their rifles and raised their arms. They slowly turned around as a group of six German schütze ran into the café, guns aimed.

They ordered something in German; Gunderson and Deac didn't require a translation. They quickly but cautiously walked around the end of the bar, neither looking down at the frail woman silently sobbing underneath them.

A German soldier pointed his Mauser inches from Deac's forehead. The German laughed, but Deac never flinched.

A second soldier came around and jammed the butt of his rifle between Gunderson's shoulder blades. The pain shot through his chest. Lucky it wasn't his head, he thought to himself.

Outside, the machine guns repeated their chorus. The soldiers of the 285th stood distressed. Some began fleeing to the woods, most to be gunned down. The rest threw down their weapons and raised their arms over their heads.

Within a matter of minutes, the gunfire was silenced, and the battle ended. It was brief but violent. Most of Battery B had been lost The remaining American soldiers became POWs.

1320 Hours

The German soldiers herded the POWs into a field about a quarter-mile from the St. Claire Café. Two feet of snow covered the pasture and a dense forest fenced it in, creating a human corral.

The men huddled for security as well as support. No one spoke. A few wandered until forced at gunpoint back in line.

Gunderson squatted next to Deac, who sat on his heels, as if praying. He stared off in the distance. He appeared as a statue, solid and composed. His body didn't shake.

The Sergeant worried. He knew that Deac was on edge and couldn't predict how he might respond to the stress of their current situation. If Deac lost it, he'd end up dead.

Back at the crossroads, Captain Beyer unfolded maps and papers on the hood of a jeep. He looked over to Lieutenant Colonels Joachim Peiper and Otto Skorzeny who sat with a few other officers in a Kübelwagen a few yards away. The Captain had never spoken, directly, to either Lt. Colonel. To Beyer, they represented the crowning achievements of the Reich. He admired their unabashed fighting tactics and undying commitment to the Führer. He knew their mission and resolved to ensure its success. He would prove himself before his idols. Hauptsturmführer Hans Beyer would stop at nothing.

He knew that once the Kampfgruppe had pushed through enough of the American front line, Skorzeny would lead a small band of his handpicked commandoes deep into Allied-held territory where they would turn the key to the Führer's plan to retake Europe.

While Beyer visualized Skorzeny's mission, a Major approached the jeep.

"Hiel, Hitler."

"Hiel, Hitler," Beyer returned, arm stiffly raised in salute.

"Skorzeny is ready. He and Peiper will be leaving as soon as the other prisoners arrive."

"Very well."

"How many prisoners are here?" the Major asked, looking to the field where the Americans sat cold and shivering.

"One hundred and two."

"And those coming behind?"

"Eighty-four, sir." Beyer spoke with pride.

"What about officers?"

"One captain and a lieutenant. The others are sergeants and corporals and privates." Beyer knew that this would displease the Major.

The Major evaluated Captain Beyer as if he were being considered for a promotion. Beyer sensed the scrutiny and stood erect and quiet. Beyer knew the Major was the right hand of Peiper. What the Major thought, Peiper would think.

Behind the Major, Captain Engel approached with the Americans captured the day before.

"Skorzeny's men need more dog tags."

"Yes, sir!"

"After you have collected them from the prisoners, send someone forward. Do not delay; the tags are imperative to the mission. Is that clear?" The Major rhetorically asked as he saluted, turned and left Beyer still standing at attention.

Beyer watched as the Major jumped in the Kübelwagon with Skorzeny and Peiper. The driver cranked up the engine and the group of Germans roared past Beyer who saluted his commanding officers. The only reciprocation came in the form of mud splashed at the hem of Beyer's coat.

Without interruption, Beyer turned and yelled down the road. "Engel, move the prisoners with the others. Over in the field. And hurry."

1348 Hours

"Hey, boss, check that out." Walker pressed his glasses further up the bridge of his nose and motioned to the left.

As the POWs came around the bend in the road, they witnessed the mirror image of themselves: young men, scared, shocked, cold, huddled in masses, wondering what would happen next.

Corporal Gould thought the scene surreal, like emerging from a picture show to the daylight, unsure about what images were solid and which were created by light through celluloid.

He rubbed his eyes. Being a prisoner figured very differently than seeing one. Gould saw his face on that of every soldier in the field, dead or alive, hundreds of himself, scattered everywhere. He watched himself cry, shake, stare, drift, pray. He despised what he saw.

He squeezed his eyes shut then refocused. They were cowards, he thought. Hoping killed them, or would kill them.

Seeing the prisoners in the field, Gould understood the reality and accepted it. He could remove himself from it while the others, imbedded, denied it. Separation, he thought, allowed him control, and control removed the expectation for help.

"Huh?" Gould asked, pulled from his thoughts by Walker's voice.

"At least there are others," Walker repeated, with an odd optimism.

"Yeah, they look like they'll be of real help."

"Strength lies in numbers," the Lieutenant cut in.

"You're not planning something, are you?" Walker inquired of his boss.

Gould said nothing. He realized that the Lieutenant was distracting his men.

"No. I'm just saying that more friendly faces means more protection."

"Well, I'm glad they're here. Do ya think this is where they're going to keep us?" Walker asked. He walked shoulder to shoulder with his Lieutenant and head held high.

"Looks that way."

The Americans with Engel moved off the road and into the clearing. The air went silent. They now saw the soldiers of the 285th that had been killed less than an hour earlier. A large group of bodies lay to the north. Single bodies lay face down scattered away from the group, shot in the back as they tried to escape. They silently joined the other prisoners.

The Lieutenant saw Sergeant Bowen's body off to the right. It had been dragged some distance from the cluster. His tag chain was exposed on top of his uniform, tags missing.

At the entrance to the field, a row of Tiger I heavy tanks sat idling, their 88mm guns pointed at the Americans. Smaller sturmgeschütz III assault guns rested at the feet of their bigger brothers. Other artillery were still arriving from the south. Captain Beyer placed a line of MG42 machine guns between the tanks and prisoners. Hundreds of infantry, M1s in hand, patrolled the perimeter.

The Lieutenant quietly ordered his men-all but one still accounted for-to the center of the field. Gould followed, walking right past Gunderson and Deac. Walker remained at the front of the mass with his Lieutenant.

1355 Hours

"Search the prisoners," Captain Beyer ordered. "You may confiscate anything you want. Bring weapons or information to me directly. Keep the rest. Shoot any prisoner that resists. Go!"

Captain Engel began to accompany the soldiers when Beyer ordered him to stop.

Engel turned, and again the two captains faced each other.

"You'll stay with me," Beyer demanded.

Engel was not about to start taking orders from Beyer. "I'm going to the prisoners." Georg Engel spun around without saluting, an obvious act of defiance.

Beyer merely smiled and stroked his sidearm.

When Engel reached the American congregation, the German soldiers had already begun harassing and toying with the prisoners.

"Bum!" one German soldier vocally popped off and jabbed his Mauser at a young POW in an attempt at puerile jocularity.

The Private gasped and fell over backward.

One schütze ordered the few prisoners with snow capes to take them off while another bundled them up.

The Germans pushed the prisoners into groups only to pick one man out and separate him from the rest. They had been taught how to intimidate.

One such group included Walker and the Lieutenant. Five Germans, brandishing their rifles, encircled the group. One eyed the L.T.'s officer insignia and commented something in his native language. The recipient of the information left his comrades and returned to Beyer.

Another German removed Walker's glasses. He put them on and pretended to cry. Laughing, he tossed them into the snow. Walker went pale but didn't move. As soon as the soldiers moved on, the Lieutenant cautiously walked over and picked up the glasses. He shook off the snow and handed them to Walker. Like always, they didn't need to speak to communicate.

Further back, a German was frisking Corporal "Deac" Greer. Gunderson had been pulled aside but managed to watch.

"Was ist dies?" the German asked Deac, pulling out a packet of lemonade.

"Ein Getränk. Limonade."

The German looked startled. "Du sprichst Deutsch?"

"Ja." Deac appeared calm, but he noticed his fingers beginning to tingle.

"Hast Du noch was anderes?" the German asked as he patted Deac's right chest pocket.

"Nur ein Buch!" Deac's whole arm now vibrated and his breathing shortened.

The German pulled the small, brown book out of Deac's pocket. He flipped through the pages and a picture fell to the ground. "Hebe das auf!"

Deac obeyed and bent over to retrieve the photograph. "Meine Frau," he said as the German took it from his shaking hand.

The soldier noticed the twitching. He stared at the picture of Deac's wife, noticed the similarity to his own wife and smiled. "Sie sieht wie meine Frau aus." He handed the picture and book back to Deac.

"Danke!" he replied as he put the intimate possessions back into his pocket. Deac felt his chest relax, and his breathing slowed.

Gunderson witnessed the episode and also relaxed. He caught Deac's eye and winked. Deac looked upward and mouthed the words "thank you."

Meanwhile, Engel pushed his way through the POWs. He headed straight towards Gould. As he grabbed the Medic by the arm, just above the white armband with the red cross, he ordered him to follow.

The German Captain led the Medic to the far side of the prisoners' temporary camp where a wounded American soldier lay writhing in the snow.

"You can help him?" Engel asked in broken English and a look of concern.

Gould looked down at the man. It didn't look good. "I can try," he answered.

"Please, God. Oh, please help me." The wounded soldier looked up to Gould.

"I'm sorry pal, but it looks as if I'm all you've got." Gould crouched down beside the G.I. who's right leg was nearly torn off. The blood only trickled now, but a large, red pool underneath indicated a great loss. The Private's face appeared blue and beaded with sweat. This man shouldn't even be alive, Gould thought to himself.

Gould pulled a new scalpel from his medical kit. Before he could unwrap it, a German guard kicked it out of his hands.

"Hey!" Gould almost stood up to retrieve the blade.

With his rifle, the guard slapped Gould on the back of the neck.

Control, Gould thought as he grimaced in pain.

Engel yelled at the guard in German and then returned to Captain Beyer at the jeep.

Gould calmly went back to his bag and pulled out some bandages. He thought about the morphine at the bottom of the bag-the gift from that Colonel to the Lieutenant. Gould knew two things: it wouldn't help the soldier, and the guard would surely confiscate it. He left the morphine in the bag and began to wrap the soldier's leg.

The leg was literally shredded through the thigh. The muscle was sliced in half, and the femur was broken at the midpoint. The intact femoral artery may have been the only thing that kept the boy from bleeding out.

The soldier began to cry.

"I'd be quiet if I were you. This guard here may decide to put you out of your misery."

"Will I keep my leg?" he asked, still shaking but trying to calm down.

While knowing the boy would lose more than his leg, Gould refused to lie to another wounded soldier. "I'll get it wrapped as best as I can and stop the bleeding."

"The pain's gone. I can't believe it but it doesn't hurt any-more. Thank you. Thank you."

Gould recognized the appreciation. He had heard it before. He also knew what it meant.

"Yes, the pain's gone," Gould repeated back to him.

The young soldier closed his eyes and laid his head back on the snow. He took one shallow breath and died.

1403 Hours

Captains Beyer and Engel argued by the hood of the jeep.

"The orders come directly from the Führer. I will obey."

"Surely the Führer didn't mean this," Engel retorted.

The soldiers who were searching the prisoners returned to the convoy.

Engel continued, "I will not allow you to do this!"

Pulling out his sidearm, Beyer ordered, "Werner, remove the Captain's gun!" Beyer had his weapon pointed three inches from Engel's face. "There are things you do not understand, Georg. The plans are brilliant. This is necessary to carry them out. Soon, you will see."

The Sergeant immediately obeyed and took Engel's pistol from its holster.

"You do not understand the consequences, Hans."

"Please, Georg. This will win the war. I will be honored in the Reich for this. Please, sit in the jeep." Beyer motioned with his gun. "Werner, shoot him if he tries to leave. Heil, Hitler, Captain." Beyer saluted and left.

1420 Hours

The Lieutenant and Walker stood in a line with the other POWs. Most of them now realized what the L.T. had feared. The guards had left the prisoners and begun to ready the machine guns.

A young G.I. stood next to Walker. He was short, dark haired and only eighteen years old. He looked around, twitching his head left and right. He scanned the Americans, then the Germans while he muttered Hail Mary's under his breath.

The other prisoners began to shake. They looked to each

other with blank and queried expressions. A few began to step away from formation.

"Zurück in die Reihe!" a guard yelled, pointing his Mauser towards the center of the mass, unsure of what was unfolding. The other Germans also seemed to become nervous.

The dark-haired Private was one of the prisoners to break the line. He didn't run, at first. In fact, he merely ambled forward.

"Private!" the Lieutenant warned.

The young soldier continued to walk, lazily, looking up to the sky.

"Zurück in die Reihe!" the same guard ordered, this time aiming directly at the deserting American. He tried to steady the gun's sight on the boy but found his muscles and mind uncooperative. The tightness in his throat told him that this was wrong.

"Kill them" were the only words Beyer spoke.

The guard shot first, uncontrollably, as if the order forced his trigger finger to pull back.

The bullet just missed the dark-haired G.I. and hit Walker squarely in the chest. The thin, blond boy fell over backwards with the force of the blunt trauma. He landed face up, arms and legs spread, like a snow angel. The wire-rimmed, army-issue glasses remained true to their owner.

The Lieutenant gasped.

The guns ignited in unison, light flashing from their tips. The roar was almost deafening.

The Lieutenant took two bullets to the right side of his abdomen. One tore into the large intestine; the other pierced his liver. Holding the wound, he turned and began to run.

A dozen American prisoners of war were killed instantly.

The rattle of the guns continued, spraying thousands of bullets in the first few seconds. The fusillade scythed into the prisoners, cutting some clean in half.

A few German soldiers refused to fire and stood to the side, watching the massacre, secretly wishing this wasn't happening.

Gould saw the Lieutenant running towards the woods and followed with his medical bag over his shoulder.

Americans and Germans dispersed with chaotic quickness. Many prisoners succeeded to the forest, hunted by their counterparts. Deac, followed by Sergeant Gunderson, sprinted to the St. Clair Café.

A small band charged headfirst through the line of machine guns and tanks. Most died before crossing. The remaining men reached a small, abandoned building a few hundred yards behind the German troops.

Beyer watched as the group barricaded the door. He whispered to Sergeant Werner.

The two-story structure had brick walls and a slate roof. A set of double windows framed the door, some of the glass still intact. The floors were wood.

Inside the escapees ranted incoherently as they realized they had only accomplished entrapping themselves. Two soldiers, mere teenagers, crouched in the back corner, holding their knees against their chests. A few others ascended the staircase to the second floor. The rest paced with anxiety.

Werner recruited a few other soldiers and sauntered over to the building. One carried a blowtorch.

A cloud of smoke now hung over the firing line. Bodies covered the field in random clumps. Blood and gunpowder discolored the snow. The gunfire slowed, but occasional bursts could be heard from the forest and town.

Werner's entourage strode right up to building like a group of teenage ruffians.

"Burn it," Werner commanded.

The soldier with the torch turned on the fuel source and lit the burner. The others stood back. In large sweeping motions, the torch threw red and orange flames against the building's wall. The whip of fire arched over the roof.

Inside, the prisoners huddled together, away from the windows. A few began to cry.

The door and window frames caught on fire.

The Germans, waiting outside, readied their rifles.

The few that had gone upstairs flew down, screaming "the floorboards are burning!"

Smoke thickened and embers dropped down from the ceiling.

A few shots came through the window, shattering glass onto the floor.

Choking on the blackness, the ensnared men coughed and resisted the impulse to exit.

The front door, nearly burned to ashes, fell from the hinges. The light attempted in vain to enter the building.

One soldier's jacket caught on fire. He ran out, tripping over the remains of the door.

One shot found its mark, and the soldier fell in the mud.

The fire traveled down the staircase. Step by step it advanced on the men, a hot wall pressing from behind while the Mauser rifles pressed from the front. The prisoners became squeezed in a suffocating hell.

Before taking their final breath, the American soldiers exited from the black cloud.

Target practice ensued. Each man dropped as he entered the daylight. The pile of green uniforms grew in front of the burning building.

In the confusion, Gunderson and Deac skirted past the line of MG42s and retreated into the café with a handful of other soldiers. No one pursued.

The soldiers took positions behind downed tables, the bar and walls, anything for protection. Once hidden, the open doorway and broken windows gave the appearance of an abandoned building. For the moment, they were safe.

Gunderson didn't stop until he reached the back door. He cracked it open and peered outside. A few German soldiers milled around, darting in and of trees, apparently not too motivated to really search for escapees.

Gunderson shook his head. "Not out the back," he whispered to Deac, who remained poised. The Sergeant was relieved to see that Marie was not behind the bar anymore.

"They're preoccupied out front," reported Private Shaw of the 285th as he came around the bar. "What's out back?"

"More Krauts," Gunderson replied.

"There're guys running all over the place out there. But it won't be long till they figure out we're in here."

"I think they already know," Deac interjected. "That old guy is talking to some of the soldiers and pointed right at us."

By the green jeep, Luc Gravot, who learned German from his days as a banker, was informing Captain Beyer that some Americans were hiding in the café.

"Danke," Beyer replied.

Luc smiled at the prospect of currying favor with the German officer.

Beyer raised his gun and shot the old man between the eyes.

"They're in the café!" Beyer yelled.

Deac stared out the window. "Here they come!" He reported this like he was referring to the neighbors coming over for a barbeque.

"Deac, come on. This way!" Gunderson flew out the back door.

Deac immediately responded. He looked at the other soldiers in the café. They remained crouched and hidden, shivering with fear.

"There's a back door. Come on!" he calmly ordered at the other men.

A few pale faces turned but didn't move.

Deac glanced out Marie's cinematic windows. A horror film now played on her screen. The memories of her childhood burned with the trees in the background. The first bullets came whizzing into the café.

"THE BACK DOOR!" he screamed, straining his lungs.

Still, they didn't respond.

Another shot nearly hit Deac. He turned and fled out the back. Shaw was right behind him.

Gunderson ran through the small clearing behind the café. The few Germans keeping watch ignored him. He pumped his arms, reminiscent of his days trying to cut weight by running through the snow on the high school track. This time, however, he was running for his life.

He reached the forest wall and jumped over some fallen logs. "Hey, Deac, over this way." Gunderson spoke without turning around.

"I'm . . .," a voice behind him huffed just before a shot rang out. The voice disappeared into the snow.

"Deac!" Gunderson stopped his body by grabbing a tree and spinning around. A few other shots echoed through the pines, but he didn't hear them. He stood next to the tree with his eyes closed. For hours it seemed that the Sergeant remained there, fearing what lay in the snow. He took a deep breath and opened his eyes to the shadows in the forest. Private Shaw lay in a slide of snow, turned on his side and facing Gunderson.

The Sergeant scanned the area. Far off to his right he caught a glimpse of Deac running into the woods. "Good man, Deac. I'll get you to St. Vith," he reassured the trees as he took off.

No other soldier, German or American, came through the back door.

Not far from Sergeant Gordon Gunderson, and hidden in a thicket of fallen limbs, Marie St. Claire wrapped herself in a blanket. She would smell the lavender again this spring, she thought to herself, no matter who won.

Corporal Gould managed to overtake the wounded Lieutenant. They were well into the woods, and the air remained quiet.

Gould grabbed the L.T. under the armpit and crutched him over to a large fir tree. The Medic removed his blood-covered hand from the wounded man's side. The Lieutenant's entire uniform was dyed red clear down to his boots.

"You don't have to tell me. I already know. I'm not even sure why I bothered running. I was mad, I guess."

"I know. He was good kid," Gould replied as he unbuttoned the L.T.'s overcoat.

"They all are." The Lieutenant's breathing was shallow and labored. He was in great pain.

Gould removed a pair of scissors from his pack. He held them momentarily in his hand. He looked around but saw and heard nothing. Gould couldn't even count the number of times he had been in this exact same position. Men all around him got shot and died, and he was always there with a pair of scissors in his hand.

"What's wrong?" the Lieutenant inquired, his eyes squinted from the pain. A tear drop squeezed out one side.

"Nothing." Gould began to cut away the bloody shirt.

"You should take off. It's not safe here. They'll be out looking, if not now, soon. There's nothing you can do."

"Let me decide that."

The L.T. winced. "You're good at what you do, aren't you."

"Not good enough sometimes."

"That doesn't mean it's your fault. My shoulder hasn't bothered me at all." The Lieutenant attempted to smile but only coughed.

Gould saw a few specks of blood around the Lieutenant's mouth. "That was just a scratch."

"This is much worse, huh."

Gould exposed the L.T.'s abdomen. A six inch slice opened right underneath the rib cage. Another smaller hole oozed just below it. Gould took some gauze from that pack and blotted inside the larger wound. For a brief second the gash was clear. Gould peeled off his gloves with his teeth and probed with his exposed finger. The liver felt like fruit preserves, an amalgamation of chunks of organ tissue and coagulated blood. Deeper proved worse. Gould knew that bullets may enter clean, but they tore and shredded as they passed through tissue, sometimes leaving a melon size hole on the other side. This shell had stopped somewhere deep inside.

"Seen anything that bad before?" The Lieutenant now arched his back and neck in agony. He gripped Gould's knee.

"Same day in, same day out," Gould answered.

The L.T.'s eyes opened. He remembered Captain Ridgeway had made the same comment. His heart now felt more pain than his body.

Gould removed his hand and said nothing. The look on his face spoke what the Lieutenant already knew.

"Today's my birthday," the L.T. said as he turned to his side trying to find relief from the burning.

"No kidding."

"Tonight, really."

"How old you gonna be." Gould knew that talking helped, but in the back of his mind he worried about the Germans.

"Tweny-one."

Gould suddenly understood the Lieutenant-the occasional looks of desperation, the hints for advice, the relationship with Walker, how his men responded so dutifully toward him. Stephen Gould sat awed, looking at the dying soldier, the dying officer. He felt almost ashamed.

"Don't think I'll be celebrating tonight." He coughed up more red chunks. The blood pooling in his intestines was working its way outward. "Hey, Gould, merry Christmas."

"Thanks, but I'm Jewish."

With the last bit of strength to open his eyes, the Lieutenant spoke. "No kidding. We both learned something today."

Then the Lieutenant's body began shivering uncontrollably. He could no longer pretend the pain didn't exist. He cried. He felt his body temperature oscillate between burning and freezing. Searing torture invaded his torso. He felt the pang of knife wounds throughout his stomach, jabbing in and out, over and over. He pounded the snow with his fists.

Gould pressed two fingers against the Lieutenant's neck then looked down at the wounds. Damn it, he thought. There was a steady beat and the bleeding only trickled. Death would creep into this man, slowly, forcing him to endure agony before taking over, like a cruel, endless monologue.

He may take hours to finally pass, Gould thought. Or, if he were found by a German, he would lay there helpless only to watch a gun pressed to his head. Unless . . .

"Unless," Gould now articulated out loud.

The Lieutenant couldn't speak but stared back at the Medic. Gould had seen those eyes before but had never felt what he felt now. He felt . . . sad, maybe. He rummaged to the bottom of his medical bag and pulled out a packet of morphine.

The Lieutenant saw and understood.

Gould took the packet and laid it on the L.T.'s chest. He unbuttoned the man's right cuff and rolled up the sleeve.

The Lieutenant was still laying on his right side, his head slumped onto the ground. He watched Gould work and saw the anguish on the Medic's face. His breaths became shorter and more intermittent.

Snow began to fall.

Gould worked meticulously and calmly. He had successfully completed the same procedure many times before and even under gunfire. But never did it mean as much as it meant to him now. Never before did he care about the patient.

He picked the packet of morphine up and punctured the needle. He gently felt for a vein.

He rubbed the bend in the L.T.'s arm until a faint blue line thickened.

The needle inserted smoothly.

The Medic administered over half of a grain of morphine, eight times the amount used for surgery.

In a few seconds, the Lieutenant's body relaxed, and he slid over onto his back. He eyes opened wider. He took a deep breath.

The Lieutenant raised his hand and grabbed Gould's.

"I'm Stephan," the Lieutenant whispered.

Gould sat stunned. But before he could introduce himself, the Lieutenant fell asleep.

He'll never know we shared the same name, Gould thought.

Gould would never know they shared more than that.

Back in the field, dozens of American bodies lay strewn about the snow-covered meadow, more in the St. Claire Café, a few by a smoldering building and still more to be found in the woods behind.

While Gould attended to the Lieutenant, Captain Beyer ordered some of his men to hunt down the prisoners and shoot them on sight. Small bands of infantry, fearing the Captain more than God, entered the forest to continue the massacre.

Corporal Gould found some branches and covered the Lieutenant's sleeping body. Soon he would be covered with fresh powder. Gould knew that the L.T. would die before the morphine wore off.

Gould looked down. He felt something but didn't cry. This bothered him.

A gun shot rang through the trees, and Gould sped off, leaving the Lieutenant to sleep.

Winley Remembers

Captain Oberon Winley ran for what seemed like the entire morning alone in the woods. The sight of Larsen slumped against the tree with the same dumb grin on his face powered his legs. He didn't stop to check the compass, and he had no idea that he headed south west, away from Elsenborn. He was in the middle of the Ardennes forest and running blind.

He cursed the information in his breast pocket, and he cursed his role in delivering it. He wished he had never heard the name Otto Skorzeny, or his plan. He wished he had given his snow cape to Larsen. Winley wished a lot of things as he ran through the woods.

Soon, his run degenerated into a slow walk. Winley never pretended to be an athlete. He didn't have the physical stamina or mental fortitude for competition of that sort. He never joined a team, nor did the other kids choose him. But that didn't bother Oberon.

Winley's parents, Winnie, short for Winifred, and Oberon II reared their only son and daughter in a quiet and structured home. However, etiquette tutors and nannies actually raised Josephine and Oberon III in the west wing of the house while their parents resided in the east, and at parties. Being twins, the two Winley children learned to rely on each other.

As he stopped to catch his breath and rest his legs, Winley felt for the handkerchief in his pocket. He then felt for the other wad in his breast pocket. Since his sister's death, Winley preferred being alone. Now the solitude with his thoughts bothered him.

"I want it gone! All of it! Do you understand me?" Winnie screeched at the servants. Winifred Winley tore through her daughter's room, opening closets and throwing clothes onto the floor. Her eyes were red and puffy and her hair was disheveled. She had obviously been crying but now screamed in anger.

Her husband stood in the doorway, silent and watching. The young Oberon heard everything from his own room.

"Do you hear me!" she yelled and hurled dresses at the maid.

The frightened girl picked up an armful of clothing and ran out of the room. Other servants did the same.

Winnie swiped across Josephine's, desk with her arm knocking the articles off. A glass vase shattered against the wall. Water and petals dripped to the baseboards.

Obee, sitting on his bed, winced as he heard the crash. He placed his hands over his ears.

Shaking, the woman ran her fingers through her hair, pulling strands out from the roots as she looked into a full-length mirror. The tendons in her arms were visible underneath the taught skin. She stared at her own corpse-like pallor.

"Get in here! I want this room cleared out!" Winnie returned to spastically dumping the contents of drawers out onto the bed. "I demand that you get back in here, now!"

Oberon II turned and walked away.

Winnie pounded on a stack of boxes in the corner of Josephine's room, crushing the Christmas presents. A few packages remained to be wrapped. She threw the cardboard containers and gifts into the hallway.

"I can't, I can't," she cried. Her body began shaking. "I can't have these in my house!" These last words echoed throughout the Winley's quiet home. "I want no memory of her left in my house!"

Obee began to cry. "No memory left in the house," he repeated as he tightened the grip on the white handkerchief in his hand. He knew there would never be a second gift from his sister.

Captain Winley tried to distract his preoccupation with his sister by focusing on Larsen. Two days earlier Larsen figured nothing more than a stupid, clumsy private with a bad sense of humor, a sense of humor that led to his current predicament.

"Hey Macon, check this out. Bedrolls!" Larsen yelled over to the other Private just making his way into the crumbling barn.

"You're kidding, right? I can't believe our luck," Macon replied looking around the interior of the barn.

"They're probably infested," interjected Private Guthrie as he jogged passed the other two privates toward the prize.

Larsen quickly replied, "Not in this cold weather. Boy are we gonna sleep tonight."

The Captain walked around the outside of barn and surveyed the landscape. The foursome was headed on a reconnaissance expedition when they stumbled on an abandoned homestead. They had heard rumors from some locals that the Germans had been stockpiling weapons and armament off the east side of the ridge. Captain Winley led three privates to verify the information.

"Hey, Winnie, you gotta see what we found inside." Larsen carried a bedroll out the back door.

"I have spoken to you on repeated occasions on how to address a superior officer. I suggest you pay attention." Winley glared at Larsen. He tried to stand as tall as possible, but Larsen still towered over the Captain.

"Uh, sorry, sir." Larsen hung his head. He knew better than to mock a superior officer, but for some reason he couldn't control what came out of his mouth. He meant no offense.

Winley walked passed Larsen and into the barn.

Turning and following, Larsen said, "Bedrolls. Some Jerries left 'em. Sure beats the foxholes we've been in."

"Do not become too comfortable, we may not be staying. Is all the gear inside?" Winley asked to no particular private under his command.

"Yeah. The lantern, radio and rations are over on the shelf. Yeah, it's all inside. We won't be staying here tonight?" Larsen inquired.

Winley thought. Recon would be more dangerous during the day but impossible at night. "Yes. We stay here tonight and leave before daybreak."

"Hey, Winley, you can take the third bed roll. The dirt will be fine with me. Anything beats the snow," Larsen offered with his characteristic grin.

"No. Thank you." Winley knew he couldn't sleep.

"Suit yourself," Larsen replied as he hunted around for something entertaining.

"What are you looking for?" Guthrie asked, holding the cigarette between two fingers of his right hand, the light from the tip of the cigarette providing the only artificial light in the barn.

Moonlight entered through a hole in the roof, windows and gaps in the siding, creating a star-like pattern on the ground around the soldiers.

"Anything. I'm bored." Larsen pushed around a pile of fallen debris with his large boot.

"There's nothing else here, Larsen. Come sit down and eat some food. You've got to be hungry," Macon said chewing on a tough piece of dried meat.

"I'm not hungry. I'm bored."

"If you soldiers have the energy, we can leave right now." Winley had lost his patience.

"No, no," the pair sitting on the bedrolls insisted.

Larsen ignored the Captain. His interest was focused on some wood near the rear door.

"What did ya find, Johnny?" Macon asked.

"Tonight's fun!" Larsen picked up a four-foot long, twelve inch plank, former siding, and a short, cylindrical tree limb. "Watch this."

Larsen placed the limb on the ground near the shelf, then the piece of siding on top, making a home made teeter-totter.

"You're gonna break that," Macon said, looking on in disbelief at what the big guy was doing.

"That or you're going to break your neck," Guthrie corrected.

"I used to do this as a kid," Larsen began to explain. "The point is to see if you can roll the board from one end to the other without falling off."

Macon inquired, "Were you any smaller as a kid, Johnnie?"

"Nope."

Larsen raised his arms out to his side, balancing on the board. Slowly, he began rocking. He appeared as a giant bear in a circus act, balancing on a ball. His stubby arms waved wildly.

Macon and Lewis began laughing.

Larsen moved his hips from side to side, and the plank rolled over the log. Soon it traveled nearly tip to tip.

Winley finally took notice. "Larsen! Watch out for the . . ."

Before the Captain finished his warning, the oversized torso of Private John Larsen fell over like a large tree trunk hewn down by a lumberjack.

"Oh, . . ." Larsen instinctively held back the expletive.

As he crashed on the ground, his thick arm smacked against the shelf holding the lantern and radio. The radio toppled over and fell to the ground.

The four simply stared at the instrument and said nothing.

Larsen made the first move. He rolled over and pressed himself onto all fours. He crawled over to the radio and picked it up. Shaking it he heard the sound of broken glass inside. He looked over to Winley.

"You absolute imbecile! One day you will get yourself killed by your stupidity."

Deac Encounters Gould

The afternoon digressed into a deadly game of hide and seek in the woods outside of Baugnez. Scores of prisoners spread out in all directions followed by fresh-and fortunately unmotivated-German infantry. Whether from inexperience or insolence, many of the seekers only pretended to hunt down the hiders. A few even shot at trees only to report later of having killed escapees.

Some Americans attempted to hide under logs, in thick firs and even buried in the snow. One thin private actually stood behind a tree, arms at his sides and eyes closed as four Germans passed within two feet. Others, with greater stamina, simply ran, drawing their pursuers deeper into the forest.

Without success, Nathan "Deac" Greer tried to induce the other G.I.s in the café to escape through the back door. Not so deep down he understood their fear and reservations, but his faith taught him not to give up so easily.

He hurdled a few logs as he entered the thick growth. He surveyed the terrain as he ran. In a few seconds he noted several places to hide, but his search for Gunderson failed.

Through the trees Deac noticed a medic attending to a wounded soldier. He thought the man courageous given the circumstances. The medic was injecting something into the man's arm. He handled the needle with the composure and dexterity of a seasoned surgeon.

Deac didn't realize he had stopped running. He watched the injured American roll onto his back. After the medic covered the man with branches, Deac saw the medic place a hand on the officer's chest and whisper something. Then a shot rang out.

A German soldier had spotted the medic and fired on him. The medic took off, chased by the Germans. Deac began to follow as the two raced deeper into the woods. The German ran passed the man hidden beneath the branches.

Deac sped as fast as he could, trying to keep an intercepting angle. From the corner of his eye, he saw no other Germans.

The hunter was nearly upon the medic.

"Halt," the German ordered and fired his gun.

The bullet whizzed past Gould's head, close enough for him to feel the air brush against the skin on his face.

Gould stopped and raised his arms by a dead pine tree. Slowly he turned around to face his pursuer.

The German pulled the trigger at point blank range. The weapon only clicked.

The two eyed each other.

Gould reviewed the previous two days. He had been fleeing for almost thirty-six hours with a German rifle at his back. He was tired; his mind was tired. He thought about the Lieutenant and Walker. He thought about the battle at St.-Lô and Madeleine's death. He didn't want to think anymore. He simply stood and faced his enemy.

The German expelled the empty clip from his Mauser and pulled another from his belt.

Gould watched the hot metal box land in the snow with a hiss.

The German fumbled with the full clip until he finally managed to load it in the rifle chamber.

Gould closed his eyes.

The German lifted his head and took aim, bewildered at the American who didn't run. With the Medic in his sight, his finger refused to pull the trigger.

The pair could have been statues in a war museum, neither moving, both thinking about someone else.

Before either man realized the other's consternation, a figure leaped from behind a tree, shouldering the German and knocking him to the ground. The Mauser rifle landed between them.

Deac grabbed the weapon by its stock and in a single motion spun around and aimed the barrel at the German attempting to crab-crawl away.

"Nicht schießen" the boy pleaded, eyes bulging and still moving away. "Nicht schießen."

Deac tried to steady his shaking arm.

Gould opened his eyes and saw only a German cowering in the snow. He lost the image of Madeleine. "Shoot him," Gould yelled.

The German listened in horror.

"Shoot him! You've got the shot."

"No," Deac calmly replied despite the panic that was settling in his stomach.

The German began to cry as he got to his feet.

"He'll be back with others. Shoot him!"

"I can't. I . . ., I won't."

"Then give me the gun!" Gould lunged toward the rifle.

Before Gould reached him, Deac spun around and pointed the gun directly at the Medic. He felt his breathing shorten and accelerate.

The German hastily turned and ran back toward the killing field, never looking over his shoulder at the two Americans arguing in the woods.

"You're crazy. Why didn't . . ."

"Shh!" Deacon's eyes focused. He dropped to the ground. His anxiety quickly dissipated.

Corporal Gould mirrored Corporal Greer's actions.

The forest was still, and snow lightly fell through the trees. The early Belgian evening had begun to fall, and the sun's little light entered at a sharp westerly angle.

Deac felt the snow penetrate his uniform and cool the perspiration on his chest. Cautiously lifting his head, he skimmed the horizon in the fading light. The air appeared hazy and dim, like his mental fog. His other senses, however, were heightened. He had heard something.

The Medic tried to get Deac's attention but found the attempt useless. The young Corporal had become fixated on a sound in the distance.

Then it came again. "Hi-ho."

Gould heard it this time as well.

Deacon remained alert.

"Hi-ho," a voice whispered just loud enough for it to carry in the wind.

"Silver," Deac finally whispered back, honing in on the location of the source of the voice.

Sergeant Gunderson slid out from underneath the branches of a large spruce tree, inching out his head just enough for Deac to recognize him.

Deac didn't move but only eyed the Sergeant who hid about forty feet away.

The young Corporal from Arizona tapped the Medic on the shoulder and began crawling towards the large spruce with the newly-acquired Mauser rifle in his right hand. Gould shadowed him in the manner taught at boot camp with his medical bag still attached to his shoulder.

The blue spruce measured over ten feet in diameter and its lowest branches hung less than a few inches off the ground. The sharp evergreen needles kept the snow out and the ground dry.

Gunderson lay near the perimeter where his torso pressed up against the thinner branches. As Deac and Gould reached the haven, their thinner bodies penetrated closer to its center.

All three took a moment to breathe.

"Good to see ya, Deac." Gunderson smiled at his friend.

Deac couldn't force out a smile but said, "Good to see you, too." His face appeared tense.

Gunderson winked and nodded back. "Glad you brought a medic along. He'll come in handy," Gunderson remarked in a friendly manner to Gould.

Again, Gould felt like a piece of armament attached to a unit but not part of it. "Thanks," he replied.

The Sergeant surveyed the forest. A group of Germans were returning to their regiment, never having fired their weapons.

"They're moving out and it's getting dark. I'm not sure I want to be stuck here all night when the temperature drops. I say we move on until we find shelter or some friendly faces." Gunderson took charge of the two Corporals.

The three men emerged from the spruce tree into the lightly falling snow and setting sun. Deac and Gunderson walked side by side; Gould took the rear.

"What were you guys arguing about back there?" Gunderson inquired.

"I don't know what's wrong with your friend here, but he choked," Gould sternly said from behind.

Deac didn't reply.

"He had a chance to kill the Kraut and wasted it. Those guys were slaughtering us back there. He could have killed a murderer."

Interesting choice of words, Deac thought to himself.

"You don't know that he was one of the ones. There were a bunch that did nothing from what I saw." Gunderson didn't know if he was defending Deac or the Germans.

"Yeah, but you don't know that he wasn't."

"I do," Deac broke in. He spoke with such a calm authority that Gould couldn't respond.

The three walked awhile in silence toward the setting sun.

Gunderson was the first to break the peace. "Uh, since we're stuck together, let's try and make the best of it. I'm Sergeant Gordon Gunderson and this is Corporal Nathan Greer, but he goes by Deac."

Deac passed the German rifle from his right hand to his left. Twisting around, he stuck out his arm.

Gould relaxed and shook hands. "Sorry, Corporal. It's been a rough couple of days. I'm not sure where my head's at."

"I know the feeling." Deac grinned.

Winley Crashes

Winley reached inside his pocket and pulled out the white handkerchief with the initials stitched in the corner. Holding it in his hand, he realized he had walked for miles. The woods had finally thinned, and the sun was just beginning to set. An orange glow slid underneath the pink clouds.

Winley stopped behind a thick clump of fir trees and spotted a small town. He saw a few farm houses and cows meandering about in the snow. A slush-covered road disappeared into the setting sun on the far side. The Germans must have passed through without acknowledging the small town's existence, but they did leave something.

A German Kettendraftrad sat idly at the eastern edge of a field. The half-tracked motorcycle looked like a mini, open-air tank. One wheel in front controlled by handlebars directed the tracked wheels behind. The cycle carried one driver and three or four other men in a box above the tracks. It moved well through the muddy, forest roads of the Ardennes even if steering often proved difficult.

Winley assumed it had broken down or run out of gas, but it was still worth a try. He decided to wait until nightfall to commandeer the vehicle.

The Captain found waiting in the snow easy compared to the last forty-eight hours. The day remained mostly clear with only a few short bursts of heavy flurries. The snow was packed and the evergreens provided protection from the wind as well as humans. He heard only the growl of his stomach.

When the sun had completely set and darkness consumed the clearing, Winley ventured toward the half-tracked. He folded his snow cape and tucked it under his arm. It was only now that he realized that he didn't have his rifle. His thoughts had been too preoccupied on Larsen and his sister. His only weapon was the .38 in its holster.

It began to snow.

He walked around the vehicle in a pointless inspection. Placing a hand on the side, he jumped into the driver's position. He looked around.

"Odd, there's no one here," he remarked to the motorcycle.

No lights emerged from the farms; no vehicles passed by; no person yelled out for supper. Only a few cows wandered among the fields.

"At least they have each other." This time he spoke to the cows.

Winley fumbled around for the starter and depressed the clutch. He pushed, pulled and twisted any knob he could find. Not knowing which appendage worked its magic, Winley felt the cycle jerk and heard the engine groan. With his right foot, he gave the machine some gas. The cycle rumbled and cranked over. The engine started.

"I can't believe it. Larsen must still be praying for me."

The half-tracked settled into its mid-pitched hum as Winley attempted to engage the gears.

The cycle shot forward, nearly throwing the man off the back. Grabbing the handle bars he regained control. The vehicle moved at a fast jog. It could, perhaps, go faster if he could prevent the tracks from slipping in the freshly falling snow.

The cycle's rear slid side to side, and Winley realized that controlling the tracks proved harder than the wheel up front.

He felt, and at times appeared, like a bronco-rider at a rodeo. He had never seen one, of course, but assumed it was similar. He bounced in the saddle as he made his way over drifts and mounds in the snow. A few ditches nearly capsized the vehicle. One particularly deep one ejected his snow cape, the last of his belongings not secured in his pockets or to his body, out of the cycle.

He knew that the roads ran west, exactly where he wanted to go. However, he also knew that the Germans were following the roads, and he certainly didn't want to surprise them from the rear. He decided to continue southwest, cutting through the forests. As long as the snow didn't fall, the cycle should function well.

Winley entered the growth of pines again. He felt safer and drove as fast as he felt comfortable in the darkness. Soon he had mastered controlling the vehicle.

He continued the drive for almost thirty minutes when suddenly he emerged from the forest and crossed a road. In the moon's light he appeared as a silver button clinking and bouncing its way across the divide. Had this occurred ten minutes earlier or ten minutes later, he would have run over a few German soldiers leaving the Baugnez massacre site and headed toward Malmédy.

The panic of being in the open momentarily blinded the Captain. Instinctively, he floored the gas on the cycle and shot across the road.

Driving at this point was all luck. The cycle roared and sped through trees, the branches hitting Winley in the chest and face.

The rear slid-out from the machine, and the cycle began sliding down a hillside backwards.

Winley turned to witness a large tree slam into the side of the half-tracked.

To keep from being ejected, Winley grabbed the handle bars with his right hand.

The cycle kicked back around and continued down the steep slope.

Winley's body hung almost completely outside the vehicle. Hitting another tree flung him into the back seat with a loud crash. The collision broke off the front wheel.

The cycle snowplowed its way toward the bottom of the ravine.

With a near silent thud, Winley and what remained of the Kettenkraftrad landed against a large rock.

Winley ricocheted off the stone and landed, unconscious, a few feet away.

Kendrick Escapes

Captain Beyer hadn't finished disposing of the American "weight" and gathered some of his most trusted men to his side. His instructions were clear, and these soldiers were willing.

They moved as a unit, Beyer out in front, five others behind in formation like a flock of birds. They crossed the road, almost bouncing, arms swinging at their sides. They looked like a big city's neighborhood gang, bold, brazen and overconfident, young thugs following their leader. As they arrived at the edge of the field, the entourage appeared at ease with their grim task.

Captain Beyer strode up to an American soldier sprawled in the snow, motionless. The dead man was thin, blonde and wore wire-rimmed glasses. His face pointed heavenward, lips parted in a voiceless plea. Beyer slid his pistol from its holster, gripped it in his right hand and let it hang loosely by his leg.

The German officer glanced down at the pale figure below him and tilted his head. He aimed the gun at the boy's forehead, barely widening the angle at his shoulder, elbow locked. Without emotion, he pulled the trigger and shot the cipher in the snow.

The barrel of the gun flashed, smoke rose and powder residue fell, evidencing the crime. The thin body barely registered the impact, only pressing the back of the boy's head deeper into the slush. The only further indication of the post-mortem execution was a small dark hole in Walker's brow and his slightly skewed glasses.

Captain Engel witnessed the event from the jeep where he sat under guard. His anger heated as the thoughts of Christmas day one year earlier invaded his mind. He had successfully locked out that day since burning the letter-the letter that informed him that his only son had died. He had successfully locked everything else out as well.

Watching Beyer's latest act of brutality, however, broke Engel's apathy. He saw his son's face with a bullet hole and felt a burning deep inside, the first emotions to enter his heart in a year. He leaped from the car and charged toward Beyer. His guard did nothing.

"I'll die before I allow you to continue this!"

Beyer was ready for him, expecting it. With a swift motion, Beyer turned around and held his arm horizontally. He smirked and fired one shot. Engel fell in the mud. Beyer holstered his weapon and continued the survey of the field.

The entourage fanned out and systematically verified the status of each body. Walking down the rows, they kicked heads with the toes of their boots, jabbed guts with the barrels of their rifles and shot any body the moved, and some that didn't. Their inspection was methodical and callous. The soldiers didn't speak. Only the occasional muffled shot blast echoed against the forest wall.

In the final row of bodies, nearest the line of trees, a German soldier approached a pile of three prisoners face down in the snow, one underneath the other two. The soldier fired his gun twice, sending bullets through the two corpses on top. One round grazed the side of Private Kendrick, still alive and hiding underneath. He concentrated his strength to remain motionless. The German continued his duties.

As they moved through the field, the German gang pulled dog tags and removed overcoats, combat jackets and even shirts and pants. The articles were taken to the vehicle where Captain Engel once sat. Two soldiers jumped in the front seats and left to deliver the bounty to Lieutenant Colonel Otto Skorzeny who was already nearing Stavelot.

On December 17, 1944 over eighty American prisoners of war were massacred on a field near the Baugnez crossroads by the German Army. It would later become known as the Malmédy Massacre for the larger town just a few miles away. It was not an isolated occurrence during the Battle of the Bulge.

As the sun set, Private Kendrick waited for the right moment. The sky was darkening, and he no longer heard German voices. He inched his head out from under the jacket shroud, leaving his body motionless. Twisting his neck, he freed his left eye. He lay obscured in the long shadow of the forest.

The Germans had moved across the road and into town. Kendrick slowly slid out of his morbid confines, worming his way in the snow. His muscles were stiff from the cold and wouldn't respond. Undulating his body in waves, he made his way toward the harbor of the forest. Minutes passed, and he had only covered a few feet. He continued slithering, now arms and legs spread like a spider. He wanted a cigarette.

He pushed himself onto one knee, then placed his weight on his right foot, his eyes never leaving the enemy. On both feet now, he wobbled for a brief second until gaining control. His legs felt as thick and heavy as concrete. He grunted as he forced one leg forward, then the other, hunched over and pulling up on his thighs.

He ran west but looked back towards the road, hoping he wouldn't hit a tree or stumble on a fallen log. Step after step he came closer to the forest line. The Germans spotted nothing. He entered the forest and stood behind a tree.

The setting sun cast strange light through the woods, reflecting off the flurries falling through the branches. The Private expanded his lungs, stretching his chest and filling his blood with oxygen. His body slowly warmed. His mind, however, was still frozen with the thoughts of what had just happened.

Private Kendrick starting jogging, the best his legs would do.

The Company Grows

The three escaped soldiers sat in a large depression on a hillside. A number of fallen trees had landed crosswise on the uphill edge of the hole, providing a small barrier between themselves and the massacre field still not more than a half mile away. The notch provided a bench on an otherwise steep slope. The Sergeant sat between the two corporals, each sensing the other's troubles.

Snow continued to fall in occasional heavy bouts, and the sky quickly darkened. Yet the men still considered themselves lucky. Not one inquired or questioned about the afternoon; they crouched in silent recognition of the alternative. Until . . .

"What was that?" Gunderson asked, nearly jumping out of the hole.

Deac sprawled his body on the snow at the other men's feet. He aimed the rifle toward the sound.

"Sounded like tree limbs breaking," Gould informed. He looked down at Deac and wondered if the boy could actually provide cover.

"There!" Gunderson bent over Deac's shoulder, his right arm in alignment with the rifle.

Both instruments pointed down the slope and to the left from where the three sat. The last brightness of day reflected off a twenty-foot slide in the snow, ending at a large pine tree growing crooked out of the ground. A green figure lay balled at the base of the trunk.

"A Kraut?" Gould asked, squinting to see in the waning light.

"Don't know," Gunderson replied. "He's half covered in snow. You make anything out Deac?"

Deacon remained fixed on the clump of olive fatigues, not much darker than the pine needles above it. "Not yet, sir."

"Gould, look out over the logs and see if anything else is sliding down the hill," the Sergeant ordered.

Gould stood with his body pressed against the hillside. His arms just reaching above the fallen logs, he pulled himself up and peered over the damp wood. Darkness had completely covered the hill. "Nothing," he said, slumping back down. "It's too dark to . . ."

A single expletive rang out through the ravine.

"It's not too dark to hear that that was English," Gould finished, almost laughing at the break in tension.

"Many Germans know more English cuss words than I do," Deac interjected.

"Really, how many Jerries do you know?" Gould questioned more than Deac's knowledge of Germans.

"Considering that Deac doesn't know any cuss words, I don't see how this is at all relevant." Gunderson was losing patience with the Medic. Helping his friend up, the Sergeant said, "I think we're okay, Deac. I doubt that word would be the first out of a German's mouth when he hit the tree."

The body began moving. It appeared like a dark mass against the snow. The man stood and braced himself against the solidity that stopped his decent. He slugged the trunk with his right hand and swore again.

"That boy's gonna get himself killed," Gunderson said.

"And us as well," Gould fired back, looking down at the soldier in a tirade. "We've got to shut him up."

"Gould, you stay here. Deac and I will go get him."

Gunderson and Deac cautiously headed across the hillside.

"I think the Medic knows something's up," Deac whispered when the two were out of earshot of Gould.

"How do know?"

"Just a feeling that he's looking through me, like he can see inside my head."

"He is a medic. I don't know; maybe he can help."

"I already saw field medics. They're not trained for, well, for whatever it is. Besides, he doesn't look like the kind that wants to help."

"I know what you mean."

"You won't say anything, to him, I mean." Deac turned and looked his Sergeant in the face. "Okay?"

"Don't worry, I promise I won't say a thing."

As the two approached, the Private shaking snow out of his jacket nearly fell over. He began to run.

"Hold on. We're Americans. Hold up, soldier." Gunderson spoke the last sentence as a true sergeant.

Deac scanned back up the hillside with the rifle, slowly pivoting left and right.

The Private stood as a statue, too scared to even turn around.

"It's okay, Private. We escaped too."

Private Kendrick held his side as he turned to face Gunderson.

"You injured?" Gunderson asked.

Deac continued his surveillance.

"Yeah, I'll tell you later. You got a smoke?" Kendrick acted like he had just walked into the mess tent back at boot camp and asked for a cup of coffee. Suddenly, not a hint of trepidation was heard in his voice.

"No, but we've got a medic. I think that's a little more important, don't you?"

"Uh, yeah. Sure."

"You ready, Deac?"

"Let's go," he replied as he lowered the gun.

The night sky had fully settled over the woods, creating a shadowless world of blacks and blues. Gunderson struggled to find their way back to the large divot in the hill.

"Who's this?" Gould asked, standing in wait for the return of the gun's protection.

"Private Kendrick. 285th Field Artillery."

Deac took interest. "You guys were headed to St. Vith." He contemplated how quickly his life had been changing lately. He wasn't sure if could get any worse.

"Yeah, at least this morning. Who knows now." Kendrick began to shiver. "Anyone got a smoke? I could really use one."

"Sorry, the Krauts took everything, or didn't you notice?" Gould felt the irritation swell inside him but couldn't determine the cause.

"He's hurt. Gould, why don't you check him out," Gunderson said without inflecting the tone of a sergeant.

Kendrick lifted his shirt to reveal a small cut on his side. A thin line of dried blood marked the small wound.

Gould pressed his fingers, not so gently, along the slice just under Kendrick's rib cage.

"Ouch. Easy big guy. You've got the light touch of a bar bouncer."

"You can call me Gould, Corporal or Medic. Not big guy! Understand, Private?"

"Sorry. It doesn't feel all that bad, kind of like the sting of a mosquito bite."

"No, it's not that bad. You'll be fine. The bullet only tore at the skin."

Kendrick poked his finger through the hole in his uniform. "Yep, I'm proud of this one. Somethin' to tell the guys back home." He smiled.

Gunderson and Deac glanced at each other and sat down on the ledge.

Kendrick tucked his shirt back in his trousers and buttoned his jacket.

The four men rested a moment on the ledge without further conversation, preoccupied with other matters. Deac sat with the confiscated Mauser across his lap. His hand trembled slightly, and he concentrated on the book in his pocket and the picture it contained. He used the image of his wife to push out the other faces that crowded his mind.

Gould watched the troubled young man from the corner of his eye.

Night fell as expected, dark but warmer. Thick clouds hid the moon and stars, only occasionally peeking around with a silver lining.

Gunderson finally took charge of the group. "Look, I would feel much more comfortable moving than sitting here."

"Me, too," Kendrick added nearly jumping off the snowy ledge. "I didn't join this man's army to hide out on some hillside. Let's go." Kendrick began to climb up the slope.

"Easy, Private. We're not headed back to the battle. I want to get as far from the Germans as possible. I say we stick to the woods and head west. Let's finding shelter, if possible."

"No problem. As long as we're doing something, I'll be happy," Kendrick replied and reversed his course.

The newly formed foursome headed down the hillside and into the gully.

Winley's Awakening

"Hey, Deac, how many rounds are left in the Mauser?" Gunderson asked.

"Eight. A full clip."

Kendrick jogged up beside Deac. "Ain't' ya got any more clips?"

Deac shook his head.

"Sorry, Kendrick. We forgot to pick a few up at the supply depot we just passed. But, hey, if you want to run back and grab a few, we'd all appreciate it." Gould trailed immediately behind the other three.

The night sky hid the men traveling in dark green uniforms. Gunderson and Deac wore waist jackets with hoods; the other two had longer coats that covered their hips. All four fortunately escaped with gloves and helmets, except Kendrick who wore a wool cap pulled down to cover his ears.

"What's your problem, Medic." Kendrick dragged out Gould's title. "I was just askin'. I wanna be ready for whatever action we meet up with is all."

Shifting his medical bag to the other shoulder, Gould replied, "Try a little respect and you might get some in return, Kendrick."

Gunderson and Deac exchanged glances that communicated their growing irritation with their new traveling companions.

Gunderson broke in. "I don't want to have to baby sit you guys until we reach a platoon. Is that clear?"

"He started it," Private Kendrick pouted. "Don't anyone have some cigarettes?"

They all looked at Kendrick.

"Ya'll don't need to answer that. I'm just itchin' for a smoke, and I'm tired. Give me a break."

Gould had also tired of the Private's voice. "Sergeant. You got any idea of who else is around these parts?"

"Not really. Deac and I had come down from Elsenborn on a . . ." Gunderson paused just quick enough to eye Deacon. ". . . transfer to St. Vith. We were waiting at the crossroads for Kendrick's group when we, well, got hit."

"I can't be much help either," Gould said. "I was with the 2nd Infantry Division headed toward the Roer Dams when the Germans started bombing us on the line. We scattered. I ended up with another division, and we got overrun again." While speaking, Gould remembered the Lieutenant and Walker. "We were taken prisoner and herded to that field."

The snow measured deeper at the base of the hill, but the flat terrain made easier walking.

"Don't look at me, either. I'm just a private and follow along. You officers don't tell us much."

"Got stripe envy, Kendrick?" Gould mocked.

"Sorry. I don't wanna be no officer. Just fight. Give me a gun and let me go at 'em."

This statement worried all the other members of the group.

"I'll carry the weapon if it gets too heavy." Kendrick looked to Corporal Greer with eagerness.

Gunderson stated with authority: "I'd rather Deac keep the gun."

This worried Gould. Rather than pursue the issue, he stated, "Well, we still don't have an answer to the big question."

The Sergeant strained his eyes and scanned the area even though there was nothing to see. "I don't think Command had any idea."

Gould added, "I don't think so either. But they should by now."

"Hold on." Deac whispered and held up his hand.

Kendrick nearly tripped.

"What? What do you see?" Gunderson asked.

The four now crouched in the snow. Only a slight breeze whistling through the pines broke the silence. The men looked in all directions.

"Over there," Deac said, pointing about a hundred meters up the ravine.

"What? Germans?" Kendrick almost sounded excited.

"A vehicle. It looks turned over."

Gunderson moved closer to Deacon. "I see it, too."

"Anyone with it?" Gould asked.

The Sergeant replied while Deac fixed his sight on the wrecked half-tracked. "Don't think so. You guys wait here."

Gunderson and Deac kept low and moved slowly. Gunderson watched the perimeter while Deac eyed the cycle.

"It obviously came crashing down the hill. It's German," Deac reported.

"Anyone with it?"

"No. No wait! There's a body lying in the snow."

The two halted.

"Is he moving?"

"No. I think he's dead."

"Still, let's be careful." Gunderson grabbed Deac's shoulder. "Wait here and cover me."

"I always do, Sarge."

Gunderson's body warmed as he moved toward the vehicle. He heard nothing and felt more confident.

The front wheel had been ripped from the cycle and the right side smashed. He knelt down beside the figure, half-buried underneath a thin shroud of snow. The chest moved.

"Deac! Get Gould!"

That was all Deac needed to hear. It didn't matter to him that the man was German. A soldier was injured.

It took only seconds for Greer to skim over the snow back to the Medic and Kendrick. He startled them.

"What? What is it?"

"Gould, come on and bring your bag. There's a German soldier who's hurt pretty bad."

"A what?" Gould nearly shouted as he looked around. His body began to shake with the fear that if there was one, there were others. "You've got to be kidding! We've got to get out of here."

"Pansy," Kendrick said, turning his head.

Gould nearly leaped toward the Private.

Deac, for the second time in his life, pointed a gun at an American soldier, the same American soldier. "That's an order, Corporal!" Deac felt firm in his stance and breathed with the realization.

"Come on, Gould." Kendrick started moving toward the Sergeant.

Lowering the gun and with a softer voice, Deac said, "I saw you back there."

"What are you talking about?" Gould shouldered his bag and began walking.

"With the other soldier, by the tree."

Gould tried to walk faster and get ahead of Deacon. It wasn't working. The young man with a gun seemed to float on top of the snow.

"What?" Gould wasn't really asking a question.

"In the woods. I saw you attending to another soldier. It was right after we fled. The Germans will still shooting, and you sat there helping."

"It was just another soldier," Gould lied. "There wasn't anything I could do."

"Didn't look that way to me. You were, I don't know. You were focused. I was. . . ." Deac was about to say proud.

"The man died. There was nothing that could be done."

Kendrick had already reached the fallen Kettendraftrad while Deac and Gould lagged just a few feet behind.

"There is always something that can be done," Deac tried to add.

Gould felt a split in his head. It hurt.

"Get over here, Gould," the Sergeant commanded.

Gould sidled next to the fallen man. "He's American?"

Kendrick stood over the others. "Duh, Doc."

Gunderson stood and jabbed a finger into the Private's chest. "One more crack and I'm tying you to a tree and leaving you to freeze to death. I'm your commanding officer, and you'll speak only when ordered. Is that clear?" Gunderson hated barking orders but had lost patience.

"Yes, sir."

Gould began his assessment of the unconscious soldier. He removed his gloves and the man's woolen cap. He felt around the man's scalp and neck. A medium-sized swelling was prominent on his head. Gould looked at his hands. "No blood, that's a good sign."

Winley's breathing was shallow but steady. Although the man was cold, Gould felt a strong pulse. He opened the overcoat and jacket. He pushed the buttons on Winley's uniform to the side of his chest, a bulge appeared in the breast pocket.

Gould made a fist and rapped the man's chest as hard as he could with the knuckle of his index finger.

"What are you doing?" Gunderson asked.

Before Gould could answer, Winley awoke.

"Ah, God, what happened?"

"Are you really asking Him?" Gould made a rhetorical comment and placed his hand on Winley's chest, keeping him down.

Winley rubbed the back of his head.

"You're lucky you've been lying in the snow. It probably kept the swelling down."

Winley's body stiffened as he became cognizant of his surroundings. "What? Who are you?"

Gould looked at the others, perplexed. "We're Americans. What'd you think?"

"Prove it!"

"Excuse me?" Gunderson asked, kneeling again beside Winley. "Look at us."

"We're not speaking Kraut," Gould added.

Deac kept a surveillance while Kendrick kept quiet, at least momentarily. Deac felt on edge; he wanted to move on. His right arm shook, but no one noticed.

"Doesn't mean anything. Who was the third president of the United States?" Winley tried to push himself away from the Sergeant and grab his pistol still holstered to his side.

"Boy he sure hit his head pretty hard," Kendrick said.

Gunderson grabbed the Captain with his right hand.

Winley tried to swing at the Sergeant, but the blow thudded into Gunderson's hand.

"Easy, Captain. It was Thomas Jefferson." Gould surprised himself that he remembered that piece of information.

"And the fourth."

"I have no idea. Do you bright guy?" Gould demanded. "You were the one riding around in a German motorcycle! We should be asking you the questions."

Winley relaxed. "Sorry. You're right. I had to ask."

"Why?" inquired Gunderson.

"I'll tell you later. Where's your H.Q.? I need a phone, immediately!"

All four escapees stared at the man in amazement. He could not be an escapee from the massacre-he still had his sidearm.

"I hate to tell you this, but we've got a long story. And it's kind of ugly." Gunderson lowered his head.

"Mine as well." Winley realized his journey wasn't over.

Revelations and Resolutions

Gunderson did his best to parlay as much information as he could. It was getting late, and colder, the temperature falling below freezing. The group sauntered through the white-sprayed pines with Gunderson out front and speaking to Captain Winley. The others followed quietly but listened.

"I don't know how many fell. There were well over a hundred of us at the field."

"I am sorry," Winley said, "But not surprised."

"The four of us just ran into each other in the woods. Well, Deac and I were together at Baugnez and then fled. Gould and Kendrick also escaped. I assume there are others out there in the same position as us."

"We are near Malmédy, though, correct?"

"Yes. We should be only a couple of miles away. If we headed in a more northerly direction we'd run right into it."

"I thought that would be our best plan," Gould interjected from behind.

"But I didn't," Gunderson continued. "The Germans split,

most headed south, but I also saw a large group with artillery headed west, toward Malmédy. I'm sure they're already there."

"I can confirm that they are following all the roads west with a minimum of three army groups all along the Belgian border. They are trying to get to the Meuse and cross it," Winley explained. "Then on to Liege, the ammo dump and finally to Antwerp. From there they could control the ports. Hitler thinks that will win him the war."

"That's impossible. They'll never get across even if they make it to the river. We control those bridges, have for awhile. They'll blow 'em and the Germans will be trapped from all sides. I don't know much about strategy, but that seems pretty idiotic to me." Gunderson slowed to a stop.

The others circled around Winley, waiting for more information that might explain the last forty-eight hours.

Deac still carried the Mauser, keenly alert. Kendrick looked too tired to speak.

"They might make it. If Skorzeny makes it."

Gunderson remembered hearing that name, back at the field. "Who's Skorzeny? And if he makes what?"

"That is my story and the reason for the interrogation back there." Winley felt his breast pocket and the thick wad of papers still hiding in it. "Two days have passed since they broke the line. It was supposed to over by now. At least according to Hitler's plans. But if you say the spearhead was only to Malmédy this afternoon, then they been slowed to a crawl. That may have bought us some time."

Looking at Winley with suspicion, Gould abruptly asked, "How do you know so much about the Krauts?"

"Look, I don't care if this guy is a Kraut." Kendrick could only hold back for so long. "It's late. I'm tired. We need to either build ourselves some shelter or find somewhere to rest."

"The Private is correct, Sergeant. I will finish explaining later."

"How're you doing, Deac?" Gunderson inquired of his friend.

"I'm fine."

"Doesn't look that way to me," Gould said.

Deac repeated, "I'm fine, really." His voice didn't sound convincing. "Besides, I think we've found the answer to our prayers." Deac lifted his chin, a directional indication.

Winley paused on the coincidence of Deacon's and Larsen's words.

"How'd ya see that? You must have radar or something." Kendrick kidded.

"Something like that," Deac humbly replied.

"Let's go, but move quietly. That means you, Kendrick." Gunderson wasn't in the mood to wake anyone up and didn't want any more scuffles between the Private and Gould.

The five moved with ease through the snow pack measuring only a few inches deep. The thought of finding shelter buoyed their spirits. Only Deac remained uncomfortable.

They approached a small, wooden structure, apparently many years abandoned.

"What is it?" Kendrick asked.

"Looks like a shed," Gunderson answered.

"Duh, but a shed for what?" Kendrick said back to the Sergeant. "There ain't nothin' else around here. No farm or village. It's a shed in the middle of the forest. Seems creepy to me."

"Could have been used for hunting. Like an outpost or something," Gould said as he was about to enter the building.

"Hold on, Corporal." Gunderson tried to grab the Medic's arm. "We don't know that it's empty."

"Well, it'd be too late now." Gould pushed the door open.

The shed smelled like old leather and wet wood. A stone foundation enclosed twelve-inch floorboards. The one large room contained a table, a few wooden crates and an old wood-burning stove and pipe. There were no windows.

"I can't see much, except that there's nobody here." Gould entered the shed first.

The other men followed him into the darkness. Kendrick accidentally kicked the table and cursed.

"Watch the volume, Kendrick. And your words," Gunderson warned. "Something, or someone, has to be near by."

Winley added, "In this darkness, we could be just a few yards from a German camp."

"That's what I'm afraid of." The Sergeant scratched his arm. "Hey, Deac, take Kendrick and Gould to scout around a bit before we settle in."

"You got it," Deac responded and immediately headed out the door. Kendrick followed.

Gould held up a moment. "Uh, Gunderson. Something's up with your boy there. I think I know what it is."

"Don't worry about Deac. He'll watch even your back. Go."

Gould shook his head and left.

Outside, the night engulfed the men in blackness; none remembered a night so dark. With no moonlight, they seemed to be walking through oil, not snow, and tree limbs hit them in the faces before they ever saw it.

"Let's spread out. Kendrick, take about twenty feet to the right. And Gould, about twenty to my left."

Gould studied Deacon. He didn't notice any of the twitching he had seen earlier, but the boy wasn't right. "You know, you're the only one with a weapon." Gould hoped to commandeer the rifle.

"I'll cover you," Deac responded.

The three spread out and continued their search. They had put less than a quarter mile under foot when Deac began seeing faces in the darkness.

The night turned into a dream and the dream to a nightmare. He watched a woman cross his path. She stopped, turned and stared back at him before moving on. Another woman, leaning against a tree, held a child in her arms, crying.

Deac rubbed his eyes with the back of his left arm. He held the gun in his shaking right. They're not there, they're not real, he mumbled to himself. Focus, concentrate. He pressed his eyes tightly shut.

He heard someone scream out.

His eyes popped open. There was nothing but darkness. He made out Kendrick's figure, then Gould's. Neither seemed to notice. His arm tingled, but he kept moving through the trees.

Gould whistled. Deac and Kendrick stopped and turned. They suddenly realized that they were standing in the middle of a road. Gould looked down at something. Kendrick and Deac ran over to him.

"An American ambulance," Gould stated calmly. "Engine's still warm, too."

Deac scanned the area.

Kendrick asked, "Any, uh, bodies?"

"Two that I've seen."

"There's more over here," Deac added.

"Let's get out of here. I've had enough death and recon for one night." Kendrick began shifting his body like ants were crawling in his pants.

"Look for food, weapons or anything else. Quickly!" Deac ordered. Deac wanted out as well. He still sensed that the faces were out there, watching him. "We could use some supplies."

The men started searching the vehicle. The overturned truck spilled six wounded and a driver into the snow bank.

Gould began patting down the body of the driver. The man wore a red cross on his arm. Gould looked at his own arm band and continued searching. He found no weapon, shells or personals. A canteen lay next to the body. Gould tucked it into his coat.

The wind began to pick up, and the clouds parted. A beam of moonlight hit the truck like a spotlight. All three soldiers tensed.

"Hurry up, while it's light." Deac spoke from inside the back of the ambulance.

Kendrick kicked through the mush of icy snow. He found a couple cans of c-rations.

Pulling the overcoat off the driver, Corporal Gould saw something fall into the snow. He picked up the object and examined it. He felt a cold, but thick, billfold. He shoved the wallet into his pocket and looked around. Deac was standing by the rear of the truck watching him.

Deac returned to searching through the ambulance without a word.

Gould knelt beside the body and lifted the arm. A silver watch had stopped working at 1605 hours. The man forgot to wind it, Gould thought to himself. He removed the timepiece from the dead medic and put it on his own wrist, replacing his broken watch.

Kendrick rummaged through the rations. The cigarettes had been removed. "Damn it," he muttered. He threw the rest of the contents into a sea-bag now slung over his shoulder already filled with gloves, a wool cap and an extra pair of winter underwear.

Deac handed a flashlight, a few more rations and a deck of cards to Kendrick. "Put these into there, would ya Kendrick."

"Sure." Kendrick stuffed the bag but kept the cards in his hand.

A cloud passed in front of the moon, and darkness again covered the wreckage scene.

Kendrick looked up and began to cough. He hacked up some phlegm and spit the wad against the ambulance.

Gould shook his head and scolded the Private. "Nice manners, Kendrick."

"What?"

"Let's go, you guys." Deac hitched the rifle over his shoulder and headed back across the road to the forest.

"You know where we're going, Deac?" Kendrick asked, looking around, lost.

"Yeah, the shed's not far."

The Medic twisted the new watch on his wrist. "Your radar again?"

"No, I just remember."

The three disappeared into the dark woods.

"What more can you tell me, Winley?"

"About what you men have been through, not much. The German Lieutenant did say that their orders were to take no prisoners and move as fast as possible to the Meuse. He used the word ruthless, I think. They were to cause enough havoc on this side of the line for Skorzeny to slip passed and infiltrate deep inside Allied territory."

Gunderson and Winley sat across from each other and spoke in the dark.

"Who's this Skorzeny? I heard his name back at the field."

"I do not quite know. The Lieutenant didn't elaborate on the man, just his plans. Do you think he was there, at the field?"

"Don't know. I just remember hearing the name."

"We should hope so, and that he has not penetrated further into Belgium."

"Why? What could one man do?" Gunderson repositioned himself on the crate.

"He has a band of hand-picked soldiers, many of whom speak English."

"What?" Gunderson suddenly became nervous, like he had a premonition of something evil about to happen.

"They speak English. They are wearing American uniforms

and driving American vehicles. They supposedly have convincing identification." Winley spoke slowly.

"Now I get your interrogation when we met."

"I had to protect myself."

"I still don't get what they could accomplish. They certainly couldn't make it too far or get any kind of intelligence. Someone would figure it out."

"They are to pretend to be retreating from the front with the others. They only need to get past the checkpoints and make it to the Meuse."

Gunderson jumped in. "There they would secure the bridges and wait for their own ground troops. Once they get across the river, we're in trouble."

"Precisely. As we speak, Skorzeny could be masquerading his way across Belgium."

"Do you think it could work?" Gunderson sensed the education of the Captain.

"Lieutenant Lucht admitted that the other officers in the High Command considered the plan ill-fated and rushed. However, they have certainly provided major ground forces."

Gunderson sighed. "And we weren't expecting anything like this, either."

"No. And the men at the bridges . . ." Winley began.

Gunderson finished, "Our boys will welcome a group of murderers with open arms. And the longer it goes on, the more Americans that die."

"Exactly." Finally divulging the information didn't provide the relief Winley expected. He now felt more fear and anxiety.

The two officers sitting alone in the dark nearly jumped off the crates as they heard the sound of movement from outside their new shelter.

"Wait here!" Gunderson rushed to the door and peered outside. Three figures came toward the small cabin. The Sergeant whistled.

Deac whistled back.

"It's them."

Kendrick entered first, trailed by Gould. Deac paused just outside the door to scan the perimeter.

"Where'd you get that?" Gunderson asked pointing to the sea-bag over Kendrick's shoulder.

"We sort of ran into an ambulance," he replied.

"Theirs or ours?" Winley asked.

"Ours."

Winley stood. "Apparently, we are not lost in the middle of nowhere."

"No," Deac said as he entered the room. "We're less than half a mile from a road that's obviously being used. The Germans must have just passed from the looks of things. They must have been in a hurry because they didn't take much." Deac looked to Gould.

Kendrick watched the Medic setting a silver timepiece. "New watch there, Doc?" Kendrick began removing the contents of the sea-bag but watching Gould.

"Trust me. He's not going to miss it."

Kendrick dropped the sea-bag on the table and straightened "If I take a bullet, ya gonna to take my personals?"

Before the two could go at it, Gunderson interrupted, "Anything useful in there, Kendrick?"

The others also felt the tension mounting in the room. Kendrick pulled out a flashlight and switched it on.

"That'll help. What about matches?" he asked, continuing the distraction.

Kendrick shook his head.

"Probably wouldn't be safe lighting the stove anyway."

"We were lucky to find the truck." Gould finished setting the watch and turned his attention toward the rations on the table.

Deac stood by the door speculating about Gould. He thought about the irony of the Medic and wondered what caused such a contradiction. Deac didn't believe in luck. He believed in the book in his pocket and the picture it contained. "We found just what we needed," he corrected.

Kendrick pulled out the clothing and rations. "They took all the cigarettes out of the rations but left the food."

Speaking quietly and facing the woods, Deac said, "Food we need. Cigarettes we don't."

"Speak for yourself." Kendrick had everything out onto the table. "I could really use a smoke."

"And some sleep," Winley added.

"Hey, Winley, what happened to all your personals?" the Medic asked walking over to the table. "All you had was your side arm."

"I just finished explaining that to your Sergeant."

Gould held back the impulse to correct him that Gunderson wasn't his sergeant. "Do we get to hear the story?"

Gunderson said, "Let's just say he's been running from the Germans as long as we have. And he's got some important information that we need to get to H.Q."

This last statement garnered everyone's attention.

Winley set the maps down on the table and the others gathered around. Even Gunderson stood over to see the papers with the help of the flashlight. They ate what was left of the rations and listened. With less detail than earlier, Winley explained Hitler's plan to retake Europe and Skorzeny's role in achieving it. The men appeared stunned and worried. The last few days began to make morbid sense.

"We're the only ones that know about this?" Gould asked, breaking the silence.

Deac felt something under his foot.

"To the best of my knowledge," Winley answered. "I also believe that the Germans have at least a half-day advantage."

Gunderson had been thinking. "If we move quickly and stay off the roads, we might be able to slip ahead of them. Then we try and find the first friendly camp and get this information over the wires."

Gould broke in, "I don't care about the information. I say we stay hidden until the P-51's blow the Krauts back to Berlin. We'd be too late to help anyways. It'd be a dangerous waste of time. The Jerries don't have the man power to last very long against us, and it'll be suicide for us to try and out run 'em. I don't see the point in taking such a risk."

"There are lives at stake," Gunderson said staring at Medic, "that's the point."

"Our lives are at stake!" Gould looked to the others.

Winley almost agreed with Gould but didn't say anything. The remaining men listened in silence.

Deac toyed with a loose floor board. "We can't force anyone to do this." He pulled up on the strip of wood with the toe of his boot. The board easily came off.

Gould's eyes widened as he heard Deacon's voice. "That's the first reasonable thing you've said."

Without acknowledging the Medic's comment, Deac spoke directly to the other soldiers standing around the table, faces lit from below by a single flashlight. "I'm going. I think we'll make it. It's at least worth the try."

"Deac and I stay together." Gunderson smiled at his friend.

"Hell, sounds like fun to me," Kendrick followed, shuffling the deck of cards like a poker dealer. "I'll do anything to see a little action. I'm tired of doing nothing but march around in the snow and sleep in them foxholes."

Winley's mind raced. He wanted to be done with the responsibility and the guilt. Sergeant Gunderson could take over from here. Then, Winley reached inside his pocket and felt the handkerchief. He paused. "I'm going, too," involuntarily came out his mouth.

Gould shook his head. "I'm not staying around here unarmed and alone. Besides, I've got the medical bag."

"It's settled, then. We get some sleep and leave just before dawn." Gunderson felt the light of hope in the dark air.

Deac Freezes

The group possessed one confiscated German rifle with eight rounds, Winley's pistol, plenty of warm clothing that they divvied up according to need, combat helmets for all, a canteen and just enough rations to fill each man's stomach, a compass, one flashlight and a full deck of cards.

"Watch this!" Kendrick worked the cards with skill. He spread them out on the table in a half circle, flipped the entire stack from face down to face up and back again. In one hand, his fingers cut the deck and reversed the two halves with ease. "Anyone for poker? We can play for smokes."

"Better make that lemonade packets." Gunderson chuckled as he lay on the floor boards.

Deac positioned himself at the doorway, alone with his thoughts.

Getting up, the Sergeant mildly ordered, "Hey, Deac, come get some rest. I'll take the first watch."

"No, thanks. I'm fine. I'd rather be looking out."

Gould repeated the command. "Deac, I think you need to get

some rest. Give the Sergeant the gun. And Kendrick, turn off the flashlight. We should save the batteries."

Kendrick obeyed. "Anyone get the feeling we're traveling with our mom." Kendrick began stacking the cards.

The others silently laughed.

"Then stop acting like a child and start acting like a soldier."

"I'm more of a soldier than you any day of the week and twice on Saturday."

"Shh!"

"What is it, Deac?" Gunderson asked in a whisper.

The others, now on alert, crouched on the floorboards.

Kendrick started to move toward the door, eyeing the rifle in Deac's hands.

Gunderson took him by the ankle and pulled him back. He shook his head.

Without speaking, Corporal Nathan "Deac" Greer moved over to the loose floor board and pulled. Underneath the shed floor was an eighteen-inch crawl space. Deac pulled at another board; it also came up. He waved to the others.

Understanding, the men grabbed the gear and slid below. One of Kendrick's cards, the ace of hearts, floated to the floor, landing face up.

Gunderson, the last to enter the dank hiding place, replaced one wooden plank, pulled a crate on top and then laid the other strip of wood in place.

Five American soldiers hid underneath the floor of an abandoned shed in the middle of the Ardennes forest as three German soldiers entered it.

Flat on their backs, the men held their breath but not their worry. A lantern floated above them, sending rays of light through the slits in the floor and scanning their dilated pupils. Inches from their ears, the sound of bending wood from boots pressing on the floor boards seemed deafening. Dust fell through the cracks, and the smell of dirt and dung filled the crawlspace, nearly choking them.

Captain Winley held his pistol across his chest. The only rifle lay next to Deac's right arm. With their current position, neither man wished for the occasion to use his weapon. Despite the cold, each man began sweating.

Above them, the Germans seemed to be arguing. One even pushed another against the wall. Their voices rose in anger. One kicked the crate covering the loose boards. It crumbled into pieces.

At the other end of the shed, the ace of hearts cast a shadow over Gould's eye. He closed his eyes as a boot came to a rest right on top of the conspicuous giveaway. Kendrick, he angrily thought.

Suddenly, the three German soldiers ran out of the shed, heading towards the road and disappearing into the dark night.

The men underneath the floor waited in silence and fear. In time, their bodies began to chill.

"I believe we are safe," Winley whispered.

Gunderson pushed up on the floorboard and pulled his body out of the crawl space. "Wait here."

The night continued black and moonless. Inside the shed was no exception. The Sergeant peeked out the door. He barely saw the trees just three feet away. Closing his eyes, he concentrated on sounds: a voice, a car, footsteps, anything. The world outside slept in the cold darkness.

"Alright, come on out."

Winley lay prostrated next to Deac. "Corporal. You can get out."

Deac didn't move.

"Corporal Greer, it is safe now. You can get out."

Still, nothing.

"Deac, you okay?" Kendrick added.

Deac didn't respond.

Gould nearly shouted, "Deac, move it!" The Medic now understood the boy's condition. He had seen it before.

Deac appeared dead.

"Hey, Sergeant. Your boy's freaked out and won't move," Gould said through the floor boards.

Kendrick now stirred, uneasy. "What's wrong him?"

Gunderson knelt by the opening and lowered his head into the dark. "Deac, it's Gordon. You alright?"

"I think my arms are frozen," Deac finally replied.

"You've just lost circulation. Try wiggling your fingers, then rotating your wrists. Start to get the blood flowing again."

Deac obeyed his Sergeant. Soon, he was able to move his arms and back muscles. He inched his way, sliding on his back, over to the hole in the floor.

"Just go slowly, Corporal. Don't worry. Time we have plenty of." Winley spoke in fatherly tone. He remembered Larsen and that stupid grin on his face. He remembered his sister and the look on her face when she gave him the handkerchief. He didn't like seeing the current look on Deac's face.

When Deac's chest appeared through the opening, Gunderson reached down and grabbed his coat. With a single arm and the strength of a former wrestler, Gunderson lifted Deacon clean out of the crawl space and stood him on his feet.

The others quickly exited. They all breathed in the cleaner air above their hiding space. Kendrick pulled out the sea-bag and removed the flashlight. The light filled the room.

Supporting his friend, the Sergeant asked, "How're your legs? Think you can stand?"

"Yeah, I'm fine now." Deac went and stood between the table and wall.

Kendrick brushed dirt off his uniform. "Don't sweat it. One morning back at camp, I woke up after sleeping funny on my leg. It completely fell asleep, dead as a piece of wood. Crazy thing is, I didn't notice it. I just got up and started walking around. I was half way to the mess hall when I figured out I couldn't feel my leg. I dropped to the ground like a rock. The other guys started laughing. They thought I tripped over my own feet. But I couldn't stand. Every time I got up, I dropped back to the ground. I was so hungry that I hobbled to chow. Funny, huh?"

"Yeah," Deac responded. Deac felt his body relax, even though he knew the cause of the paralysis didn't result from lack blood supply.

Gould didn't think it was funny. "I've seen guys shot in the leg do the same thing until they got shot in the chest. Only then did they stop hobbling."

Deac suddenly realized something about Corporal Stephen Gould, the Medic.

Gould turned and glared at Gunderson. The glances they exchanged spoke the truth. Gould knew that Deac had shell shock and was seriously disturbed. The boy could loose it at any moment. He was a danger to himself and possibly to the others as well. Gunderson now understood that Gould knew.

Gunderson walked over to the table where Deac was leaning. "Could you make anything out?"

"Just that they were out scouting. One of them had a problem with their mission."

"What are you saying?" Winley asked as he spun Deac around by the shoulder.

"That one of the Germans had a problem with the mission you've been talking about. Wacht am Rhein he called it."

"No, what I mean is how do you know what they were saying."

"Come on, Winley," Gould said. "He speaks German. Isn't that obvious?"

"We've all had enough of your attitude, Gould. The question remains how he knows German."

"Thank you!" Kendrick felt validated that someone else had become irritated with the Medic.

Deac moved across the room, trying to hide. The attention made him nervous. He focused on Gunderson. "They said they had to get to Malmédy. I think they were behind the others. One seemed anxious to get going."

"What'd they leave so quickly?" Gunderson spoke directly to Deacon.

"I don't know. They just left." Deac bent over to pick up the playing card still on the floor.

"You haven't answered the question, Deac." Gould now stood next to Gunderson at the table trying to look the troubled man in the eye.

Deac ignored the Medic and handed the card to Kendrick. "I think you were one short."

"He's not the one . . ." Gould started.

Gunderson interrupted. "You know, Gould, we've all got stories to tell. It's late, and we all need some rest."

"Amen to that." Winley closed the conversation.

DECEMBER 18, 1944

Journey

The morning dawned cloudy and gray with nearly a foot of fresh, white powder. The men had received just enough sleep to feel groggy but not rested. They all rubbed their eyes to alleviate the burning.

The remainder of the night had passed uneventful. Corporal Gould had planned on continuing his watch until morning, allowing Deac to sleep a little longer. Deac, however, relieved Gould on schedule and without a word.

Kendrick pushed hard on the door which had become jammed with the new snow. His breath frosted in the cold, outside air. "Looks like another great day, boys."

Gunderson stretched. "More snow I take it." He removed his gloves and rubbed his bare hands. "I could have slept the rest of the day."

Winley was awake and packing the sea-bag. Gould readied his own bag.

"Yep, more snow and not a German in sight."

Deac ventured first out the door, rifle in hand.

Kendrick followed.

"Uh, Sergeant. I'd be more comfortable if someone else carried the rifle." Corporal Gould picked up the helmet with the red cross against a white square and placed it on his head.

"Don't worry about Deacon. He'll be fine. And I'll keep an eye on him."

"Still, I'd be happier if anyone else had the gun."

"That boy has covered my back more times than I can count. I've never seen him miss a shot."

"That may be true, but obviously . . ."

"I know where you're going. I'd still rather have his eyes and ears attached to that rifle than anyone else's. I think you'll be surprised at what he can do, even now."

Winley heard every word but pretended not to listen. Deac and Kendrick were already outside.

"What happened to him?" Gould asked.

"It's a long story, and I promised I wouldn't say anything. His trust means everything to me, and I won't betray that."

"Maybe I can help."

Gunderson unknowingly gave the wrong response. "I don't know there's anything you can do."

Winley shouldered the sea-bag and left the shed. He also resolved to keep an eye on Deacon.

The sun had barely risen by the time all five had left the cabin behind and began their journey to anywhere.

Winley pulled out the compass and checked the needle. Lifting his head to the west, "That way," he said. He had studied the maps before sleeping. Stavelot was the nearest town but he figured that Skorzeny and the Wehrmacht had made it at least that far the previous day. Bastogne was too far south to arrive in time. Manhay numbered third in his line of choices. It was only twenty miles away in a straight shot if the maps were correct. Winley held little hope of their success, but he held that to himself. He simply nodded towards Manhay and walked.

What Winley didn't know was that pockets of American troops all along those muddy roads proved a greater resistance than Hitler had planned on. The Germans barely moved.

Winley led the group, all marching in single file and silence. Deac took the rear. Unshaven and haggard, they appeared as a bunch of vagabonds traveling along a railroad, hoping to find a boxcar to lighten their load.

The snow was soft under their feet. Large drifts often dictated their direction. Other times dense trees or steep slopes rerouted the entourage. Wind blew flurries of tiny flakes, accumulating on their shoulders. More snow invaded their tightly laced boots.

They traveled most of the morning, accomplishing only a couple of miles. The route had become more circuitous than Winley had predicted.

"I believe I'm a bit fatigued," Winley admitted, turning around to the others. "You men need a rest?"

"I think that's best." Gunderson agreed. The two senior officers seemed to share the role of leader. "There's a fallen tree just over there. We can sit on something dry."

They picked up the pace and arrived at a large oak tree. The interior of the trunk had rotted out, but still supported the weight of the tired men.

Deac wandered around until coming to a rest at a nearby oak tree. He took the small book out of his shirt pocket and began reading. Gould sat alone at one end of the forest bench. Kendrick, removing the deck of cards, squeezed between the Sergeant and Winley at the other end.

"How far you think we've gone?" Gunderson asked Winley but stared at the cards in Kendrick's hands.

"Difficult to assess." He pulled out a map and scrutinized the unclear markings. "I admit I've never excelled at orienteering."

"None of us have. There always seems to be someone else in

charge who knows where to go."

"That does seem to be true." Winley believed this to be true in life as well as the army.

Kendrick shuffled the cards against his thigh. The sound of flipping cards felt familiar to the soldiers.

"How long have you been a Sergeant?" Winley asked over to Gunderson.

"About six months, just after we got to the beaches."

Gould perked up. "You were at the invasion?"

"No, didn't get there until a week after. You there?" Gunderson bent forward and looked past the two men sitting next to him and over to Gould.

Gould stared off into the forest. His thoughts lingered on Madeleine. "Yeah. I was there."

"Quick game of poker?" Kendrick interjected to Gould's relief.

"I prefer games of intelligence," Winley answered.

"Don't look at me. I'd lose." Gunderson nodded in recognition of his own shortcomings. He knew he wasn't very educated. He barely made it through high school and only with the help of his wrestling coach. But he had other strengths.

"You play cards?" Kendrick asked Gould.

"A little." He still thought about Madeleine and searching for her in that bombed-out apartment building. The Medic stood without saying another word. Intentionally leaving his medical bag and helmet leaning against the fallen tree stump, Gould walked over to Deacon.

Corporal Greer drifted in and out of daydream, and almost consciousness, as he read the small book in his hands. He remembered its stories well. They always made him feel at peace.

The Medic slowly approached the reading soldier. He seemed distant, and Gould didn't want to startle him.

"How're you doing?" he asked, tilting his head in a

sympathetic gesture and his hands in his pockets.

"Fine."

"You get some rest last night?"

"Yeah." Deac hated to lie but didn't want to involve Gould in his affliction. The Medic was still something of an enigma.

Gould realized the lie and decided to change topics. "You married?"

"Yeah."

Gould didn't take the brevity of communication as an indication of apathy to his presence but rather the man's mental state. Gould made lines in the snow with his foot as if he were going to play tic-tac-toe.

Deac watched him

The Medic made an X in one box and then an O in another. He continued until all the boxes were filled.

"Draw," Deac said, still holding the book in his steady hand.

"Kind of a dumb game, huh," Gould replied.

"I don't know. I used to play all the time as a kid. We didn't have much else in the way of games."

Gould erased the snow with his foot. "No one ever seems to win at the game."

"Does someone always have to win?" Deac had become the interrogator.

"Somebody wins in everything but tic-tac-toe."

"So winning means beating another person?"

Gould began to feel as he were caught on a witness stand being trapped in his own words by a savvy lawyer. "Yes, in one sense I think it does."

"What about the other sense?"

"I'm not sure if there is another sense." Gould wanted out of this conversation. "Take this war, it's a game."

"Kind of a bloody game."

"The worst kind. And we're not getting out of here until

one side loses."

"You must see a lot of death, being a medic and all." Deac began to feel something for Gould. It wasn't pity. It was something much deeper.

"Too much."

"Like the guy you were helping yesterday. That must have been hard for you, to leave him, I mean."

"He was just a lieutenant I ran into before we got captured." Gould certainly didn't want to discuss the Lieutenant. "You never told me your wife's name."

"Mary. I've got a picture if you'd like."

"I'd love to see it."

Deac opened to the end of the book between the last page and back cover. He removed the worn photograph of his wife. The one the German soldier didn't confiscate. He handed the picture to Gould. "Be careful. It's kind of worn."

"She's very pretty. How long have you been married?"

"Almost two years."

"Really?"

"Yeah, why?"

"You just seem like the kind of guy that's been married all his life."

"I get that a lot."

"I didn't mean anything by it." Gould sounded apologetic.

"I know. Don't worry. In one sense, I guess I've always been married."

"You don't have a bunch of wives, do you?"

"No. Just one. Why?" Deac laughed.

"You speak German. So I just assumed that maybe you were one of the German protestant religions, Amish or something. I guess I really didn't know. I've only been wondering how you learned the German language."

"I was a missionary in Germany before the war."

"Like helping the poor build sewage trenches, that kind of thing?"

"Some of that." Deac laughed. "Mostly we taught about God and Jesus."

"You taught about God to the Krauts?"

"To the Germans, yeah."

"What for?"

Deac didn't know how to answer that question, at least not in a brief way. "Well . . ." Deac began before getting cut off.

"You've got to be kidding me. They're the most Godless people on earth."

Deac heard more in those words than Gould meant to imply. "They're not Godless."

Gould felt a swelling in his chest. He raised his eyebrow in disbelief. "Where were you yesterday? Were you out to lunch when they gunned down prisoners!?"

"Not all are like that."

Gould moved a bit closer to Deac's face. "All the ones I've run into seem to be that way."

"There are good people in Germany."

"You do know that you are killing Germans every time you shoot a rifle." Gould couldn't restrain the anger he felt inside.

"Yes." Deacon now felt the tide of the conversation turning, and he wanted out. He knew very well that he had killed Germans, and others. Innocent others. His demons began to creep down his right arm. The tingling disturbed his concentration.

"How do you justify killing people you tried to convert?"

Deac didn't respond.

"And how do you sleep at night? Oh, I forgot. You don't sleep at night."

Deac fought to keep Gould's words out of his head. "I could make you understand," he finally said.

"What? Try and convert me. Don't even try."

"That's not what I meant." Deac felt the control again in his arm and mind.

"I'm sorry. But don't talk to me about God. God certainly wasn't in that field yesterday. And as far as I'm concerned, He hasn't been around at all lately." They both looked down in silence.

Shaking his head, Gould walked back to the others sitting on the fallen log. Part of him regretted blowing up at Deac.

Pity now crept into Deac's heart. He followed the Medic over to the bench.

Kendrick had been showing the other two a card trick when Gould and Deac returned.

"Three of diamonds, right?" Kendrick exclaimed holding that card up to Gunderson.

Smiling, he replied, "Nope. Not the three of diamonds."

"Come on. It's the three of diamonds. It has to be. I did the trick right."

"No, it's not. Ask Winley."

Winley nodded in agreement. The two officers shared a secret. Winley then took out his handkerchief and sneezed.

Kendrick looked perplexed. "Really?"

"Really, it was the jack of clubs," Winley confirmed.

Kendrick stared at the deck of cards in his hands. "I don't get it," he mumbled. He continued speaking to himself and reshuffling the deck. He cut the stack in half and lifted the top card. "Four of hearts. Hmm. I'll try it again."

"You two getting along?" Gunderson asked looking up to Gould and Deac.

They both replied in unison, "Just fine." They looked at one another.

"I guess so." Gunderson smiled at Deac.

"You guys know that Deac here lived with the Krauts, teaching about God," Gould informed the others.

"No kidding. That explains how you speak the language."

Winley sneezed again into the handkerchief. "I thought perhaps you had been educated abroad."

"No. I was a missionary."

"Damn it all. Seven of hearts. I don't get it." Kendrick's face started turning red.

"Ever thought of revising your vocabulary, Private Kendrick," Winley scolded. He folded the handkerchief and replaced it into his pocket.

"Ever thought of revising your face."

Winley laughed. He remembered Larsen's humor and now realized that it wasn't as witless as he thought.

"Oh, and nice hanky there, Captain Winley." Kendrick failed in his attempt to imitate Winley's New England accent.

Winley kept laughing. Gunderson and the Medic joined in the levity. Deac worried about the volume. He thought he heard something off in the distance.

"Well, excuse me mister e-ti-kett. I may be a dumb ol' boy from North Carolina but at least I don't snot into a napkin and put it in my pocket.

Winley pulled the linen back out. "It's clean."

"Ooh, don't show me that. It's disgusting."

"It's the polite thing to do."

"This is the polite thing to do." Kendrick turned his head, placed a finger closing off one nostril and shot mucus from the other with a quick, hard blow. The yellow wad landed like a bird dropping in the snow.

Winley just shook his head. "Lovely, Kendrick."

"Whose initials," Gould asked, noticing the blue stitching on the corner of the handkerchief. "Your wife's?"

"No, my sister's." Winley hurriedly stuffed it back into his pant's pocket.

Deac wandered a few feet away from the others. "Uh, guys. I think I hear trucks," Deac reported.

Snow Storm

They all could now hear the faint roar of engines coming from behind them. However, the vehicles seemed to be a good distance away.

The men replaced helmets, bags and gear and quietly moved away from the sounds.

The soldiers walked through a forest without shadows as the light from the sun diffused through the mist. The sky still threatened snow, but hadn't yet followed through. The clouds darkened, and the wind blew cold from the west.

Winley again led the group, compass in hand. He looked up at the thickening sky and sighed. "That's not looking good," he mentioned to Gunderson.

The Sergeant agreed. "If that thing comes in, we're not making it to Manhay anytime soon."

"Then neither will the Germans," Winley added.

"Anymore more snow and we're not making it period," Gould remarked from behind. He walked next to Kendrick. "Anywhere else around here?"

"I believe that we are nearing Trois Ponts, a small town according to the maps. Hopefully we've avoided Stavelot. However, Corporal Gould, with my orienteering skills we might be headed back to Berlin."

"Don't kid around like that," Kendrick said.

"I thought you wanted to see a little action, Kendrick." Gould turned to the boy next to him.

Kendrick stared straight ahead and said nothing in return.

The others were too preoccupied with the weather to notice that Deacon had lagged behind.

The same faces raced through Deac's mind, but this episode was different. This time he saw Mary's face amid the others. She looked distant and troubled.

Deac fell to his knees and dropped the gun.

The other women screamed. The children cried. Everything turned dark.

They yelled in French with high pitched and frantic voices.

Grabbing his head, Deac closed his eyes.

He saw women pressing together in a corner, holding babies, children clinging to their skirt hems.

"No!" he yelled.

The other men stopped in fear.

Suddenly, Deac found himself in a dark hallway, his gun sight to his eye. He moved slowly against a wall. There were no more gunshots, but the sniper could still be in the house. In front of him was a closed door.

Gunderson was the first to turn around, even before he heard Deac's cry.

Deac saw no moonlight enter the only window in the hall; outside the snow fell hard. The handle to the door was barely visible. It was still silent as he reached his left hand toward the knob.

"Deac!" Gunderson yelled as he witnessed his friend bend

over backwards in the snow.

The knob felt cold to the touch. Deac's heart pounded against his chest. He didn't have to volunteer for this assignment. He knew as soon as his company was fired upon that he would be the one to go. With his skill, much was expected. It was his duty.

The snow began to fall, thick and heavy, in both worlds.

The four soldiers ran back to where Deacon fell with his arms spread and shaking.

The lone soldier in a dark hall turned the handle, ever so slowly. It clicked as the bolt retracted and the door popped open. He pushed against the wood. No light or sound came from the room.

Gunderson came upon the sprawled soldier first; Gould landed right next to him.

Deac peered through the crack. He couldn't see anything but blackness. The gun stock was pressed firmly against his shoulder; his right index finger caressed the trigger. Only this time it wasn't his automatic but a German Mauser rifle. Deac didn't understand and felt his body begin to shake.

A gunshot echoed from outside the home. Deac was certain he heard it.

Deac closed his eyes and fired the weapon through a small slit in the door. A single bullet left the barrel and entered the dark room. Time stopped.

"What's wrong with him? He looks dead!" Kendrick yelled, the last to arrive.

Gunderson and Gould knelt over the comatose man.

Deac felt nothing. He dropped the gun and tried in vain to open his eyes.

"He's in shock!" Gould replied, looking not to Kendrick but to Deac.

Suddenly a sense of calm flowed though Deac's body. He relaxed. His eyes opened.

The room was lit and empty.

Gould raised his arm.

Deac scanned around the room in relief. He was about to breathe when he heard: Honey.

In complete clarity, Corporal Nathan Greer saw his wife. She held a child in her arms.

Mary, he spoke in his mind.

The woman closed her eyes.

Deac saw blood on her blouse.

The Medic brought his arm down in a swift motion. He slapped Deac across the face.

"NO!" Deac yelled, opening his eyes into the blizzard that was above him. His chest heaved.

The men hovered silently around the man lying in the snow.

Deac began breathing, quickly at first, then more slowly. He couldn't move. His eyes were blank. His comrades were stunned.

The snow nearly buried the men standing over Deacon. The scene appeared as a funeral, only the mourners wore green fatigues, and the deceased wasn't dead. Deac still lay back in the snow, breathing deep and aware of his surroundings. The gun was still at his side.

"Help him up," Gould ordered Kendrick. "Before this storm buries him."

Gunderson had already taken one side. Kendrick came around the other.

"Let's move. We need to get him out of here and into some shelter. He needs to rest, and in a few minutes we'll all be frozen." Gould motioned as if he was directing traffic.

"This way." Winley headed west, now carrying the sea-bag.

"Are you sure?" Gould asked the Captain.

"Yes. I am sure," Winley answered with confidence.

Gould picked up the gun and hoisted it onto the opposite

shoulder from the medical bag. He followed behind.

In the shape of a diamond, the five American soldiers, stranded in the Ardenees, forced their way headfirst into a snow-storm. The cold, wet moisture fell in clumps blown horizontal by the wind. Tiny chunks stung the men's down-turned faces. They moved as if pushing against an invisible wall. They traveled almost an hour through the storm, and Deac still could not carry himself.

The weather turned worse.

"Stay here, I'll run ahead and see what I can find." Winley almost had to yell to be heard above the wind. He dropped the bag next to Gunderson.

"Okay," the Sergeant replied and watched Winley disappear over a small crest.

The remaining men stopped.

Gould came around. "How you doing?" He tried to look Deac in the eye.

"A little weak, but I'm fine."

"Don't worry. We'll get you to shelter," Gunderson reassured his friend.

"I think I can walk now. Sorry for the trouble." Deac tried to free himself from his two supporters.

"No you won't, Nathan. Let's just wait until Winley gets back and see what he says." Gunderson continued to hold his friend.

Wiping snow off his eyebrows Kendrick said, "You ain't that heavy anyways."

"As soon as we get to shelter, I've got some stuff that will help you sleep," the Medic reassured.

"No, I don't want anything. Please, Gordon, tell him I don't want any drugs," Deac pleaded with the Sergeant.

"Don't worry." Gunderson looked to Gould and nodded. The Sergeant was no longer sure how to help Deacon.

The four men stood in silence as snow accumulated around their boots.

"Hey, how'd ya get the name Deac?" Kendrick yelled into the wetness.

"A long story but it's just a nickname." Deacon was too tired to speak.

"No one has ever given me a nickname," Kendrick hollered back.

"Give me time, Kendrick. I will secure a fitting soubriquet before this mission is accomplished," Winley broke in. He returned nearly stumbling on the group in the white-out conditions. He picked up the sea-bag and shook off more than an inch of snow.

"You find anything?" Gould immediately asked the Captain.

"A farm is just over this hill. There are other homes further down and a road that passes in front. I doubt anyone will be traveling down it tonight."

"Sounds like our best option. Let's go." Gunderson hadn't finished speaking when Deac started moving his legs.

Secrets

It didn't take long for the men to reach the perimeter of the farm. Even through the storm, the home appeared large and, more importantly, empty. Across the short field, a storm door seemed to lean against the side of the house, just barely accessible through the snowdrifts.

Captain Winley pointed to the hatch. "There. We should have no problem reaching it. But I suggest moving individually."

"Why don't you lead first and see if it's open. I'll bring Deac once I see you inside," Gunderson added.

Winley reached inside the bag around his neck and felt for the flashlight. After pulling it out, he handed the knapsack to Kendrick. "Here, do you mind?"

"Nope." Kendrick seemed to ease his personality around Winley.

The Captain ran across the field, a green speck that faded through the falling snow and then disappeared underneath the farmhouse.

"That's it. You ready, Deac?" Gunderson wrapped an arm

around Deacon's back.

"Yeah."

Kendrick and Gould watched as the hobbling pair of soldiers also disappeared.

"Truce, Doc?" Kendrick asked, turning his face against the wind.

"Yeah, truce. Let's move."

Inside, the cellar was large and lined with mostly empty shelving. A few glass jars filled with preserves lined a shelf by the door. While two small windows near the ceiling provided some light, the wood burning stove might offer aid of a more urgent nature.

"Someone certainly lives here," Winley said, shining the spotlight on the jars and reflecting speckles of reds, blues and greens around the room."

Gould gently closed the door, shutting off the howling wind outside. "Let's hope they don't decide to have some jam and toast."

Five adult men sat cross-legged against the walls as if around a campfire. The snow on their uniforms melted onto the floor as the world outside melted away into memories of friends, faith and family. Even without the stove lit, the cellar warmed enough for the men to share.

"So, you're a hunter." Kendrick looked across the brotherhood at Deac.

"Ever since I was a little kid. Got my first four-point when I was only ten."

"No, way."

Gunderson laughed. "Kendrick, do you even know what a four-point is?"

"Well, yeah. It's a male deer with four points on its antlers. My dad's got a five-point stuffed and hangin' on the wall in our front room."

"Why does that not surprise me," Winley added.

Deac smiled. "See, Sarge. There are other people who know about deer hunting."

"Okay, okay. But you never explained to me about the bees."

"You keep bees?" Gould asked, trying his best to take part in the conversation.

Deac replied, "I bet Kendrick knows why."

"Shi . . ." Kendrick held back the profanity. "Shoot yeah, to fertilize the fruit trees."

Winley stared at Kendrick. Education comes in a variety of forms, he thought to himself.

"They're also good if you're not scared to harvest the honey." Kendrick spoke with pride.

Gunderson shook his head. "I never would have guessed."

"So, Nathan, you grew up on a farm in Arizona, is it?" Gould intentionally used Deac's real name. "And you're married. Any kids?" Gould didn't realize the import of his question.

In the dim light they all noticed Deac's face change. "Not actually," he whispered.

Gould felt a bit embarrassed and didn't know how to proceed. Not even Gunderson understood Deac's reply.

With a deep breath and hoping to exorcise his demons, Deac explained. "My wife just lost our first. Died in child birth a few weeks ago."

"Oh, Deac. Why didn't you say anything?" The Sergeant's heart felt heavy in his chest.

"I didn't want to worry you."

The Sergeant couldn't believe that Deac was worried about him. "When did you find out?"

"Last Thursday."

Gunderson realized his eyes began to swell. "Oh, God," was all he could manage to say. The former state champion wrestler began to cry.

"It's okay. Death isn't an end."

Gould had the sensation of gears crunching, like metal inside his head had twisted. Death was an end; it was the cessation of life, verifiable. He sat unresponsive, thinking about Madeleine.

Winley also sat in silence. His similar thoughts were on his sister, Josephine. He rubbed the handkerchief, feeling the silk slide against itself deep in his pocket.

Only Kendrick appeared unmoved. "Back in North Carolina, when I was a kid . . ."

"When you were a kid?" Gould chided, grateful for the detour in emotion.

"Yeah, when I was kid, we'd steal cigarettes from the corner store and go out into the fields and smoke until we got sick. Once I puked all over my friend's foot."

"And that didn't teach you a lesson?" Winley asked.

Kendrick again stopped himself short of his habitual language. "Heck no."

Deac smiled.

"I spit, wiped my mouth and lit another one. Been smoking ever since."

Outside, the snow continued to drop as the sun began to set. Another day was ending.

"Amazing what stupid things we do as kids," Winley said, trying to detour his own thoughts.

"Stupid?"

"Nothing personal, Kendrick. I mean we all did stupid things. What other secrets are you hiding? I imagine you're full of them."

"What makes ya think I'll tell you?"

"Oh, come on, Kendrick."

"No. It's someone else's turn to embarrass himself."

Deac cut in. "I never kissed my wife until we got married."

Four pairs of eyes bulged and four jaws dropped. Not one

had a response. All five started to laugh.

Gunderson stepped up to the plate. "It was my first day of high school. I wrestled in junior high and done pretty well. Wrestling was a big sport in my school. I was a big kid. Still am, I guess. Everyone thought that I was pretty tough.

"Everyone knew me and expected me to do well in the high school tournaments. And so, I show up on the first day, and I've got this huge fat lip. I mean the thing was black and purple and swollen the size of an orange. Everyone noticed and was talking about it.

"I told all my buddies that I had been hit playing stickball. They believed me, and I saved my reputation. Truth is I got hit by Alice Piasecki's fist."

Kendrick chirped, "Alice Piasecki," enunciating every syllable.

"Do we want to know how this Alice came to hit you?" Winley asked.

"I think I'll save that story for the next campfire."

"All right, I can beat that." Kendrick straightened up as if he were about to expose some important information. "I was workin' with my dad one day, and I found this rubber tubing in the back of his truck." He began laughing. "And so I'm playing around with it. You know, blowin' through it, makin' whistling sounds." Kendrick really began laughing.

"Easy there, soldier," Gunderson said.

"Anyway, I'm playing around with this hose thing and I figure out that I can stick one end on my skin and suck the other."

"Why would you do that?" Winley raised one eyebrow.

"To give myself hickies. What else?"

"What's a hicky?" Winley honestly inquired.

Even Gould stared at Winley.

"Are you kidding me? A hicky is when a girl sucks on your neck and makes it bruise."

"Oh. You learn something new every day, I suppose."

Kendrick went back to his story. "So I suck on this tube and give myself hickies all over my neck. I tell my friends that I've got this girl friend from another town."

The men laughed.

Winley thought of something. "Well, I've found a nickname for you, Kendrick."

"Yeah, what's that?"

"Hicky."

Kendrick stopped laughing. His face looked hurt. The others could only try to hold back their own giggles in feigned respect.

"Okay, Winley. What's your secret?" Kendrick asked.

"My secrets I keep secret." Winley surprised himself to even admit he possessed a secret.

"You can't do that," Kendrick said and began to stand up.

"Please, Shirl."

"How'd ya know my name, Winley?"

"Another secret, I'm afraid."

"What's your first name, then?" Kendrick asked, sitting back down.

"Captain." Winley smiled at his new-found ability to jest.

"Enough of you. Who cares." Kendrick shook his head in frustration. "What about you, Doc? What's your secret?"

"I don't have any."

"Come on. Even Winley's got secrets. He's just too much of a pansy to talk about 'em. What's yours?"

"No, really. I don't have any. Sorry." Gould thought about his big secret, the secret that he had fallen in love with Madeleine and never had the chance to tell her.

"Hey, Gould," Gunderson interrupted.

Almost leaning on his Sergeant, Deac had rolled over and fell into a deep, regenerative sleep.

The Medic simply replied, "Let him sleep."

Winley decided to ask Gunderson the question they all wanted the answer to. "While he's asleep, would you mind explaining what happened. I believe if we proceed as a team, we all have a better chance of succeeding."

Gunderson accepted that they would have to rely on each other before this mission was over, and Deac's condition had worsened. These men deserved to know.

"First, you've got to understand something about Deac. He's the best soldier I have ever met. He's a natural. Some say gifted. He hears things before others do, sees things that most don't. It's crazy, I'm telling ya. And his shot? I've never seen him miss. Maybe it's all that hunting he did, growing up with guns and stalking things. And even in his current state, I'd rather have him watching my back than anyone else in this army."

Gould became concerned. "I still don't want him carrying the rifle."

"I'll carry the gun," Kendrick said. "I'm a pretty good shot myself. Did my own share of huntin' back home."

"That's fine with me. As long as it's not Deac." Gould sounded emphatic.

"Okay. But try and cut him some slack. I wouldn't want to have gone through what he did."

"That bad?" Winley asked.

"Yeah. Last week our company got sent out from Elsenborn. Just spreading out the line we were told. We didn't expect to see any action. It was a Thursday morning, and mail had come just before we headed out. Deac got a letter. It seemed to bother him, but he never said anything about it."

"And now we all know." Gould stretched his legs and leaned against the wall. "That alone could do a guy in."

"Would have done any of us in," Winley added, also relaxing his posture.

"The kid is tough, though. Just like you'd guess a guy from

a farm is like. Take it all in stride, pull yourself by the boot-straps, carry your own load, that sort of thing. Deac works harder than anyone. I've never seen him slack off. And he's a good friend, too."

Winley began to lie down. "That we can all see."

"But a guy's got to learn when to rest." Gould couldn't let go of being a medic.

"I agree," Gunderson admitted, "but you can't force him. Besides, I've learned that he knows how to take care of himself. Like now, his body finally made him sleep. This is the longest he's been out since last Thursday."

Kendrick showed his impatience. "What happened?"

"We got sent out from Elsenborn to set up camp somewhere to the north. It was a standard march. In a word, boring. And cold that day. Very cold and snowing. Most of us didn't even pay attention to where we were going. We just kept our heads down, tucked away from the wind.

"We marched along this road and there were homes and farms on both sides. I didn't see anything. It was night, dark, snowing. I could barely see my own boots. I couldn't see anything. But Deac did.

"He tried to warn us but the shot came too fast. We lost a good man. We scattered like a bunch of sheep. Most of us made it into a drainage ditch of some sort on the other side of the road. A couple of more shots came from the upstairs window of one of the farmhouses. The sniper didn't hit anyone else, but it certainly trapped us in the ditch.

"The sniper went quiet. Deac said he had seen where the flash had come from, and he'd go in. Our C.O. agreed. I don't know how he did it, but Deac scrambled across the road and up to the farm house without being hit. The sniper shot at him three or four times. Then he went quiet again.

"At the time, we didn't know if it was a crazed local or a

renegade German. Deac just volunteered and took off. I didn't worry about him. He had always come out clean from whatever he got into."

Gunderson stopped and looked at Deac. He still slept on his side with his right arm underneath his head. His breaths were deep and regular.

"Our company waited until we heard something. Deac was in the house for maybe five minutes when his automatic started firing. We could see the flashes from the window. That's all we heard.

"A second later, someone yells 'Deac scared him out.' This German comes flying from around back. Our entire company starts shooting at him. It was almost funny. They guy drops.

"We get up out of the ditch and there're no more gunshots so we assume everything's alright. The entire company crosses the road. Some go to the German and others to the house. I head straight for the front door. Deac didn't come down. I got this real strange feeling in my gut.

"At first I thought that maybe Deac had been hit. But I never heard another rifle shot, just the spray of the automatic. I tried to look inside but everything was dark. There were no lights or fires. I yelled his name, but he didn't respond. I began to panic.

"I ran up the stairs which were by the door. I started looking in the bedrooms off the upstairs hallway. There were all empty. When I got to the last, I could just barely make out Deac's silhouette standing in the doorway, the automatic hung in his right hand."

Winley placed his palms over his eyes. The story had made its way to his regiment in Elsenborn. He knew what had happened.

Gunderson continued. "When I got inside the room, there were three women and five children. Deac had killed them by mistake.

"It was very dark, and I had to move within inches of them to tell they were even women. There was no way Deac could have known. I had to pry the automatic out of his hand."

"Has he talked about it?" Gould inquired.

"Not one word. He didn't speak at all for two days. He was given leave to go to St. Vith. Our C.O. said there were facilities there. I asked to go with him. We were in Baugnez waiting for transport when, well, you know the rest."

Before any of the men could speak, Deac awoke. Then they all heard the footsteps above their heads.

Beyer and Ochmann

Captain Hans Beyer had met resistance at Stavelot a few hours after leaving the massacre site. They fought through the night, and both sides suffered heavily. The Americans retreated as capture became eminent, wiping out a bridge on their way out.

Beyer worked his men like slaves to lay down new tracks so the tanks could cross. The repairs took most of the morning. Peiper and Skorzeny moved more quickly and were further west. Feeling left behind, the Captain continued to drive his men the rest of the day.

The remnants of Beyer's company arrived in Trois Ponts just as the snow storm hit that afternoon. The Germans looked more worn than the prisoners they had killed at the Baugnez crossroads. Hans was furious at the delays.

The road led through the center of the small village and continued on to Manhay, about twelve more miles due west. Many of the locals had fled with the Americans, and others banded together at various homes, hoping the Germans would move through their town just as quickly.

Captain Beyer headed his men on their march into town. The snow fell hard and blindingly. The Captain realized his predicament and entered the first building he came to.

The store was locked, and Beyer shot the handle and again near the jamb until the door swung open. He went inside with two of his junior officers.

"Look around. Bring anyone you find here and wait for me," he ordered. Beyer left the men to their search.

Outside, he yelled through the snow at his troops. "Head out to the north. Find any shelter you can. Confiscate any food, equipment, weapons you can claim. Shoot anyone who resists. It is your right and duty as soldiers of the Reich. We leave at first break in the weather."

The soldiers began to fan out to the north, taking homes, barns, shops. Some only kicked-out the occupants; a few killed them. But most of Beyer's men simply found places to rest.

Beyer returned to the store. His officers had found the proprietor and his family hiding in a back room.

He pointed his pistol at the man's head and laughed. "Over there, into the corner."

The family of four moved as a unit and huddled together in the corner of the general store that sold mostly out-of-stock sundries. What the establishment had available was stacked on a few tables near the front windows.

Beyer shot at a bag of wheat, spilling its contents onto the bare floor. The grain streamed down like sand in an hour glass, making a cone-shaped pile below.

The two children, a boy about seven and a girl about five, winced and hid their faces against their mother's breast.

First Lieutenant Kurt Persin and Sergeant Major Rudolf Ochmann stood near the doorway.

Beyer ran his hand under the cascade of wheat. "Tic, toc. Tic, toc," he mumbled.

The two officers exchanged glances. The family huddled.

Beyer moved about the store. He flipped lids on canisters and kicked at a few more bags of grain. "Oberleutnant Persin, take these out to the trucks," Beyer ordered, pointing at a few loaves of bread on a counter.

Persin obeyed, and the other officer followed.

"Not you, Ochmann. You stay here. You're going to earn your rank." Beyer knocked glass jars off a shelf. They crashed to the floor.

Ochmann stopped and put down a loaf of bread. He felt a heaviness in his arms. Persin smiled and left. He knew the lesson Rudolf Ochmann was about to receive.

"Your sidearm!" Beyer demanded of Ochmann.

The man removed his pistol and held it out for his Captain.

"No, I don't want it. It's your honor."

The store's proprietor eyed the Captain.

"Ochmann, dispose of the prisoners!" Beyer then continued his perusal of the shelved items.

Rudolf Ochmann pointed his gun at the family, but sickness pervaded his stomach. He watched the mother cringe. She buried her face between her children's. The father stared at him with a wounded look on his face.

The Sergeant Major waited, hoping the family would charge out a back door or behind a counter. They didn't move. The kids whimpered. The father put his arm around his wife. She began to sob.

Ochmann sweated. A bead of water dripped into the corner of his right eye, momentarily blurring his sight on the family. He wiped it out with his shoulder.

"Come on, Rudolf! Earn it!"

The thickness swelled into his chest and lungs. He felt nauseous, and his body went numb.

Rudolf Ochmann dropped the gun to his side.

"Coward," Beyer yelled coming over to the officer. He grabbed the gun and hit Rudolf across the face, splitting his upper lip in half.

Ochmann turned his back and tasted salt on his tongue.

Captain Beyer fired two rounds, killing the adults. Then he sneered, "The children are worthless."

Beyer pushed Rudolf Ochmann out the door. The children cried, still hanging onto their parents.

Gunderson and Catherine

Catherine drank coffee and nibbled on bread in her parent's kitchen. Sophie played with a doll in the other room.

Catherine Thierry and her daughter Sophie were visiting her parents when American troops charged through Trois Ponts. Information passed from neighbor to neighbor until it reached the Thierry homestead. The Germans soon followed. Catherine thought of nothing more than protecting her daughter.

The adults spoke softly over their coffee.

"Please, Catherine, stay here tonight. Until we know what is happening," her mother pleaded.

Catherine refilled her cup. "I want to get Sophie home, to her own bed."

"But she is happy here."

"And safer," her father added, looking concerned. He got up and went to the window. "The snow is falling too heavy. Yes, stay here for the night."

"It's just down the road, Papa. We'll be fine."

"Then I'll come with you."

"No, really, Papa. We'll be fine. You stay here with mother. We'll come back in the morning. I don't want Sophie to become concerned." She gulped the coffee and placed the cup in the sink. "Time to go, Sophie."

The little girl bounced off the chair with a doll in her arms. "I'm ready, Mama."

Sophie was six years old. Her long, blond hair hung in curls like her mother's. With pale skin and eyes, she appeared very much like the other children in Belgium. She wore a petticoat and simple, black shoes. The girl never walked. She trotted or bounced her way around the neighborhood. Her curls were always set in motion.

Catherine pulled a shawl over her head and shoulders. "Off we go, little one."

Sophie jumped off the front stoop and into the freshly falling snow. She nearly disappeared.

"Careful. I may not be able to find you."

"I'm right here, Mama." Sophie waved her arms in the air, her red gloves signaling like aircraft ground crew.

"Come on. Let's get home before you turn into a little snow princess."

Sophie ran though the snow, her light weight and youthful legs barely making a depression.

"Wait. I can't run as fast as you. It's dark, be careful." Catherine appreciated the moment. Her daughter existed in a world without war or death. The girl's greatest preoccupation was what she might be getting for Christmas only a week away. "Don't drop your doll."

"I won't."

Sophie was nearly home when Catherine thought she heard something. The wind hummed though the trees carrying no other sounds. She never took her sight off her daughter.

"Wait, Sophie. Wait for me." Catherine jogged as fast as she could. Her black boots sunk deep into the snow. She held her arms out to the sides for balance, almost tripping twice.

When she finally arrived at her front gate, Sophie was already standing on the porch, barely breathing. Catherine was out of breath.

"You'll be the death of me, young lady. I'm not six years old anymore."

"But you're pretty."

Catherine smiled. Her daughter was too young to be patronizing. It was an honest, and true, compliment.

"You are precocious, young lady," Catherine said, coming up the walkway to the front porch.

"I'm what?"

"Nothing. Let's get inside and dry off. I think it's time to bake that bread that's been rising all afternoon. What do you say?"

"Yes. And can we have some chocolate, too?"

"Certainly." Catherine had one, very small tin of cocoa left that her parents had given to her. She wouldn't be able to buy more, not even for Christmas. She decided to make a cup of hot chocolate for her daughter on this snowy winter's night.

Sophie had burst across the threshold before her mother finished opening the door. The girl stamped the snow off her boots on the hard wood floor. The sound reverberated throughout the house.

"Shh!" Gunderson stood up and tilted his ear toward the wooden beams above head.

Deac also listened. The others didn't make a sound, content to allow the Sergeant and Deacon to assess the situation.

"At least two people are up there."

"Yeah," Deac confirmed.

"You hear any voices?"

"Sounds like a woman. Sounds French."

"I'll go outside and check things out. Deac, stay here with the others. Keep the flashlight off until I come back down. Clear?"

"Clear."

"Winley, if you don't mind, your pistol?"

Winley complied. Private Kendrick held the Mauser. Gunderson moved to the hatch door.

Winley switched off the light as soon as Gunderson opened the cellar door. Snow blew in and swirled around, the cold snapping the men back to a state of alertness.

Outside, the storm was beginning to subside. Even the wind calmed. Light angled out from the kitchen windows above Gunderson's head, casting shadows of a figure moving inside.

The Sergeant pressed himself against the house, watching the movement on the snow. Sliding underneath the rays of light, he made his way to the front porch, noticing the footprints leading inside. There were two sets of prints, one obviously a child's. The other appeared to be a pair of women's boots. He breathed in relief.

Gunderson quickly glanced into the front room through the small glass panes set in the door. Nothing. He tried the larger window to the side. The glass was beginning to mist from the heat inside. Just like the store windows in New York at Christmas, he thought to himself. The warmth of childhood filled his body.

He peered in the window. Through an open doorway inside, he saw a woman standing in the kitchen kneading dough with her fists. She was beautiful. She wore her curly blonde hair tied in back. She also wore men's trousers and a loose blouse. A coat hung on a hook behind her. She dropped a chunk of dough onto a pan and placed the bread into the stove. She then turned toward the front room.

Gunderson spun around, his back to the wall. He could hear her coming towards the door.

"I'm getting some jam from the cellar, Sophie. I'll be right back," Catherine yelled to her daughter playing in her room. She warmed her hands by the stove before leaving the kitchen.

"Okay," the girl chirped in reply.

In the front room, Catherine looked out the window before leaving, just in case. She saw only flurries, and the road was empty. She unlocked the bolt and opened the front door. Shuddering, she grabbed the shawl draped over a chair. She flung the wool knit over her shoulder as she stepped onto the porch. She slipped on a small patch of packed snow.

Instinctively, Gunderson moved to catch her. She screamed with the touch. She swung her arm around and caught the Sergeant on the shoulder. It barely registered, but he released her anyway. Scuffling on the floor board, she ran into the house.

"Dang it!" Gunderson said out loud. She's probably getting a gun, or worse, he thought. He decided to put the fire out.

Gunderson ran into the front room just as Catherine was shutting herself and daughter into a room.

"Sauvez-vous, mon mari a un pistolet!" she screamed through the door with no lock. Sophie clung to her side.

"You don't understand."

"Sauvez-vous!" Catherine was too scared to think. She had no husband nor gun. She didn't know if her ruse was working. She felt her voice crack. She pulled her daughter closer.

"You don't understand. I'm American. Américain!"

Catherine recognized the language. This man was not speaking German. She knew a few words, but she still couldn't be sure. "Sauvez-vous, s'il vous plaît." Her voice rang more fluidly now.

"I won't hurt you. I'm an American and stuck behind enemy lines." Gunderson didn't know why he explained that. He also didn't know if she and the child lived alone. Then, he thought. If she had a husband, he'd be yelling through the door, not her.

"I'm coming in. I won't hurt you." Gunderson turned the knob on the bedroom door. He slowly opened it.

Catherine and Sophie huddled in the far corner. The woman's eyes bulged as she saw the pistol in Gunderson's hand.

The Sergeant looked down. "Oh no, no. I didn't know if you were Germans." He stuffed the gun into his pocket, presuming they were alone.

Sophie cried out as she saw Deac come in the front door.

Gunderson cranked his head around then back to the woman. "He's American, too. We're friends."

Catherine understood the word friend. Her shoulders relaxed but she still held tightly to her daughter. "Américain?"

"Uh, oui, Americans." Gunderson also breathed again.

"Everything alright?" Deac asked running into the room. "We heard screams."

Catherine's eyebrows squeezed together. She looked at the two soldiers in her home. Americans had been in her home before and treated her well.

"I'm Gordon." The Sergeant pointed to his chest. "This is Deac. What's your little girl's name?" Gunderson smiled as broadly as his facial muscles would allow. His cheeks bulged.

"Sophie," she tentatively permitted. Then she said, "Catherine" and pointed at herself.

"Deac, go back and tell the guys that everything's all right. I'll be down in a minute."

Deac obeyed, but the order seemed to bother Catherine.

Gunderson held up his hand with his fingers and thumb extended. Then pointing again to his chest, he said, "There are five of us in your basement." He counted five on his hand and signaled below where he stood.

Catherine understood. They both relaxed and entered the front room. Gunderson noticed that the wool shawl was lying on the porch in melting snow. He walked outside to retrieve it.

Sophie stood next to her mother.

Gunderson cautiously approached the two, holding the shawl out to Catherine. She smiled.

Gunderson sniffed. He could smell the dough. "Fresh bread?" he asked.

"Oui, uh, bread." She pointed and moved toward the kitchen. The Sergeant allowed her to pass. He held his stomach.

"Are you hungry?" she asked and brought her pinched fingers to her mouth.

"Oui, madam, very much." Gunderson's accent hadn't improved in the last few days, making Catherine giggle.

Sophie walked straight up to the Sergeant and shook his hand. Her smile broke any remaining tension.

The two made attempts at communication despite the language barrier. He was able to learn that Americans had gone through earlier, and the Germans had arrived not long before the storm. She hadn't seen any and didn't know if they were still in town.

Catherine understood that Gunderson and the other four were trying to get back to their leaders and were hiding in the cellar, tired and hungry. The guns made her nervous, but she felt comfortable helping them. She handed the Sergeant a small oil lamp.

Downstairs, light from the lamp filled the room, as Gunderson entered. The men, pacing anxiously around the cellar, froze in the brightness.

Winley appeared the most agitated. "What have you been discussing up there all this time?"

"I got a knitting lesson," Gunderson joked.

Winley felt knots in his stomach and suddenly lost his burgeoning sense of humor. "Seriously, Sergeant, does she have a phone?"

Gunderson glanced at the faces of his companions who seemed worried. "No, there's nothing nearby, either. It's been out for a long while. And it's highly likely that the Germans are here. We're on a farm fairly south of the main part of the town. She hasn't seen any movement."

"Good," Winley concluded.

Kendrick stepped forward into the light, still holding the Mauser. "What do you mean? How is that good."

"If they're here now, that means they are moving as slowly as we are."

Gunderson added, "It's been quiet outside all night. I've seen no evidence of any movement, especially troop movement."

Gould asked, "But, are we safe here?"

Neither Winley nor Gunderson could answer that question, at least not with any degree of certainty. The group debated their options.

Winley silently felt the fatigue of carrying the weight of the information and wanted this journey to be over. He debated leaving on his own.

Gunderson noticed Deac smiling.

"What are you grinning at?"

"I smell bread."

"Catherine was baking when I was upstairs."

The same thought occurred to all five men as Catherine gently tapped on the cellar door.

"Bonjour, messieurs. Est-ce-que je peux descendre?"

"Please." Gunderson was the first to greet the owner of their hideout.

Catherine carried a basket draped with a towel, steam rising from the edges. The aroma of warm yeast, flour and a mix of herbs filled the basement. Catherine tipped her head as she held out the bread. Sophie stood by her mother's side.

"Mercy," he said, inhaling like it was his first breath. Then the Sergeant began the silent introductions.

She approached Oberon Winley. Before he could extend his hand, she leaned forward and kissed him on the cheek. Having a better understanding of the culture, he kissed hers. The others followed Winley's lead. Kendrick was so excited that he nearly knocked her over as he hugged her. She laughed in surprise.

Catherine smiled at Deac and Gould. She was sensitive to the despair in their eyes.

"Prenez de la confiture aussi," she said, pulling one of the few remaining glass jars off the shelf.

Gunderson began breaking apart the bread. Kendrick used the knife in the basket to spread the blackberry preserves. The men finished the two loaves in a few minutes and returned the empty basket to Catherine. She nodded.

Sophie, who had remained quiet but smiling, stepped forward without reserve. She seemed to know who to approach. She passed by her mother and stood directly in front of Corporal Greer.

"Joyeux noel!" Sophie spoke with the clear voice of a child. Her blushed cheeks brightened her wide eyes. She held out a small figure made of folded tin foil.

Deac received the Christmas gift. He felt the pressure of generosity swell behind his eyes. His body tingled, not with fear, but with love. The image of his wife settled in his mind. He knew, or felt, that she was happy now. There were no other images plaguing his head.

He held up the figure. It was a Christmas angel, simply folded with leftover tin foil. Deac felt the release as a tear slid down his cheek.

DECEMBER 19, 1944

Winley's Decision

Deac slept on a full stomach and, for the first time in a week, undisturbed. He awoke just before dawn.

"Sergeant, wake up." Deac shook his friend.

"I know. I'm getting up."

"No, it's Winley. He's gone."

"What?" Gunderson jumped up and scanned the cellar. He saw two other lumps. The third was gone.

"Wake the others. I'll check outside."

The sky was clear and bluing. Hints of daybreak sliced through the trees. A blanket of clean white snow covered the homestead on the outskirts of Trois Ponts. Not even the road was distinguishable from the fields. The only flaw in this perfect picture was a set of barely visible footprints leading from the basement to woods behind the home.

"Winley, what were you thinking?" Gunderson muttered to himself.

Lowering the hatch, Gunderson reported back to the others. "He's gone ahead without us. Must have left some time ago. His tracks don't look fresh."

"He's got the compass," Gould said with a concerned look on his face looking directly at Gunderson. "And what about the rifle?"

"He left us that. And all the gear in the sea-bag," Kendrick reported. He held the deck of cards in his hand. "Do we go after him?"

"Yes." Gunderson buttoned his coat.

"Wait a minute," Gould spit out. "He'll make much better time traveling alone than we will as a group. We should reevaluate our plans. We're safer here than out there."

"There's nothing to reevaluate. We can follow his tracks."

Suddenly, Catherine threw open the door to the cellar and yelled down. "Attention! Il ya a une vehicule allemagne qui approache!"

The men didn't understand the warning, but they could hear the sound of an engine.

Catherine shut the door and left.

She'll be fine, Gunderson tried to convince himself.

Deac picked up the Mauser and moved to the hatch. "I'm fine," he insisted before Gould could make a comment.

Knowing Gould's concern, the Sergeant confirmed, "He'll be fine."

Deac searched inside the cellar until he found a small chunk of concrete. He opened one side of the hatch and placed the jagged lump in the opening.

The sun's low rays began to flood the cellar. Deac could barely see through the glare. He heard the jeep pull up to the front of the house.

Fishtailing down the road, an American jeep with a Nazi flag on the hood carried two German soldiers. The driver, First Lieutenant Kurt Persin, noticed Catherine running back into her home. An officer with a swollen lip sat in the passenger seat.

The jeep slid to a stop.

"We should be looking for deserters," Ochmann insisted. "Those were Beyer's orders."

"Do you see anything? I don't! Except the woman."

"Then we should catch up with the group. They left over an hour ago." Rudolf sounded insistent.

"Let's see what the girl's got for breakfast first. I'm hungry." Persin hopped out of the jeep and sunk a foot into the snow. Lifting his knees, he began waddling to the front porch. He didn't notice the footprints on the side of the house leading into the forest.

Deac watched until the German disappeared in front. The other remained in the jeep. Deac stared at him.

"There are two. One went inside," Deac informed the others.

Gunderson walked to the center of the room and listened above. "Hang tight, Deac. Let's wait and see what happens."

Deac returned to his surveillance. The second German simply sat with his arms folded across his chest, looking at the house. Deac took aim at the man, just in case.

Gunderson heard the faint patter of feet and a door shutting. He assumed Sophie had hidden in the same room as the night before. Two other adults walked around in the kitchen. He heard voices but not loud enough to guess at a translation. Kendrick and Gould positioned themselves next to Deac.

A pot crashed to the floor. Gunderson tensed.

Catherine screamed. Pounding made its way to the front of the house.

"Something's happening, Deac."

Deac held the gun with Ochmann in his scope. Not one muscle in his arm twitched; his breathing was slow and steady. He panned, searching for the other soldier. Catherine appeared first in his sight, running toward the street. Her blouse was torn.

Ochmann got out of the jeep, angry at his companion. "Was machst Du?"

"Halt Deine Fresse!" Persin came running behind Catherine, grabbing at her loose clothing.

Deac controlled his anger at the scene playing out before him. He could fire on both Germans in less than one heartbeat. Leave her alone. I'm watching you, he thought to himself.

Persin seized Catherine by her blonde curls and spun her around. Tears streamed down her face.

"No, no." She tried to shake herself free. She screamed again.

"Lass Sie gehen!" Ochmann shouted.

Deac understood that the one in the jeep was trying to stop the other German. He refocused the rifle on Catherine's attacker.

"Deac, what's going one?" Gould quietly demanded.

"Shh," he whispered back.

Kendrick heated up. "There's only two. Let's take 'em!"

"Shh!"

Deac kept the sight pinned on Persin. The attacker's face was reddened with anger. He drew his arm back and slapped Catherine across the face. She fell into the snow.

Deac shrugged his shoulders and aimed. "Stop right now," he whispered out loud.

Persin reached down and gripped the woman's arm. He began dragging her back toward the house.

Ochmann trudged up the path.

"Halt, Ochmann, oder Ich Schieße!" Persin drew his pistol with his free hand. He aimed at Ochmann.

Rudolf stopped and reached for his gun.

"Denke nicht daran, Rudolf," Persin warned his compatriot.

"Rudolf," Deac repeated, still aiming at the aggressor.

"What?" Deac's companions pressed their bodies against the cellar hatch trying to see through the crack.

Ochmann tried pleading; Persin wouldn't be dissuaded. Catherine hung limp at the end of his arm. He started pulling her.

"It's your choice! You've been warned." Deac gently squeezed the trigger.

The gun popped, and smoke blew across Deacon's face.

The bullet flew, stopping in Persin's temple.

Ochmann gasped. He began to run.

The four Americans charged out into the morning light, squinting against the rising sun.

Catherine managed to pull herself up but shook too much to move her legs.

Deac stood outside the basement and aimed at the fleeing German.

"Shoot him!" Gould yelled.

The gun's sight traced Ochmann darting across the road.

"Shoot now! Before he makes the trees."

Deac continued to watch, and follow.

"Not again, Deacon." Gould became angry.

Gunderson and Kendrick reached Catherine.

"If you won't. Give me the gun. He's a sitting duck." Gould began to reach for the rifle.

"No. I can't"

"You can't, or you won't?"

Deac lowered the gun from his eye. "Something told me not to shoot."

Ochmann disappeared into the forest.

"You've spent too much time with the damn Krauts. I'd say you're a sympathizer." For no reason, Corporal Gould jogged toward the running man.

Gunderson helped Catherine to her feet and embraced her. He held her head against his broad chest. She began to hyper-ventilate with sobs.

Sophie appeared in the front doorway.

Kendrick ran over to the little girl and encouraged her back inside.

"Deac, you and Gould get this body outta here. Throw it into the back of the jeep and take it to the trees." The Sergeant held the weeping woman by her waist and guided her back up the walkway. "Go help the other guys, Kendrick. We don't have much time."

"I don't believe it. Look at that!" Gould stood near the road with his hands on his hips. Coming toward him was the German soldier, hands over his head, and Corporal Winley behind. "Deac, your runaway is back."

Gunderson turned around. It was true. Winley held his pistol pressed into the back of a prisoner.

Deacon was even more surprised. "Rudy, Bist Du daß?" he asked, starting to run across the snow-covered lawn to his German friend.

The bright day provided plenty of light in the cellar. Rudolf Ochmann and Nathan Greer sat on the dusty floor talking, oblivious to the other soldiers around them. Standing over them, Kendrick held the rifle. While Sergeant Gunderson was disposing of Persin's body, Gould and Winley sat on the stairs.

"So, Winley, why'd you come back?"

"I was worried about you guys out here by yourselves. I thought you might need my help." Oberon smiled.

Gould shook his head. "You're a real comedian."

"Thanks, I've been working on it."

"Well, keep working on it. Why'd you really come back?"

"I guess I felt guilty," Winley lied.

"For what?" Gould didn't understand

"It might sound strange to you, Gould, but I think of you men as my company. We started together and should finish together." What Winley didn't say was that being alone in the dark forced him to confront the death of his sister. He had to come back.

"You're right. That's crazy. But no more crazy than that." Gould pointed over to the two soldiers chatting on the floor.

"That is strange, meeting some German he knew from before the war. I can't imagine the odds. And Deac's had that book out since they sat down."

"I think that I saw them praying," Gould said. "That was too much for me. Praying with a Kraut? I'll never get that."

"I think there's a lot you don't understand, Gould."

Gould struggled with the justice of Deac running into an old friend while he lost the only woman he'd ever loved-all in the same war. His head ached.

"You okay, Gould?" Gunderson asked, returning from his morning errand.

"Huh?"

"Doc, you look nauseous. You okay?"

"Yeah, I'm fine. I've just got a headache."

"Too much mental input in the last few days." Gunderson's faced showed sympathy. "I've felt it, too. We all have."

"Yeah, I guess." Gould lied. Deep down he didn't believe anyone felt the way he did.

"Monsieur," Catherine interrupted. "Some food." She brought the food wrapped in wax paper.

"Mercy, Catherine." Gunderson held the woman in his gaze. For the moment he forgot the war.

Winley finally interrupted. "Let's go, boys. Either we make it to Manhay first, or the Germans do."

Gunderson accepted his fate.

"And how are we going to outrun the Germans dragging a prisoner along?" Gould asked to no one.

The Sergeant pointed to the jeep. "There are a few guns and plenty of rounds in the back. At least we'll all be armed."

"We can't take the roads," Gould reminded the others. "We'd

be traveling straight through the middle of them."

Deacon spoke up. "Rudy told me which roads the spearhead was taking."

"He goes by Rudy?" Gould moved closer to Deacon.

"Yes, that's his name. He said that the advance was seriously slowed by the storm and roads. He said it would be hours before they reached Manhay."

"And we can trust him? Trust a Kraut?" Gould continued his interrogation.

"I trust him."

"What about the rest of us?" Gould looked to the others.

The soldiers nodded in agreement with Deac.

"Fine. But what do we do with him?"

Deac didn't hesitate. "We let him go."

"What? I give up." Gould threw his hands into the air. "The Jerries are killing prisoners, and we're letting them go." He stormed around in circles.

"Deac, are you sure?" Gunderson asked his best friend.

"Yeah. We talked about it. He'll take the jeep back to town. There are a few other soldiers there."

Winley asked the obvious question. "How will he explain the dead one?"

"He said not to worry about it. His superior officer wouldn't be there, and no one else knew that they were together."

"I'm satisfied," the Captain approved. "Let's move."

Deac and Rudy exchanged a few more words in German. "He says to follow this road south for about a half mile and then head west through the woods. In about seven miles there's another road that passes just south of Manhay. It'll get us around the advance."

Winley overheard the conversation. "It's not on the map."

"But it's worth a try," Gunderson stated. "You guys get what you can carry out of the jeep."

Catherine had been standing off to the side, watching the men. Sophie slept inside. She didn't see anything in the early morning light.

"We're leaving now," Gunderson said. "I want you to take this." He held out a German pistol.

"No. No gun," she managed to say in English.

He tried again, but she waved her hands in front of her. She had never had a gun in the house and wouldn't start now.

"N'inquietez pas. On va se debrouiller."

From the look on her face, Gunderson didn't need a translation. He knew they'd be fine.

They stood across from each other in awkwardness, neither speaking.

Rudy left in the jeep; the Nazi flag fluttered in the wind.

The Sergeant turned his head and looked at the foursome with new rifles slung over their shoulders. How badly he wanted to stay, here, with Catherine, with Sophie. He turned back to the beautiful woman in front of him.

"I'll always remember you."

From the look on his face, she didn't need a translation.

Confrontation

Three days after the German Army began their campaign, they had traveled less than thirty miles, being delayed by roads, weather and resistance. Americans fled discouraged, and the lack of intelligence was an embarrassment. Eisenhower met with his senior commanders early on December 19th to bolster their spirits and instill confidence. It worked, from the top down. The American army began to fight with renewed vigor throughout Belgium.

Gunderson and his men were unaware of any of this. They merely knew the most dangerous part of their mission lay ahead.

As the previous day, Winley led the others with compass in hand. Although the night's storm had buried the countryside in snow, the sun now shined brightly, slowly rising at their backs. The day began warmer, and a blue sky appeared over the Ardennes for the first time in almost a week.

Kendrick trotted up to the front. "Hey, Winley, you gonna tell me your first name now?"

"It's Oberon."

"Excuse me?"

"Oberon," Winley repeated.

"What kind of name is Oberon."

"It's a character from a Shakespeare play. Ever heard of Shakespeare, Hicky?"

"Yeah. But it's still a dumb name. That must have been your secret."

"That is not my secret. Besides, what kind of name is Shirl?"

Kendrick quickly responded, "It's short for Shirley. Got a problem with that?"

The others didn't hold back the laughter.

"No," Gunderson replied, "It's my mother's name!"

Winley dropped the compass into his pocket and pulled a cigarette out. He struck a match and lit it, slowly pulling it in. Kendrick's eyes widened.

"Where'd you get that?" Kendrick almost reached for Winley's mouth.

"I've had it the whole time." He took another drag and blew out the smoke across Kendrick's face.

"I swear no jokes about your name. Just give me a cigarette. It's been two days."

"It's my last one."

"I don't believe you. Just gimme one."

"On my honor, Hicky." Winley raised his right arm, cigarette between his fingers.

Kendrick followed the burning tip like a dog watching a biscuit in his master's hand. "Then just give me one drag, please."

"I may have told you my first name, but I don't share my smokes."

The Private's face flushed. "Fine. See if I do anything for you, you . . ."

Before Kendrick could finish his sentence, Captain Winley cut him off. "And no cussing," he reprimanded, shaking his cigaretted hand. "You'll offend Deac, and me. Try stretching that Carolina brain and using another word."

"Fine, you, you Oberon!"

All the men now roared as they began to move up a steep incline. They spread out and ascended in a line. Deac and Gould took the right flank.

Gould caught Deac grinning. "You happy, Deac?"

"No, not really. But I'd rather laugh than worry."

The snow began melting in the sun.

"You've been worrying a lot lately."

"I've had a lot to worry about."

Gould began slipping down the slope. Deac grabbed the Medic's arm and propped him up.

"Thanks."

"No problem." Deac turned his feet and stepped up the hill sideways. Gould imitated him.

"How're the shakes?" Gould inquired of Deacon.

"I feel better today."

"They'll come back."

"Maybe they will, maybe they won't. I don't know. But for now I'm feeling better."

The sun sliced through the trees, creating large shadows on the snow. The men held onto branches and trunks to pull themselves up. They slid a foot down for each yard gained. They moved slowly, and this worried the Sergeant and the Captain.

Although he still felt irritated at letting the German go free, Gould tried not to sound mocking. "Seeing that friend must have helped."

"Every good thing helps."

"Is that what your book tells you?"

"Yeah, in a way I guess it does."

Gould began to sweat with the exertion of climbing the hill. The men had barely covered half the distance.

"I think that's a load of crap."

"Why do you do that, Gould?"

"Do what? You mean be honest?"

"Honest? No. As soon as you begin to be honest, you hide in your cynicism."

"You don't know anything about me. Besides, I think you're the one hiding from reality in that book of yours. And your German friends."

"What's wrong with a German friend?"

"They're the enemy. Or hadn't you noticed the war." Gould tried to climb past Deacon but couldn't get the traction.

"They're not all the enemy. Or haven't you noticed?"

"No, I haven't noticed." Gould felt vexed. "All I've seen is them killing us."

"We kill them, too."

"Yeah, I know. And that seems to be something you do very well. Isn't it?"

"You make it sound as if I'm proud of it."

"From what I understand, that's your reputation, dead-eye Deacon."

Deac began to understand that Gunderson had probably told the guys more than that as well. He didn't feel anger but, rather, relief. He didn't like carrying that burden alone and was glad the others now knew.

"I didn't ask for that nickname." Deac moved closer to the top of the hill.

"But you enjoy killing. It's like hunting, hitting your target," Gould barely managed to keep up with his counterpart.

"No. I hate it."

"Like you hated killing those women and children?" Gould's mouth misinterpreted what his brain had signaled. But he couldn't take it back.

Deac stopped. He looked up the hill, keeping his back to

Gould. The others had just disappeared over the crest.

"What? The shakes coming back? Not over it like you thought, huh?"

"No." Deac turned and glared at Gould. "I feel fine. You wouldn't understand. You have the luxury of saving lives. I'm not so fortunate."

"Luxury?!" Gould's anger escalated.

The two faced each other on the hillside.

"Luxury? You think it's a luxury running out into a field with bullets flying so close past your helmet you can hear the clinking, just to listen to a man's final cry for help. Is it a luxury to bandage and tape various body parts with blood spraying all over your uniform knowing it's not going to do any good? Then, I really enjoy it when the wounded get this look in their eye like somehow I've helped just before they die on the ground in front of me. Is it a luxury when someone you've . . ." Gould couldn't finish. His chest froze, and his eyes felt heavy with the images of Madeleine. Even the Lieutenant pressed hard against his mind. "Yeah," Gould finally went on, "being a medic is what I call a luxury."

Listening, Deac also began to feel tears. "That's not what I meant."

"I don't care what you meant."

Not knowing what else to offer the man that stood in front of him, Deac said, "We could save some lives if we make it to Manhay."

"And what? You think that saving a few lives will erase the memory of those people plaguing you? Don't count on it because it won't, regardless of what your book says. Those images will always stay with you. You're stuck with them."

Gould charged up the remaining hillside to find the others bent over and panting.

With the laughter gone, Deac sauntered up the hill.

Card Trick

"There's a burned-out home over there. We can rest inside. I'd prefer not to be out in the open," Winley suggested, wiping his forehead with the white handkerchief.

Deac approached the group in silence.

"Glad ya made it," Kendrick said looking at Gould and Deacon. "Thought we'd lost ya."

"Almost," Deac replied. "Let's get to cover."

The top of the hill presented a small clearing with melting snow, the sun almost directly overhead. Off to the north, the forest thinned, and the Germans moved.

The shelter proved nothing more than the remains of an old, stone structure, like a small castle. The roof and most of the walls had long crumbled. The men headed quickly for it.

"You okay?" the Sergeant asked, intentionally holding back with Deacon. He huffed even with the jog to the stone house. The hill took a lot of strength out of him.

"Yeah, I'm fine. Just thought I could help him, I don't know, to see things differently." Deac seemed to move more easily over the slushy snow than his friend.

"He's a stubborn one, that's for sure."

"Are you okay, Gordon? You don't look so good." Deac slowed to allow the Sergeant to catch up on his right.

"I'm stubborn, too," the Army Sergeant pronounced.

Then, Deac winced as a shot rang out, and something wet hit his face. Instinctively he dropped to the ground and readied the same Mauser he had taken from a German soldier shortly after the massacre. The other men mirrored his actions.

Wiping his face, Deac saw smeared blood on the sleeve of his uniform. If he had been hit, he didn't feel any pain. Gordon, he thought.

Sergeant Gordon Gunderson lay chest down with his face to the side and a few feet from Deacon.

"Sarge!"

"Deac, come on," Winley yelled, scrambling to the rock shelter. "They're coming on the right flank!"

"Gordon!"

"Deac, come on. Now!"

Deac shimmied along the slush. Winley and the others had taken refuge behind a short stone wall. They began firing.

"Now, Deac. Move!"

Deac threw the rifle over his shoulder and got to his feet. The ground was too slick, and he stumbled back to his knees. Shots echoed from off his right shoulder. He pressed on the mud with his hands and continued pushing with his feet.

He felt as if he were in a dream, running in a long tunnel but never reaching the end. He scraped along the ground with his fingers to gain traction but only found sopping wet dirt. He couldn't see the shelter. He clenched his eyes as much to move forward as not to return back to Gunderson.

"That's it, Deac. Keep moving. We've got you covered," Winley yelled as he changed the clip in his pistol.

Kendrick and Gould also fired at three German soldiers about two hundred yards away. They had arrived in a jeep and were using it as cover. The Americans didn't possess any automatics, but three rifles flashed in rapid succession.

Kendrick found one man in his sight. He fired. The German fell onto the hood of the jeep.

Deac reached the building after an eternity of running. He felt dazed and weak. He slumped inside the stone wall and placed his head in his hands. "It's all my fault," he mumbled to himself.

"Deac, get up here. We need you!" Winley ordered, taking control.

He didn't respond.

"Deac!" Gould yelled this time. "It's not your fault."

Deacon finally got up and aimed his rifle. The two other Germans tried to climb back in the jeep. Deac fired and hit one in the shoulder.

Deac shook his head and squeezed his eyes shut.

The wounded German managed to get in the driver's seat of the jeep and start the engine. The second was coming around the side.

Kendrick and Winley fired off round after round. Bullets ricocheted off the metal and into the snow.

Raising the butt of the rifle to his shoulder, Deac tilted his head to use the scope.

The jeep lunged, tires spinning in the mud and flinging the dead man off. The second German grabbed the windshield and pulled himself in.

Deac lined the cross-hairs and flexed his finger. He almost saw the bullet in its trajectory. In exaggerated time, it flew straight across the clearing and found its mark. The German slouched and dropped off the side of the vehicle.

Deac aimed again.

As the jeep headed back north, slush flew off the rear tires. He fired.

This round hit the same wounded shoulder. The German cocked his neck toward the pain shooting down his arm. He disappeared, leaving two bodies and a set of tire tracks.

"I tried," Deac said softly, lowering the rifle to his side.

"That was fine shooting, Deac." Winley sounded optimistic.

"Not good enough," Deac said and turned to look at Gunderson. He paused. Gould was halfway there. Deac dropped his gun and followed at full speed, even though he knew what he'd find.

Kendrick and Winley watched in silence. "Kendrick, grab the guns. We need to move fast. That guy will be back, and he'll be bringing friends."

Kendrick said nothing.

"Hey, Private. It's okay. We've got work to do. Let's get moving."

Kendrick reached into his pocket and pulled out the deck of faded playing cards. He thumbed through it. Fanning out the deck in his hand, he said, "Hey, Winley, pick a card."

Winley looked down. He sensed Kendrick needed this. He pulled out a card and noted that it was the six of diamonds.

"Put it back in the deck, anywhere."

Winley slid the card back in.

Kendrick closed the fan and skillfully shuffled the deck. Then he repeated the procedure.

Winley watched on with interest.

"Here, cut the deck."

The Captain lifted a stack of cards off the top of the deck.

"Turn the card over."

Winley obeyed and looked at the face. The nine of clubs.

"That your card, sir?"

"Yes, Kendrick. I don't believe it. But that's my card. The

nine of clubs."

Kendrick smiled. "Had to get it right sometime."

"Yeah you did."

While the two men finished the card trick, Deac and Gould reached Sergeant Gunderson.

They sidled next to the body, one on each side. Gould laid his bag in the snow and reached across. Gently, he turned Gunderson over.

Deac shut his eyes and tried to hold back the tears.

The bullet had hit the Sergeant on the side of the neck and passed clean through.

Gould sighed. He attempted to look Deac in the eye.

Deacon began to sob.

The Medic tugged at the Sergeant's collar, covering most of the wound. Then, with a handful of damp snow, he wiped the soldier's face clean.

"Deac. It's alright now. You can look."

Deac removed his hands and stared at his friend, the best friend he'd ever met.

"He shouldn't have been here. It's all my fault."

"He wanted to be with you, Deac."

Deac heaved, trying to catch his breath.

"That speaks pretty highly of what he thought about you."

Hyperventilating, Deac fell forward, tears dropping on Gunderson's uniform.

"He said that you were always watching his back. I think he was always watching yours."

Deac lost control. The pain of all he knew flooded his body. His child. The women and children in the bedroom. His best friend. He let the anguish leave in a flood of tears. He looked to heaven and cried out.

Gould lowered his head and sat. He looked at a man in more

pain than he would ever know. He looked at a soldier grieving. Stephen Gould felt confused.

Winley and Kendrick arrived and stood nearby.

"We've got to get out of here," Deac said as he regained his breath.

The others stared at him.

Deac stood up. "He believed in what we were doing. We've got to finish what we started."

Winley's Secret

Rudolf Ochmann arrived at the rear of the spearhead with three other soldiers just a few miles before Manhay. The sun had melted the road to a brown strip winding through the woods. Although barely hanging on, the Nazi flag still waved to the side of the jeep.

They splashed past the troops to the front of the column and pulled over near the other vehicles. Captain Hans Beyer barked orders, his skin reddening from anger and the sun. His troops coagulated on the roadside while the officers debated how to approach the town.

The three soldiers dismounted the jeep and disappeared into a sea of green uniforms. Rudy went over to Beyer.

"Where's Persin," Beyer asked immediately, throwing some papers into the back of the Kubelwagon.

"Back readying his men," Ochmann uncomfortably lied hoping to buy some time. "I'm just returning the American jeep."

Beyer paused on the uselessness of the jeep. He needed weapons and men.

"I'll head back to the men now," Ochmann lied again just as a second jeep skidded into the column.

The vehicle appeared out of nowhere and nearly slammed into Beyer's Kubelwagon. It stopped everyone's conversations. Even Beyer ceased his barrage of words. The driver slumped over against the wheel.

"What the . . ." Beyer stammered. "Someone get him out of there."

Ochmann and another soldier pulled the driver out of the jeep by his left shoulder. His right arm bounced loosely at his side. The blood-soaked uniform over his right chest was shredded.

They laid him on the ground next to the jeep's front tire when Beyer began questioning him.

"Where'd you come from?"

With his left arm, the soldier pointed to the south.

"How far off the road?"

"Maybe a mile. I got stuck a couple of times."

"How many?"

"Five. No, four. We got one."

Rudy held his breath. He thought about his friend and the other Americans.

"I don't want to take any chances. Ochmann, take some men and kill them. I won't have these mosquitoes slowing me down."

Rudy felt a knot in his stomach. He couldn't move.

Beyer screamed, "Go, Ochmann!" as all the spare blood rushed to his face. He pushed two soldiers into Rudy and pointed to two others. "Take the jeep and go!" Beyer stormed off, brandishing his gun at the air like a wild cowboy.

The soldiers were about to jump into the jeep that had just arrived when Rudy stopped them. His thoughts raced.

"No. Let's take the other jeep."

He felt nervous and offered no other explanation. The five soldiers obeyed and followed Rudy to the vehicle draped with the Nazi flag. Rudy drove.

"We're not going to make it over that," Winley insisted, huffing and coming to a quick stop. He wiped sweat off his forehead with the handkerchief.

"We have no choice!" Gould said. "We have to cross."

The four Americans sped through the slush and woods only to come to a wide creek. The barrier had been frozen until the warm day. The thinning ice appeared as a sheet of glass. Water rushed underneath.

"Come on, Winley." Kendrick was the last to arrive at the creek bed. "It's only water. Put your hanky away and let's go."

Winley faced his own demon and fingered the handkerchief

Gould observed Winley's consternation. "You alright? You look a little pale."

"Yes, I'll be fine. Let's move."

Deacon tested the ice first by placing one boot on the surface. He could see the blue bubbles below. He added his weight. The glass didn't crack. "I think it's okay." He proceeded to cross.

Kendrick entered the iced runway a few feet down the stream. Gould traversed behind Deacon.

Winley hesitated on the edge as he pulled the linen back out. He placed his hand over this heart and closed his eyes. He saw Josephine smile. He took a step onto the ice.

Deac reached the other side with ease, but Gould slipped and crashed into the embankment. Deac reached down to lift the Medic up.

Gould accepted the gesture as he re-shouldered his medical bag.

"Not so bad," Kendrick bellowed from downstream. "Just a little ice skating." He shuffled his feet in the melting snow.

The three turned to observe Winley. He was paralyzed in the middle of the ice.

"Winley, keep moving, or the ice will crack," Kendrick joked. "I'm sure that water's pretty darn cold."

Winley glanced down. The handkerchief was still in his hand. He rubbed the JAW stitched in fine, blue thread. Inhaling the cool air, he lifted his right foot.

The weight of his body on a single leg created a hairline crack in the ice. He looked up.

The others heard the ice shift. The crack widened and spread from the epicenter, shooting cobwebs in all directions.

"Move now!" the men standing on the bank shouted, signaling with their hands.

Winley clutched at the white cloth in his hand. Fear prevented him from putting his foot back down on the ice. He never felt so alone.

The glass floor gave way. With a faint slurp, the hole swallowed Winley, and he disappeared into the blue water.

Gould nearly knocked Deac over as he raced down the stream's edge. "Come on!"

Kendrick was already running. Deac paused in thought.

Flowing downstream, Winley clutched at the ice coffin. He sucked in water as he gasped for air.

His mind fought for the control his body lacked. His mental eyes viewed the same scene they had back in the woods earlier that morning when he was alone. He saw his sister's death.

The cold water of the lake splashed on Josephine Alice Winley. "Obee, can't you please slow down," she cautioned as she clutched the side of the sailboat.

"It's powered by the wind, not a motor, Jo."

"Yes, but I know enough about sailing to know you can do something."

Oberon breathed the December air. His lungs burned with the chill. The day was clear but windy. Everything seemed more peaceful out on the lake: the sun's reflections in the ripples, the dampness of the air, the wind's whistle through the sail.

It took his mind off introducing his soon-to-be fiancee to his parents later that night. He knew the meeting wouldn't go well, despite his sister's confidence. He had coaxed her into sailing with him to alleviate his tension.

"Sorry, Jo. Just enjoy the ride."

Josephine rubbed water from her eyes and smoothed back her damp hair.

As she placed her hand back on the rail, a strong gust squarely hit the mainsail. Oberon struggled to control the boat. He failed. And his parents never met his love.

What followed had darkened Winley's mind for years. It clouded his dreams, his thoughts and his life. He tried escaping to alcohol, then to the army. Nothing alleviated his guilt. But it wasn't until he gulped the cold water that he honestly accepted what happened to his twin sister.

As his body slid underneath the ice, Winley consciously gripped the white handkerchief, the only tangible memory left of Josephine. His mother had removed every reminder of her daughter in an emotional rampage. Fortunately, she didn't know that Josephine had given the handkerchief to him the week before, or it also would have been destroyed.

Winley had held onto the white emblem since the day she died. Now, flowing down a river a thousand miles from his home, he released his grip. He felt the ice cold water against his palm as the memory floated away.

Gould and Kendrick sprinted along the bank.

"Kendrick, get downstream and blow a hole in the ice with your gun!" Deac yelled. He started to run after the other two.

Kendrick didn't understand him. "What?"

"Shoot a hole in the ice downstream!"

Winley continued to bounce in between the rocks and ice.

Kendrick managed to get far enough ahead to stop and aim his rifle. He shot off five rounds into the center of the stream. The first two almost seemed to rebound off the surface in a fray of ice. By the fifth, a large chunk broke away and vanished underneath.

Winley's dark figure neared the hole.

Kendrick jumped into the puncture just in time for Winley's body to collide into his legs. The force bruised both his shins.

Kendrick reached down and snatched Winley's water-logged coat and heaved. He couldn't extract him.

The current threw Winley's body up onto Kendrick and out of the water as Gould arrived at the fracture. The two men slid the body across the iced surface.

"Doc, he's not breathing!" Kendrick exclaimed trying to pull Winley further up the other side.

Deac stopped next to them.

"Move," Gould ordered and knelt next to the limp body. He placed his medical bag on the ground.

Winley looked as though he were sleeping with his eyes shut and a slight part in his lips. But his pale blue face indicated a more severe slumber.

Gould unbuttoned the wool overcoat and turned Winley's face to the side. Straddling him, Gould pushed on his gut. Water dribbled out Winley's mouth. The second push forced out a steady flow. Still, Winley didn't move.

Kendrick and Deac awaited instructions from the Medic.

"Private, pinch his nose and blow gently into his mouth."

"What?"

"Tilt his head back and blow into his mouth."

Kendrick looked puzzled. "Like this?"

"Yeah, exactly. Blow in two times."

Winley's chest inflated with each breath.

"Good, the air's getting in."

Winley still didn't respond.

Gould bent forward and placed both his hands over Winley's sternum. He rocked at the waist like an oil drill. He felt the resistance of he man's rib cage. "Come on," he yelled at Winley's face.

Nothing.

"Come on," Gould yelled as he depressed again.

Deac closed his eyes and began to pray.

"You're not helping, Greer. Rub his arms and warm them up. He's ice cold. Kendrick, again!"

The Private blew twice.

"Breathe damn it!" Gould pounded on Winley's chest with his fist. He continued the compressions.

"Come on, Winley, just breathe," Deac whispered.

Gould pushed one more time.

Winley coughed.

Droplets of cold water spurted out of his mouth. He coughed again then inhaled, his mouth gaped open. "Oh, headache." He tried to bring his hands to his head.

Deac held them down, "Just relax."

"Glad to have you back, man." Kendrick sat next to Winley's head, grinning with pride.

Winley looked up at his teammates. He closed his eyes and breathed.

"I can't believe he came back from the dead," Kendrick exclaimed.

"He'll be right back there if we don't get him some drier clothes. It's warm, but not that warm out here."

"Good work, Corporal. You saved his life." Deac tried to make eye contact with the Medic who avoided the connection.

"Sorry, Kendrick. I lied. I did have one left. I was going to give it to you, but now I doubt you want it." Winley carefully pulled a limp cigarette from his breast pocket and handed it to the Private. "Sorry."

Kendrick's hand shook as he took the cigarette. He ran it under his nose and sniffed. "At least I can still smell the tobacco."

"Still want to know my big secret?"

Kendrick looked at Winley. "What, now you're going to tell me?"

"Sure. It's not a secret anymore."

"What is it?"

"I was afraid of the water."

As the men lifted Winley, a bullet whizzed past his face and hit a tree to his right, splintering the bark.

They turned and looked upstream. A German soldier stood in the back of a wildly swerving jeep. A Nazi flag flapped on the hood.

Rudy's Gift

A German soldier in the back seat of a jeep began yelling at Ochmann.

Rudy had intentionally driven in circles hoping to avoid a confrontation. To his dismay, one of the soldiers had spotted the Americans. He now fish-tailed the jeep not knowing how long he could continue to delay.

Rudy cranked the wheel as the standing German fired again. The man fell out of the jeep, cursing as he slid on his back down to the stream. He hit his head and went unconscious. The bullet disappeared into the air.

"What's wrong with you?" another screamed from the passenger seat.

"Die Reifen spinnen sich."

Ochmann began to turn the jeep around to retrieve the fallen soldier.

A soldier from the back ordered, "Forget him. Go after the Americans."

Rudy continued the retreat.

The man next to him called Rudy a coward and elbowed him in the face, breaking open his swollen lip.

Rudy stepped on the brake, and the jeep slid to a stop. The passenger pushed Ochmann out the open side and hopped in the driver's seat. Slamming the vehicle back into gear, the three remaining Germans sped off toward the Americans scrambling for cover, leaving Rudy standing behind.

"Take a tree," Deac yelled.

The men found a row of large oak trees a few feet away. Each hid behind a trunk. All except Winley inserted new clips into the rifles' chambers.

Deac peered around the tree. The jeep came cruising through the slush and mud. He recognized the flag on the hood, but he didn't see his friend. "Kendrick, I'll cover you while you get Gould and Winley out of here!"

Kendrick lined his sights on the approaching jeep. "I've got the better position. I'll cover you. Go!"

Deac assessed the situation. He knew that Kendrick was right.

"Go!" Kendrick yelled again. "I've got target practice." He leaned to the side of his wooden wall and fired. He hit one of the Germans. "Got ya!"

Deac began to move over to Gould and Winley. He wondered if Rudy was in the jeep. "Come on! Kendrick's got our backs."

Kendrick took a deep breath. "Okay, let's bag another Jerry," he mumbled to the tree. He came around the trunk and fired.

Upstream, a German fired back.

The two bullets nearly collided. Had the rarest of events actually occurred, Private Shirl Kendrick would have lived through the day. As it happened, his lifeless body slumped against the tree trunk.

The German marksman shot again. The projectile pierced the side of Winley's right leg. He stumbled to the ground.

The jeep containing two German soldiers headed towards them.

Deacon and Gould picked Winley up by the armpits.

"Halt," the German brandishing a weapon ordered coming up behind them.

The three Americans conceded and raised their arms in surrender.

"Schießen Sie!" the driver ordered.

Deac understood the command to shoot and closed his eyes.

The rifleman bought his weapon to his shoulder.

Before he pulled the trigger, another gun fired, and the sound of clinking metal echoed over the rushing stream. The German's helmet flew through the air, and his body fell to the ground.

Rudy Ochmann stood upstream, smoke rising from the tip of his rifle.

Rudy fired again. He hit the driver, killing the man instantly. He knelt down by the stream and cried.

Gould cut through Winley's trousers as Deac spoke in German to Rudy.

"This is going to hurt." Gould saw the bullet lodged just underneath the connective tissue covering the muscle.

Winley lay on his stomach. "Not more than my head right now."

"You want some morphine?"

"A lot of good I'll be all drugged up," Winley replied. "Just do it."

"Then take this." Gould handed him a wadded piece of tent canvas. "Bite on it. It'll help."

The Medic took a small pair of forceps from his medical kit and inserted the tips into the wound.

Winley gasped and bit down on the cloth.

The pincers touched the small lump of lead in Winley's leg. Gould carefully pulled it out. He quickly stuffed the small hole with gauze.

"Want to keep it?" Stephen Gould held up the bullet.

"Uh, no thanks," he said, spitting out the canvas. "Can I get up now?"

"Hang on." Gould removed the last of the bandages and tightly wrapped Winley's thigh.

"What about Kendrick?"

Gould shook his head.

Winley said nothing and sat on the ground.

"There are two uniforms here and one more upstream," Deac informed Winley and Gould.

"What are you talking about?" the Medic asked.

The three remaining men stood facing each other as Rudy Ochmann ran back upstream.

"We put the German uniforms on and drive straight through on the roads."

"Are you crazy?" Gould lifted his arms in exasperation. "If you haven't noticed, we've seen a few too many Krauts already. And now you want to stroll right down the middle of their column, past their tanks and machine guns?"

"It'll give me dry clothes," Winley added, trying to pacify Gould.

"Rudy said that the Germans are preparing to take Manhay. They're leaving the main road and spreading out. There's no other way to make it. It's either that or keep running to the next town."

Winley instinctively reached his hand into his pocket. "Let's try it. Deac speaks German. I'm wounded and wet. It'll be dark, not to mention cold, in a few hours. We don't have any other choice."

Gould hung his head. "Alright, let's pretend to be German."

"All right boys, let's get changed." Although hobbling, Winley was full of vigor.

The three Americans donned the German uniforms.

"Good thing I haven't eaten in a few days. That guy was thinner than a blade of grass," Winley joked, sucking in his gut and trying to hitch the pants.

"You sound like Kendrick."

"Not such a bad thing, I guess." Winley smiled.

Gould threw his armband, helmet and bag with the red crosses into the back of the jeep. In a matter of minutes, he had been demoted to a German schütze. He felt awkward, almost dirty. He pulled at the shoulders of the uniform. It didn't fit right.

Winley lifted himself up and into the rear seat of the jeep. He stretched out his leg and retied the blood soaked bandage over the new pants, part of the ploy.

All three tunics had blood stains but not enough to rouse suspicion, they hoped.

Deac sat in behind the wheel. He'd do the talking, and the praying. The men sped off.

When his comrade regained consciousness, Rudolf Ochmann explained that the other three and the Americans were dead, and the jeep was destroyed. He presented each soldbuch as evidence. The two walked the mile back to Captain Hans Beyer and company. By the time they got there, it was all over.

The jeep moved quickly through the forest. They headed in a north-westerly direction. Deac focused on the terrain while the other two worried.

"Hey, Gould, you've never mentioned your big secret," Winley said, lying in the back seat.

"Like I said, I don't have one."

"Everyone's got a secret, even you."

"Uh, guys. Look over there." Deac pointed past a row of trees.

Off their right shoulder they could see about two hundred troops, a few tanks and a myriad of other vehicles. Clumps of men hurriedly formed, dissipated and merged again, like amoebas on a glass slide. Captain Beyer roared above the drone of starting engines.

"Be ready," Deac said as he steered right.

Although the day was still bright, the sun began its descent in the west. The forest appeared as a quilt of brown and white patches hastily sewn together by threads of green grass. A sunny spring day erupted in the middle of the Ardennes winter.

The jeep bounced through the patchwork, the red flag with black swastika still prominently tied on the hood. The men began their charade. Winley faked being unconscious, and Gould turned around to attend to him. Deacon put on a German helmet.

They entered from the side and drove through a group of oblivious foot soldiers. Deacon searched for officers to avoid. He drove the jeep back onto the road, the tires following the deep ruts.

A hundred yards ahead, Captain Beyer argued with some other officers. A guard was positioned in the middle of the road.

"Halt," he ordered and waved his arms.

The jeep rolled to a stop. Gould pressed on Winley's leg as if to prevent bleeding underneath the bandage.

Deacon leaned across Gould to speak to the guard. "Wo ist Eure Krankenstation?" he asked, nodding to the wounded soldier in the back seat.

The guard pointed to a dirt road just ahead. "Kiese Strasse nach rechts, dann 500 Meter geradeaus. Kann Man nicht verpassen."

Deac understood the directions to the aid station just a quarter mile away down the dirt road. He began to pull forward.

Before Deac could leave, the guard seemed to recognize Gould and tapped him on the shoulder. "Warst Du nicht mit mire in der Grundausbildung?"

Gould's face went pale. He stared straight ahead.

The guard waited for a response.

Deac's only option was to pull away. He put the jeep into gear and pressed the gas.

The rear tires spun in the mud. The jeep didn't move.

"Oh, nicht schon wieder! Kannst Du anschieben helfen?" Deac asked the guard. He silently thanked God for the distraction.

"Ja, klar," the German responded. He moved to the back of the jeep. "He, Ihr beiden! Packt mal mit an!" He ordered two other soldiers to help extricate the jeep from the mire.

Gould got out and pushed against the side door opening while the Germans pushed from behind. Deac and Gould exchanged incredulous looks.

"Scheiss amerikanscher jeep, was?" The guard mocked the quality of the American jeep.

"Ja," Deac said back. He slowly gave the jeep some gas.

The men pushed, and the vehicle began to inch forward. As it gained traction, Gould jumped back into the passenger seat. He turned and looked down to Winley who eyed him back. Winley was sweating profusely.

"Danke!" Deac waved as the jeep ran down the road.

The guard watched as the Americans passed the turnoff to the aid station. "Oh . . . nein. Du bits vorbeigefahren. Du must da einbiegen!" He started waving to the right.

Deac held straight down the road.

A few more Germans noticed the jeep with the Nazi flag as it approached the still-arguing officers. Beyer looked up.

Deac shifted gears and began to speed up.

"Halt," an officer ordered.

Beyer recognized the jeep and its flag. He didn't recognize the occupants. He started moving toward the jeep.

Seeing the soldiers coming at him, Deac floored the gas pedal. Mud flew from the tires as they spun almost out of control, splattering the officers. The jeep moved at full speed.

Beyer yelled something, took out his pistol and began firing. The first few bullets hit the rear of the jeep.

Winley rolled onto the back floor. Gould and Deacon slumped as far down as they could.

Soldiers ahead of them didn't react. The simply watched in confusion as three Americans in German uniforms drove an American jeep with a German flag flying from the hood.

The vehicle bounced and skidded, barely staying on the road.

"You can make it," Deac said to the jeep.

Beyer and the officers continued firing. One bullet embedded itself in the back of Gould's seat.

"That's it!" Winley snatched a rifle off the floor and sat up. He knelt on the seat, facing Beyer. He fired off all the rounds in the clip.

The officers scattered. The entire company was now aware of the infiltration. The Germans moved forward, tanks rolling.

The jeep headed straight toward Manhay and the American troops dug in there. Hundred of Germans followed.

Saints and Soldiers

The jeep floundered in the sludge that the road had become. The tires sank past the rims and the undercarriage scraped the ground. Winding through an undulating onslaught of potholes, humps, hollows, rocks and ridges, the mud path led to the final grove of trees, the last sentinels of the men's journey through the Ardennes.

The high-pitched rattle of automatics blended with the hoarse hum of the two Panther tanks. The synchronization was marred only by the occasional pops of rifle fire and bullets whizzing through the air. The jeep carried scars from those incoming rounds.

Deacon muscled the steering wheel as required to avoid capsize or collision. One correction nearly ejected Gould from his seat. He held firm to the seat back as his legs flew over his head and out of the vehicle. His feet recoiled off the ground and back into his seat like a rodeo cowboy back into his saddle. The jeep bounced off the road. The three remaining Americans held their breath as they entered the copse of aspens.

"Deac!" Winley yelled with his eyes bulging and his head pressing between the front seats.

"We'll make it."

Finger-like limbs scratched at the sides of the jeep; larger ones hammered the hood. Deac covered his face as the windshield shattered. The red flag fluttered amid the spraying twigs, rocks and mud.

Gould winced as the jeep broadsided a large trunk, the branches breaking and cutting his face. A slice under his right eye began to bleed.

The setting sun shot orange and red streaks across the pale blue sky, and melting snow froze into icicles twinkling in the light.

Winley glanced behind. The American jeep with the Nazi flag seemed to lead a small German spearhead.

"The flag!" Winley yelled.

Across the meadow, the 7th Armored Division lined the road into Manhay with rocket launchers and Browning .30 caliber machine guns. Behind the line, M4 Sherman tanks sat ready. Major John Hocken commanded the men of the Division along the tree-lined, paved pathway.

"Prepare your weapons! Just a few more minutes and it's show time!" the Major ordered looking down the road.

Men all along the road began inserting clips, magazines and rounds into their weapons.

"Major, look over there!" a private screamed, pointing to a jeep emerging from the trees, just to the north of the road.

"Samuels, the rocket launcher! Ahead left." The Major began to run across the road to Private Samuels who shouldered the large gun. He pointed at the jeep with a Nazi flag on the hood. "They're coming through!"

Samuels eyed down the long, wide barrel of the launcher and sighted the oncoming jeep.

"Take it out!" the Major ordered.

"Hold on. There's a guy climbing onto the hood."

"What?" The Major tried to focus on the vehicle.

"He's pulling at the flag. He's barely hanging on." The Private kept his aim on the men in the jeep.

The flag tore loose and slid over the top of the jeep, revealing its true insignia on the hood.

"It's one of ours, sir!"

"Shoot it!"

"They're holding their weapons over their heads."

"You sure?"

"Yes, sir."

The Major could now distinguish the three occupants. They appeared to be surrendering.

"Think it's a trick, sir?" Private Samuelson asked.

"Hold on." The Major turned back to his men along the road. "Anything coming down?"

"Not yet, Major," a soldier replied.

Suddenly an incoming mortar landed right in front of the jeep. It exploded in a cloud of dirt and snow. The jeep careened and rolled over, discharging the three men.

"Where'd that come from?" The Major now sprinted back to his troops.

"It's German. They're firing on that jeep," the same soldier informed.

"Samuels! Hold fire! Hold fire!" he screamed behind his back. Then he said to the soldier next to him, "Something tells me to protect those guys in the jeep. Cover them."

The soldier relayed the order down the road. The infantry took positions off the road to protect the fleeing men.

Tanks appeared in the middle of the road just ahead of them. Germans began spilling from the forest like gray ants. Mortars dropped from both directions.

"Gould, get Winley!" Deac yelled as he scrambled through the mud to a Mauser rifle lying next to the jeep.

Gould scuttled over to Winley and lifted him under the arm. They limped back to the jeep and took cover with Deacon who was already firing at the Germans.

"There are too many, Deac. We've got to make a run for it." Gould still braced Winley.

"Take Winley and go. I'll cover."

"No way!" Gould replied. "You're coming with."

Bullets began to pelt the jeep like hail.

"Someone's got to stay, or we'll all be killed." Deac popped his head over the jeep and fired. A German fell. "GO!" Deac pushed Gould in the chest.

Gould and Winley began the hobble across the open field.

Private Samuels watched. He aimed the rocket launcher just over and beyond the jeep. He fired the weapon. The kickback nearly toppled him.

The small mortar flew with a shriek, leaving a faint tail of smoke in its wake. It landed between Deac and the onslaught of German infantry. The soldiers fell into the mud.

Deac continued to fire through the smoke until the cartridge went empty. He threw the obsolete weapon to the side and found another in the jeep, its strap wrapped around the stick shift.

Winley took another bullet in the shoulder as the two approach Samuels.

"We're American! American!" Gould yelled.

The Private's jaw dropped.

"We're American!" Gould repeated. His legs gave out with this last sentence. He and Winley slid to a halt.

More Americans now entered the fields to ward off the attack. The gun fire became deafening. Bullets criss-crossed. Scores of men died.

Samuels dropped the launcher and ran out to the pair of

German uniforms in the snow. "Cover me!"

Another soldier followed Samuels.

Deac aimed and fired with rapidity, round after round. Each shot finding its mark. Before the Germans had recovered from the rocket blast, Deac found himself out of ammunition.

Corporal Nathan "Deac" Greer put his hand over his pocket with the small book and picture of his wife. He took one deep breath. He turned and ran.

"Americans," Gould cried again without composure. He felt the numbness of fatigue invade his body.

Winley rolled over onto his back.

Deac had covered a few yards when a bullet hit him in the back. He arched in pain. He stumbled but kept moving.

"Captain, this is suicide!" an officer screamed into Captain Hans Beyer's face.

The Captain's face reddened with the setting sun. The German officers had argued and stalled too long on the eastern side of the woods. The hot orange glow from the west blinded their advance. They were stuck.

An M4 incoming round landed on Beyer's Kubelwagon. The explosion shredded everything within thirty feet.

The two soldiers from the 7th Armored rescued the two Americans clad in German uniforms, finally dragging the exhausted and wounded men to the western side of the front.

Deac slumped to his wounded side. He continued to run amid the bombardment of bullets. His legs moved automatically as his mind dwelled on his wife. He saw her eyes, her hair. Even her smell permeated the senses in his brain. In his thoughts, she wore a simple dress and held a child, his child. She extended her arms and held the baby out to him. He stopped running and took the child in his arms. In the last thoughts of his mind's eye, he held his son to his breast and cried.

Private Samuels took Winley to the first aid tent behind the tanks where he asked for a commanding officer. Almost four days after Winley had met Lieutenant Lucht up on the Elsenborn Ridge, he was finally able to deliver the message he had carried on his back and mind. He slept peacefully that night.

The information proved invaluable to the Allies. Skorzeny and his men were caught and tried as spies after the war. The Germans never made it to the Meuse River, and Hitler's plan to retake Europe failed. The Allies crushed the Bulge.

That evening, Corporal Gould folded his arms across his chest. He stared across the field littered with vehicles and men. Twilight filled the meadow with blue light. His thoughts lingered on Deac, and he found it difficult to breathe. He looked down at the German uniform he wore. It still didn't fit right.

About the Author

Jeffrey Scott is a practicing attorney in the area of entertainment law. While raised on both coasts, his love of the mountains compelled him to choose the Mountain West to make his home where he spends his free time training and competing in endurance sports. He is currently working on two additional novels, a collection of short stories and a screenplay. *Saints and Soldiers* is his first publication.